MURDER
On A Country Walk

BOOKS BY KATIE GAYLE

KATIE GAYLE

MURDER
On A Country Walk

bookouture

Published by Bookouture in 2024

An imprint of Storyfire Ltd.
Carmelite House
50 Victoria Embankment
London EC4Y 0DZ

www.bookouture.com

ISBN: 978-1-83525-099-0
eBook ISBN: 978-1-83525-098-3

We love taking walks and so this book is dedicated to the keepers of the paths and green spaces, who ensure that walkers have a place to go.

If there was a prize for Most Enthusiastic Dog at the South Cotswolds Dog Show, Jake would have won it for sure. No one could touch him in that category. His tail whipped from side to side in a blur. He was grinning like a loon, his head swivelling around at each new delight: A little girl in pigtails commanding a clever border collie in the Best Handler Under Ten Years category; a cockapoo – a cocker spaniel/poodle cross – washed and, it seemed, blow-dried to a deep black shine, a red ribbon nestled in its curls; the smell of pastries from the refreshment tent. It was all simply marvellous as far as Jake was concerned.

He yapped, three sharp excited barks, and turned in a circle, unfortunately wrapping himself and the lead around a pole holding up an awning over the table where Pippa was selling tickets for £2.50 per event entry, proceeds to the Guide Dogs association. Pippa reached for the cash tin with one hand and the tickets with the other, as the table rocked and the awning swayed ominously over her head. 'Oh, Jake!' she called. 'You're up to no good again!' From anyone else this might have seemed a bit rude, but it was Pippa who had originally tried to train Jake as a guide dog, before she gave up and gave him to Julia.

Julia loosened her hold on Jake's lead, briefly, to release the tension and disentangle him from the pole, but Jake took advantage and made a run for it, bounding across the grass area between the church and the hall, where the dog show events were being held. He was eager to make the acquaintance of the entrants in the Golden Oldies category, at that moment being judged by a man who was surely one hundred himself (or fifteen in dog years, Julia thought, doing a quick bit of mental arithmetic). Although the day had the distinct feel of spring, the old chap was dressed for deep winter in top-to-toe tweed, with a matching cap on his head.

Jake came bounding into the arena, and the judge raised his walking stick and shouted in a stern yet quavering voice, 'Could the owner of the chocolate Labrador please control your dog!'

Julia looked over at her boyfriend, Dr Sean O'Connor, whose well behaved rescue cross-breed, Leo, was sitting quietly, not being a loon, and rolled her eyes to the heavens. Sean smiled supportively. He was used to a bit of chaos following Jake around.

'Jake, come in!' she called in her most authoritative tone, but as well as having developed a severe case of the Zoomies, Jake had apparently been struck deaf. Fortunately, the competing dogs – eight years and older – were a lot calmer than Jake, and watched with bemused indulgence as he hurtled around as if he was on some sort of manic victory lap. Julia managed to grab his lead as he ran past the second time, and he slid abruptly to a halt, but not before smacking into the back of Sean's knees and knocking him into Julia, who tried to step out of the way, but connected with Leo's lead. The four of them – two humans and two dogs – ended up in a humiliating tangle on the damp, daisy-speckled grass.

'Goodness. Is that you down there, Dr O'Connor?' the

elderly judge asked, peering down at him over the half-glasses perched on his nose. 'Are you all right?'

'Perfectly fine,' Sean said, getting to his feet and holding a hand out for Julia, who was relieved to find herself with four unbroken limbs. 'We're all good, thank you, no injuries. Please, continue.'

Julia had managed to hold on to Jake's lead as she went down, and as she staggered to her feet she brushed bits of grass off her trousers with her free hand and muttered dark words under her breath.

Jake was now quite calm, having worked off a bit of excess energy, and sat patiently through the Golden Oldies, and then the rather chaotic Musical Sit, which was like the game Musical Chairs that is played at children's parties, but without the chairs, and with dogs instead of kids. Something called a 'chug' – a chihuahua cross pug – won Little Cuties. A golden retriever won Best Paw Shaker, although Julia thought that Leo should have won, he shook hands more politely, and with great style.

The Pooch Got Talent competition raised the bar as far as skills were concerned. There was a dog that could count; a dog that could be persuaded to spin in circles, changing direction at the click of the handler's fingers; a dog that could roll over and play dead; a dog that could sing, if by sing you meant howl. The crowd pleaser – and the ultimate winner – was a pretty silver-grey Weimaraner that gently herded five chickens into a small pen without so much as a peep from them. Its owner had brought the chickens for the occasion, which a grumbler standing near Julia thought was 'a bit of a cheat, given that they were probably experienced'.

'Don't get any ideas,' Julia told Jake, although she couldn't imagine the bossy old Henny Penny, head girl of her chicken crew, submitting to his clumsy herding.

Now, as the enthusiastic clapping and whooping died down, it was finally their turn to compete. Julia had entered

Jake into only one event – Best Sausage Catcher. Julia believed in playing to your strengths. Sausages were at the centre of Jake's area of interest and expertise.

'Come on,' she said, when the event was called. 'It's your moment to shine.'

It was a popular event, with twelve contestants – hardly surprising, given the low level of skill required and the participants' high level of enthusiasm for sausages. There was a preponderance of Labradors in this line-up – eight dogs out of twelve. As a dog trainer had put it to Julia, rather euphemistically, 'As a breed, they are highly food-motivated.'

The judge for this round was a round-faced cheerful-looking woman in her late-thirties, who was, according to the voice over the loudspeaker, Eleanor Hugs, the head teacher of the primary school. Julia suspected that in such a role she would have developed just the kind of skills and attitudes required to wrangle a bunch of greedy, over-excited dogs.

'Okay then, chaps. We're going to go one at a time, smallest to biggest.' She took the lid off the repurposed ice-cream container she was holding, releasing the delicious smell of cooked sausage. She took out a chunk about an inch long and held it up. The dogs were fixated on the glistening bit of banger.

'You'll toss the piece of sausage in the air, and the dog will try to catch it. A nice high toss, at least your own head height. No easy lobs, please.' As Eleanor spoke, and moved the treat a little left, a little right, their eyes followed. 'If the dog succeeds in catching it, he or she will go through to the next round. And so we go, until there's only one left. The winner! Is everyone clear on the rules?'

There was nodding, and some drooling from the assembled dogs, as well as some of the humans.

'Right, let's have some fun!'

Round one eliminated just three of the dogs. Round two another three. Jake was still in the running, as calm and attentive as you please, his body still and quivering, his eyes on the prize. With each round, his jaws snapped shut around the sausage with a sharp slapping noise.

'I don't like to boast, and perhaps I'm biased, but Jake just has huge natural talent at sausage catching, doesn't he?' Julia said, when he made it through round three, along with three others.

Sean nodded sagely. 'Yes indeed. The focus, the confidence, the style. He's got it all.'

'It's like this is what he was born to do. His vocation, almost.'

In round four, it was down to two – Jake and a golden Lab.

'First up, Molly,' said Eleanor. 'It's a high stakes situation. Two exceptional competitors, we have here. They've both performed magnificently thus far. And now they're going head-to-head for the championship.'

Molly's owner, a teenage boy, lobbed a delicious bit of sausage elegantly into the air. Both dogs followed it with their eyes as it arced up to the boy's head height, and then fell, down, down, down...

Molly opened her mouth in anticipation, but she misjudged the trajectory, brushing the sausage with the side of her nose as she snapped thin air. She opened her mouth for a second attempt at the sausage, but it was too late. It hit the floor.

'Jakey! You won!'

He looked bemused. Where was *his* piece of sausage? Molly had got hers. The judge came over with a red rosette, and the ice-cream carton with the last few bits of sausage.

'What a very good chap you are, Jake,' she said, fixing the rosette to his collar. 'I doubt there's a better or more determined sausage catcher in the whole of the Cotswolds!'

'I think it's very unlikely. He's unusually gifted,' said Julia, fondling his silky ears while he guzzled the remaining sausage, his tail slapping hard and happy against the pole.

2

Jake was unusually subdued the morning after the dog show. Instead of bounding out of the door – like the champion dog that he was – when it was time for his breakfast, and to feed the chickens and collect the eggs, he moved slowly.

'What's wrong, Jakey? Are you tired and stiff from hurtling about at the dog show yesterday? Too much excitement? Or are you suffering from a sausage overdose?'

There was no answer from Jake, of course, but he did give her a mournful look, rolling his limpid eyes to the heavens. He cheered up a little when the pellets rattled into his metal bowl, and he managed to walk over and stick his nose into the food. He paused, and looked at Julia as if to point out that he was putting in a brave effort for her sake. As he ate, Julia noticed that the dog's tail was at a bit of a funny angle. She reached down and gently touched it. He yelped and looked indignant. A quick google of 'broken tail' found a lot of horror stories about injuries and amputations. Feeling slightly panicked, Julia phoned the vet and got an appointment for that very morning.

. . .

Julia was pleased to see an empty waiting room when she arrived. Jake was always delighted to see his fellow canine patients, but she didn't enjoy navigating his interaction with the skittish dogs, let alone the terrified cats and poorly parrots and their stressed-out owners. Even if they weren't stressed out before, Jake's enthusiastic arrival in the waiting room usually made even the calmest owners look strained.

'Hello, Mrs Bird. Dr Davies won't be long. She's busy with a patient, and you're next,' said the receptionist, from behind the desk.

'Thank you, Olga.'

Julia took a seat and surveyed the extensive range of pet foods for sale while she waited. Pellets and pouches and tins and treats. Organic, free-range, vegan, gluten-free. Good for puppies or kittens, or seniors, or pets with allergies. In flavours of tuna, beef or pheasant. The world was a strange place, if you thought about it. The exotic beasts of the air and sea being fed to domestic beasts of the shires and suburbs. Julia rather wished she hadn't had that thought, but before she had time to dwell on it, it was interrupted by the opening of the door of the surgery. A man came out, carrying a huge fluffy grey Persian in his crossed arms. The cat looked positively princely, reclining on the owner's forearms, its magnificent tail hanging down to below the man's waist. Jake avoided its eyes, and leaned a little harder on Julia's leg. He was nervous of cats as a rule, and this one was particularly alarming, what with all that fur, and those round, cold blue eyes.

Behind her, in the doorway to the surgery, Eve Davies addressed them with a smile. 'Hello, Julia, hello, Jake. Come on in.'

Jake slunk past the cat, giving it the widest possible berth, and then put on a little trot to get a bit of distance between them and reach the safety of the surgery. Ordinarily, Jake loved a visit to Dr Davies. When Julia took him for his regular injections, he had to be physically restrained from knocking Eve to the ground and licking her to death. But today he followed the two women into the room meekly, his tail hanging limp.

'What can I help you with today?' The vet had a calm, no-nonsense manner that put both dogs and owners at ease. She was one of those people whose age was hard to tell. She had a wholesome quality – slim, no make-up to hide the spray of freckles on her nose, and her curly golden-brown hair tied back in a ponytail, for work at least – that seemed somehow youthful, however old she was. She could be rather stiff with humans, but always had a broad smile and a kind word for dogs.

'I think he's hurt his tail. We were at the dog show yesterday and it seems he must have injured it somehow.' Julia paused, but couldn't help adding proudly, 'He came first in the sausage-catching category, you know. It was a pretty exciting moment.'

'Well done, Jake. I'm sure it was a hotly contested event,' said Eve with a grin as she examined Jake's limp tail, gently feeling along the length of it, checking where it was tender. He winced when she got to the sore bit, but maintained a stoic demeanour. He really wasn't himself.

'I don't think it's broken. It looks like Jake's got what they call happy tail syndrome.'

'Happy tail syndrome? That's a real thing?'

'It is indeed, an actual condition that you learn about in vet school.'

Julia mentally filed the diagnosis away to tell Jess when she next phoned from Hong Kong. She had fallen into the habit of amassing a stash of interesting and amusing things to tell her daughter on their weekly chats. Jess adored Jake, and would be sad to hear of his injury, but she would get a kick out of that funny name.

The vet continued. 'It happens when a dog wags their tail forcefully, hitting it against hard objects like walls, or furniture.'

'That makes perfect sense. He was in such good humour at the show yesterday, his tail didn't stop wagging for a minute.'

'It must be lovely to be such a happy chap.' Eve sounded almost envious of the dog. She actually looked a little glum herself, Julia thought, not as perky as usual. 'Not a care in the world except for a sore tail, and that tail will likely heal all by itself. I'll give you some anti-inflammatories for him. Five days. That should help with the pain and any swelling. Just keep him calm, if you can.'

'Easier said than done.'

'I know, he's a bit of a live wire, but see what you can do. If it doesn't get better on its own in a few days, we might have to X-ray, but I suspect it's just bruised and he will be right as rain soon enough.'

'Thanks, Dr Eve. Is it okay to take him for walks?'

'Yes, keep him on a lead, though, so he doesn't go wild. I know you like to chase those rabbits up on the hill path, don't you, Jake?'

Julia and Jake sometimes passed Eve on one of their regular walks, the one that took them up along the edge of a hill to a high point with a lovely view over the village and beyond. Eve was often with her elderly mother and her elderly mutt.

'How is your mum, Eve?'

'Oh, she is very well. All that walking keeps her fit as a fiddle.'

'She is remarkable. And she always seems in such good spirits.'

'She seldom gets stressed, or anxious. Even when she should be. It can be quite annoying.' Eve gave a sigh. 'Can't say the same for me. I wish I had her temperament.'

Julia hesitated. After all, they were only acquaintances, not friends, and she didn't want to pry, but then again, she was fond of the vet and didn't like to see her down. She said gently, 'Are you all right, Eve?'

'Oh, just got a lot on my mind. Sometimes it's hard to know what to do in a situation. Hard to know what the best outcome will be for everyone. Things aren't always black and white, are they?'

'That's certainly something I found in my work,' said Julia.

'Sometimes I wonder if it's even all worth the fight, you know,' said Eve. 'If I make any difference at all.'

'You make a huge difference to me and Jake,' said Julia, a bit thrown by what Eve had said. 'And to the whole community.'

'Thanks, Julia.' Eve smiled. 'I just can't help feeling like something terrible is going to happen, no matter what I do.'

Julia waited to see if Eve wanted to share more, but Eve said nothing. 'Well, I hope it all resolves to your satisfaction, whatever it is. Like Jake's tail!'

'That would be wonderful, I must say.' Eve didn't sound optimistic about the possibility of a simple improvement.

'You take care of yourself.'

'Thanks, Julia. And you take care of Jake.'

'Will do, thank you. You'll see us on the hill walk sometime soon, I'm sure. We seem to cross paths there quite often.'

'Yes, we do seem to have a similar schedule for the afternoon walk. Not today though, Monday's the day I play Padel. Have you tried it?'

'Is that the one like tennis, with the small courts that went up recently?'

Eve smiled. 'They've been up for a year now. I love it – only downside is that you need four people to play, so it can get sticky with finding and keeping a partner.' Eve rolled her eyes slightly, hinting at many Padel-related dramas.

'The courts do seem very busy.'

'So busy. You have to book a week in advance for the popular slots. You should come some time. It's fun and very good exercise. Gets the heart rate up, I can tell you.'

The vet did, indeed, look strong, slim and healthy. She'd

probably be one of those fit-as-a-fiddle old ladies, like her mum. 'Takes your mind off your worries for a bit, too. The game will cheer me up this afternoon, I'm sure.'

'Enjoy it, and thanks again.'

Dr Davies gave Jake a pat and a little biscuit in the shape of a bone. His tail moved limply, and he gave her his poor long-suffering patient look, or perhaps his 'Don't you think I deserve another biscuit?' look. 'Don't tell all the other dogs,' she instructed, slipping him a second biscuit. 'And, Julia, don't hesitate to give me a ring if you're worried, and if you don't see a significant improvement in a couple of days, bring him back.'

'Will do, thanks.'

'See you on the hill path.'

'We'll be there. See you on the path.'

3

Julia felt a literal and figurative spring in her step as she made her way around the village. It was such a delight to have warmer weather. The winter had seemed endless. Jess had left to go back to Hong Kong just as autumn tipped into winter, and Julia had found herself feeling rather glum. It was odd. She had become accustomed to her daughter's absence over the first two years that she was away, but after Jess's month-long visit to Berrywick, Julia missed her every day. Everything from the sight of Jake, whom Jess loved so much, to the empty spare room, reminded her of Jess. Her mood wasn't helped by the coldest, wettest winter on record. Days on end went by without a glimmer of sun. Fortunately, Jake's high spirits and Sean's loving company had kept her from falling too deeply into a full seasonal funk.

A poet (Julia could not, just this instant, recall which poet it was) had written: 'If winter comes, can spring be far behind?' The answer, it turned out, was, 'Yes, Mr Poet, since you asked, it can be *very* far behind, in England, at least. So don't get your hopes up.'

Finally, this week, the tardy warmer season had come

tiptoeing in with a couple of bright, sunny days, and Julia felt a lovely lifting of the spirits. She had left Jake at home to rest his tail – much to his disappointment – and spent the morning doing errands in the village shops.

Filled with spring ambition, she'd bought packets of tomato seeds, as well as basil and mixed varieties of lettuce. At the butcher's she'd bought four free-range lamb chops, two each for her and Tabitha, who was coming for supper and, as her best friend had put it, 'A big FAT chat.' She'd posted a letter. Dropped off a pair of shoes to be re-soled. She even remembered to buy the chocolate she needed to make the brownies for her book club meeting later in the week.

'You are a wonder of efficiency, Julia,' she told herself. Usually, she addressed her random comments to the dog, but in his absence, she talked to herself. She wasn't sure which indicated more robust mental health.

As she walked home, she admired the verges and the gardens that were coming into their spring finery. Mrs Sommers' crab apple tree was a mass of pink flowers, and snowdrops and daffodils popped their heads out of the grass around its trunk. She resolved to plant a crab apple this year. It might take a while to reach the finery of Mrs Sommers', but Julia had learned more patience in the last two years. Julia had been so busy enjoying the scenery and mulling over her list of garden tasks that she was almost surprised to find herself at her own front door. Jake's excited yelps brought her thoughts to the present. 'How's the tail?' she asked as she let herself in. It certainly looked a little perkier than it had the previous day, when they'd been at the vet. He looked a lot perkier all round. She touched the place where it had been tender, and he didn't yelp, just moved away a step.

'I know, I know. I went without you. It was all shopping. Don't worry, we'll walk a little later.'

After 'trunch' – an invention of Julia's that did the work of a late lunch and an early afternoon tea – they set off. Not wanting Jake to swim with a sore tail, Julia decided against the river walk, in favour of what the locals called 'the hill walk' – the very walk that she often saw Eve on. It involved a short drive, but was worth the effort for the lovely views over the whole county on a clear day. Half of Berrywick seemed to have had the same idea, because the dog walkers were out in force, even though the weather had turned rather nippy. The sky was still bright and blue, but there was a chill to the lively breeze that had picked up since the morning.

When they got to the hill, old Aunt Edna was tottering about the edge of the small car park, wreathed in layers of scarves and assorted drapery. Her only concession to the advent of spring was a boa of bright plastic flowers that looked as if it had been salvaged from a child's dress-up box. She stopped when she saw Julia, and addressed her in a loud voice.

'High time for a walk. Very high time, watch your step now.'

'Yes, thank you, Edna. I hope you are well.'

'Up and down, up and down, down, down. Hill and dale.'

'Well, enjoy your walk, Edna.'

Julia found it best to respond courteously and briskly, as if everything Edna said made perfect sense. Which it didn't. It was mostly fairly incomprehensible, although she did have occasional eerie flashes of what seemed like insight, or even premonition.

Edna bent down and fixed Jake with a piercing look. 'And don't let the tail wag the dog, dog.'

Jake gave Julia a worried look, which only dissolved when Edna wandered off.

'Ah, she's harmless, Jake,' Julia said with a laugh. 'Poor woman probably weighs less than you do. Now let's get moving, warm us up.' She crossed her arms and rubbed her shoulders, wishing she'd brought something warmer.

Julia left the car park along the small path between some trees that soon split into two. The higher path branched off to the right, heading up and over the hill. The lower, left-hand path continued round the bottom of the hill. It was a longer but flatter walk. Julia turned right, for the higher path and its views.

The small, sturdy figure coming briskly towards them was unmistakably Sebastian, trotting along ahead of his mum, Nicky. He dropped to his knees to press his face into Jake's neck. Jake leaned into his small friend, who whispered endearments.

Nicky, on the other hand, never whispered. She spoke loud and clear and in an endless stream: 'Oh my word, Julia, where did that wind come from? I can't stop and chat, we're on our way to the church hall. Just came up here for a quick walk to burn off some energy, if you know what I mean. Can you believe I left my coat at the hall, the very day I need it, what with the wind getting up again. Like I was saying to Kevin, you can't trust the weather until May, and even then it's liable to sneak up and... Sebastian, don't kiss Jake. How many times, I ask you, how many times have I told you: no kissing dogs? Anyhow, Julia, I'd love to stay and chat, don't think me rude, but I must be going. Come on now, Sebastian, stop dawdling.' And with that, they continued down the path, Julia having not had to utter one word of her own.

The thing about a conversation with Nicky was that when it ended, you really appreciated the silence. The path had emptied out, and Julia and Jake kept up a good pace. She started to warm up a bit and enjoy the scenery. As they climbed up the hill, the view opened up before them in the spaces between the trees, the patchwork of fields punctuated with swathes of woods, and little toy towns connected by roads and lanes. Puffy clouds scudded in from the south. They really did live in a beautiful part of the country. She'd been lucky to end up here, of all the places. Tabitha had moved here years ago, and Julia had visited, and liked it. So when Julia was retiring, divorcing, and eager for a change, she thought that if she was going to move from London, she might as well live where she had at least one good friend. And how well it had worked out.

This pleasant stock-taking of her life was interrupted by Jake, who took off barking. It must be the rabbits! Damn, she should have remembered to put him on the lead before she got to the rabbity part of the trail. She felt awful. He was supposed to be keeping calm and not straining his tail.

His tail didn't seem to be giving him any trouble. It wagged back and forth. In fact, he looked absolutely delighted with life.

'Jake, come in!'

He did stop. Not because he was obedient, but because he'd reached his destination. There at the side of the path was not a rabbit but an elderly dog.

'Hello, old chap,' she said. Walking towards him, she saw it was Eve's dog. He was an indeterminate mix of small and medium breeds, shortish in the leg, longish in the tail, reddish brown fur turning grey at the muzzle, kindly hazel eyes, and a sweet temperament.

'Are you lost, Fergus? Where's Eve?' She looked around, but saw no sign of his owner.

It was very odd for the dog to be alone. He was hardly the type to run off, and if he did, Eve would have no trouble catching him. He was hardly speedy, and she was as fit as a fiddle.

'She must be around here somewhere, she can't have gone far.' Julia directed this at the dogs, who did not seem to be listening.

'Eve!' she shouted. 'Eve, are you here?'

There was no answering call. No rustling of the bushes.

Fergus took a few stiff steps towards the edge of the cliff and turned to look up at Julia expectantly. She wasn't sure what to do next.

They were at the top point of the hill. She could see down the path in both directions and there was no sign of Eve. She walked to the edge, to the lookout point, the highest point in the area, at the top of a small granite rock face, and overlooking the whole county. She could see for miles towards the horizon. She saw a railway, and a train ferrying passengers in the direction of Oxford. A bird of prey hovering in the middle distance. But no Eve. 'She wouldn't have gone down this way, it's too steep,' she said to herself, turning back to the path.

Fergus toddled stiffly towards her, and lay down at her feet, whining.

She looked down at the dog. 'Ah, you poor old boy. Are you tired? Have you been running around looking for your mum? I'll take you home, we'll give her a ring, shall we? Come on.'

She slapped her thigh encouragingly, but the dog didn't budge. He just stared mournfully over the edge of the cliff.

'Are you going to make me carry you?' He looked briefly up at her, sighed, and returned his gaze to the bushes below. It was Julia's turn to sigh. Her afternoon walk had been altogether less relaxing than she'd hoped. And now she would be carrying an elderly dog back down the hill.

She bent to scoop him up in her arms, her eyes on the edge of the path. It would be unpleasant to lose one's footing and fall at this point of the walk. The cliff really was quite high. She glanced over the edge. The sunlight reflected off something white in the bushes below, glinting and catching her eye. She narrowed her eyes and frowned against the glare. At the bottom of the cliff face she could now make out the shape of a person, lying on the ground. Funny place to take a rest. Julia's view of the person was half obscured by the plants growing on the rock face and on the ground below, but there was something odd about the way they were lying, arms and legs akimbo.

Julia struggled to make sense of the situation. Her mind grappled with questions – How did the person get down there? Were they resting, splayed out in that strange way? Perhaps they were camping? – but produced only one answer.

That whoever was down there was dead.

And Julia had a horrible feeling that she knew who it was.

4

DI Hayley Gibson's car slid into the parking area just as Julia came down the hill with Jake and Fergus. She had phoned Hayley as she started walking down the hill, and told her about the person she'd seen at the bottom of the cliff.

'They must have fallen from the top path. They're not moving. I am going to go down and see if I can help them. I think I can find the place. It's a little off the path, close to the foot of the cliff. Will you come? And I think we should call an ambulance, too.'

Through the phone, she heard the wheels of Hayley's chair as she pushed it back from her desk. 'On my way. It's not far. I'll be there in ten. DC Farmer can phone the ambulance from the car.'

'It'll take me a little while to get down. I've got Jake, and I found a dog, he's Eve Davies' dog. Hayley, I can't see from up here, but I'm worried the body might be her.'

'Let's not jump to conclusions. I'm on my way. Meet me in the parking area. You can show me where you think the bo — where the person is.'

True to her word, Hayley arrived if not in ten minutes,

exactly, then in less than twelve. Her car door was open before Walter Farmer had quite brought the speeding vehicle to a halt. She walked briskly to Julia and said, 'Let's go,' with her customary lack of preamble.

'The dogs should stay.' Fergus was walking stiffly on his short legs, and breathing heavily. He wasn't young and already he'd been up and down the hill.

'DC Farmer, can you take care of the dogs? Maybe give them some water,' Hayley called to Walter over her shoulder, already on the move.

Julia handed over Jake's lead, and left him and the panting Fergus with the young constable.

She ignored Jake's pleading look and led the way to the lower, left-hand path, the one that ran round the bottom of the hill. 'When the medics come, send them this way,' Hayley called to Walter.

A couple of tourists, who were wandering about reading the signs on the trees and taking photos, looked alarmed.

Walter could handle them, and the dogs. The women needed to get to the fallen walker. Julia set off briskly. She should have been tired, all the walking she'd done, but the adrenaline and worry energised her. Hayley hadn't thought to change out of her work shoes. They were rather unsuitable for trail walking, but she kept up.

As they rounded the corner, the cliff face came into view a little way away. Julia pointed up, squinting against the light.

'That's where I was standing when I saw the body, near those trees. I couldn't see well because of the bushes halfway down. So I reckon she's up ahead, just below those bushes, somewhere over there.' She gestured broadly ahead of them.

'She? Are you sure?' As she spoke Hayley continued briskly along the path, with Julia puffing slightly to keep pace.

'No, but my first thought was that it was a woman. Something about the shape, the light fabric. And Eve's dog... but I could be wrong. I hope I am.'

Ten minutes later, they were in line with where Julia thought she'd been when she looked down.

'Around here somewhere, but not right on the path. Closer to the cliff.'

The two women left the path and walked over the rough ground, overgrown with thorny brambles that caught on their legs and threatened to trip them up. If Hayley was struggling with her imperfect footwear, she said nothing of it. They hadn't gone more than a few yards off the path when they saw it up ahead. The tangle of golden-brown hair amongst the brambles. The face was turned away from them. Definitely female. And the hair...

'Stop,' Hayley said, putting her arm out to bar Julia's path. 'We don't want to tramp around the scene.'

'Oh, right, but shouldn't we see if she's...'

'I'll go and look. Wait here.'

Hayley edged around the bushes to get a line of sight on the woman.

'Damn,' she muttered under her breath.

'What? Hayley, what can you see?'

'Dead. It looks like her neck's broken.' Hayley sighed deeply.

Julia walked in a wider arc, past the bushes, to a spot where she could see the body. It was awkwardly positioned, one arm under the body, the other stretched out to the side, the head at an unnatural angle. From here, Julia could see the face, with a sprinkling of freckles across the nose standing out against the pale grey skin. She recognised them, and the generous mouth that had always been ready with a smile for Jake.

It wasn't exactly a surprise, but Julia still felt a cold wave of shock when her suspicions were confirmed. 'Oh no, Hayley, it *is* Eve. You know. The vet.' Julia's chest felt tight with shock. She had seen Eve so recently, and liked the younger woman so much. She couldn't believe that she was now lying dead at the foot of a cliff.

The sound of feet on the path behind them heralded the arrival of the medics, a man and a woman, between them carrying an orange stretcher, and a bag of equipment that would be of absolutely no use at all to Eve Davies.

A frighteningly fit-looking older couple came power-walking down the path from the other direction, stopping almost nose to nose with the medics. 'Oh, heavens,' said the woman, taking in the scene. 'What happened?'

'Accident scene, keep clear please.' The couple looked at the medic in alarm and scuttled off the path to give the brush with death a wide berth.

'Walter,' Hayley barked into her phone. 'You'd better get down here. Bring the tape. We need to keep the walkers away from the scene. And we need a uniform here to start taking people's names. Maybe someone saw her fall.'

There was a brief silence on this side, during which Walter was presumably talking.

'Put the dogs in the car. Rufus can have a nap... Yes, Fergus, whatever his name is... Yes, of course, you're right. Leave the window open... And Walter, call the coroner. Yes, I'm afraid so. Very much dead.'

Hayley put her phone in her pocket, then thought better of it. She pointed it at the victim and took a photograph, and then another.

One of the medics was crouched next to poor Eve. She felt her pulse and checked for breathing, following procedure. 'Seems like she's been dead an hour or two.' She looked up to the cliff, from which the woman had fallen. 'It's quite a drop, but survivable, I would think, if she hadn't fallen in this way. Must have hit her head, snapped her neck. Very bad luck.'

'Out on a little walk, lose your step, next thing you're on the ground, twenty foot down, and CRRCK.' The second, younger, medic made a truly horrid crunching noise, and then looked shamefaced. 'Awful situation, poor thing,' he added, to make it clear that he wasn't unsympathetic, merely alert to the unpredictability of life, and to its inevitable conclusion. Julia rather saw his point.

The awkward moment was broken by Walter, who arrived with a roll of crime scene tape, saying, 'The dogs aren't too happy, but they are in the car with the window open. There was a chap there with his poodles and I asked him to keep an eye for a few minutes, until the other officers arrive. And the coroner's on their way. Where do you want the tape?'

Hayley swept her arm to indicate a wide circumference, taking in a fair bit of the path. Walter trudged through the undergrowth, waited for Hayley's nod, and affixed one end to a tree some few feet off the path. He set off again, following her pointed finger, unrolling as he went. It was a laborious process to watch, as he kept entangling the tape and himself on brambles and ferns. At one point he tripped, and only just managed to right himself. Hayley, who had gone back to the task of taking photographs – this time of the body – grimaced at the crashing about.

'Just go round, Walter. Take the easiest route.'

When Walter had secured the scene, Hayley instructed him to go back and seal off the entrance to the path.

'I'll go with you, Walter,' Julia said. 'I'd best get back to Jake. Oh dear, what are we going to do about Fergus?'

'Fergus?' Hayley's mind, now, was on the scene in front of her. She didn't have brain space for the names of random dogs.

'The other dog. He belongs to Eve's mother.'

'Eve's mother.' Hayley looked grim at the thought of what that meant. 'Someone's going to have to go and break the news to her. I can't leave here yet. I need to go up to the top of the cliff to see where Eve fell from.'

Walter stared at his superior officer, pale-faced, knowing what was coming but silently begging her not to make him go. Julia knew he'd had to do that horrible job on at least one occasion, and was devastated by it.

'Walter, will you tell the next of kin, please?'

Hayley waited for him to acknowledge her question, which was, in fact, as they all knew, an instruction. He gave her one last pleading look and then nodded, sadly. 'Yes, DI Gibson. I'll go.'

'Julia, do you know where she lives?'

'She lived with Eve. I've never been to their house, but I know it's somewhere a little out of the village, on this side. That's why they walk this path so regularly.'

'They must be close. Walter, call in to the station and get an address.'

He nodded, but didn't phone. Instead he addressed a question to Julia. 'Do you know the mother at all?'

'A little. Enough to say hello to, but not much more. I see her on the path from time to time, because she often walks with Eve. She introduced us. Now what was her name, it's on the tip of my tongue.'

Julia hated this aspect of ageing – knowing she knew a piece of information, but not actually being able to bring it to mind. Fortunately, it usually came out of hiding and slipped into her consciousness by some mysterious mechanism, and in its own good time. As was the case now. 'Kay, that's her name. Kay Davies.' It was a relief.

Walter turned to Julia. 'I was thinking, since you know her, and you're a social worker and all, maybe you could come with me.'

Just when she thought her day could get no worse, a lower bar appeared. 'Really, it's not my place, Walter. I don't have any official role here. I'm retired. And I don't really *know* her, only to say hello to on the path. It just wouldn't be right for me to come along.'

Walter could appear rather dim, but he was canny in his way, 'You could help me with Fergus. Poor boy. You found him, after all. And you're so good with dogs.'

'It's true, Julia,' Hayley said. 'You are good with dogs. And with people. Would you go with Walter? We would both appreciate it, and I'll be along as soon as I can.'

Julia felt she was being backed into a corner by the two of them, which was quite annoying. On the other hand, she was not immune to flattery. She *was* good with dogs and people, and she did feel sorry for young Walter Farmer. And for Kay Davies. She wavered, and then succumbed.

'All right. I'll come with you. But I'm just your backup person. For Fergus. This is your show, Walter.'

'Thank you, Julia, thank you.' He looked so grateful that she didn't entirely regret her decision.

'Thank you,' Hayley said, and nodded.

Julia and Walter returned to the car, where a tall, thickset man was pacing back and forth, keeping an eye on Jake and Fergus in the car, with the window open. A baseball cap was pulled low over his forehead.

'All right?' he said, looking up.

'Yes. There was an accident.'

'Ah, bad luck,' he said, shaking his head.

'Thanks for keeping an eye on them.'

'No worries, I like dogs.' He, himself, had two poodles, a brown and a black, on leads. They seemed like a rather unlikely choice of breed for the man, but as Julia knew from her extensive studies of the dogs and owners of Berrywick, you never could tell.

Walter opened the car door to check on the dogs, patting the old Fergus and speaking to him in a comforting murmur.

'What do you think happened?' the man asked.

'We don't know yet. Someone slipped from the top, by the looks of things.'

'Treacherous up there.' The man shook his head sadly. 'Very treacherous.'

As soon as Kay Davies opened the door, and saw the young policeman, and the older woman carrying her elderly dog, she knew that the news was bad. Julia had watched the same progression of facial expression dozens of times, when she'd rung the doorbells of strangers. Polite enquiry as to who might be calling unexpectedly, recognition that this was an official visit, confusion, mild concern, and growing panic.

Mrs Davies was quicker off the mark than most. 'Is Fergus all right? And where's Eve?'

She glanced behind them as if Eve might appear, but all she could see was their two cars, and Jake's mournful face looking at her out of the window of Julia's Fiat.

'Mrs Davies, I'm DC Farmer and I think you know Julia Bird. May we come in?'

'Where's Eve?' she said, not budging.

'There's been an accident, ma'am. She fell. If we could come in, please.'

Kay Davies stepped back, opening the door to give them access. Julia put Fergus down and she and Walter followed him past the older woman into the little hallway next to the front door, with its coat hooks and space for boots. Fergus stopped to give a pair of muddy walking shoes a good sniff and wandered off into the house.

Kay was all efficiency, grabbing a jacket from the hooks and instructing them. 'Wait here. Let me get my handbag. Which hospital is she in? Do I need to bring her toothbrush and her pyjamas, do you think? Or will she be home today?'

Walter's face flushed, then seemed to drain of all colour.

His sparse facial hair, badly shaved, stood out against the white skin. He had a couple of spots on his chin, and in his nervous pallor, he looked about sixteen years old. He stammered, 'Mrs Davies, she's...' He cleared his throat and tried again. 'I'm sorry to inform you that Dr Davies fell on the cliff path. Actually, from the path. The impact was fatal.'

Kay looked at him, blinking as if trying to make sense of it all, and turned to Julia, as if for an explanation. Julia took her hand and said, 'I'm so sorry, Kay. Eve fell off the clifftop path. I'm afraid she's dead.'

It was Julia's experience – and she had, regrettably, had a fair bit of experience – that there were three basic responses to very bad news. Most often, the recipient would be simply unable or unwilling to take in the terrible truth. They would seem to be confused, in denial, believing there must be some terrible mistake. Another common response was to be utterly overwhelmed, crying, shrieking, fainting, falling to the ground. The third response was to be shocked into a seemingly calm, almost unresponsive state. Kay Davies fell into the third group. 'I'd better feed Fergus,' she said, turning away from them, towards the house. 'It's past his supper time and he must be getting hungry.'

Kay, who had always struck Julia as a rather strong and forceful older woman, shuffled into the kitchen, her face blank and her eyes glazed. Walter looked at Julia, his eyes questioning. What should they do now? She gave a tiny shrug, and they followed. Kay was spooning dog food out of a tin into a bowl. Her movements had a mechanical quality, scooping up a spoonful, dropping it in, scooping up, dropping in, until the bowl was full to overflowing. It was far too much food for a little old dog, and she showed no sign of stopping. Julia took the bowl gently from her and put it down in front of Fergus.

'Mrs Davies, you've had a terrible shock. Can I make you a cup of tea? And perhaps you can tell me who I might phone. Is there someone who could come and sit with you? A friend or a relative?'

Kay looked at her in surprise, as if she'd forgotten she was there, or what for. She began to speak in a dreamy, dislocated sort of voice.

'Yes, that's a good idea. Tea. Phone.'

Walter, who was eager to have something practical to do while Julia took care of the personal side of things, turned the tap on to fill up the kettle, the sound of water drowning out a few words.

'Except, well, I don't have a lot of friends here. I only moved in with Eve a year ago. I was in Cheltenham before. The thing is, Eve is the one I would phone in a crisis, even though... even though she was very busy. Always very busy with her work. She was a vet, you know? A very good one. Loves animals, dogs especially. She'll do anything for them.'

Julia noticed how Kay slipped between present and past tense when speaking about her daughter, her brain struggling to make sense of this awful new reality.

'Can't abide cruelty or neglect of animals. She was on all sorts of committees and groups, mostly for the dogs, you know. So busy, she was. And she kept herself fit. The walking. That Padel. And something on the computer, yoga, I think. She wasn't married. I always hoped, but her work kept her so busy, and it was a bit late, I suspect. She turned forty in February. And well, now, of course, it's too... She'll never...'

Reality seemed to catch up with Kay, because she started to cry. She didn't sob, but made little sniffy choking noises. 'It's too late. Oh, I should have been a better mother. I've been awful, really. Caused her so much worry and trouble, I did. Poor girl, my poor Evie. I should have gone with her. I wasn't there, you know. I usually go, me and Fergus.'

'Yes, I know you do. I've seen you often,' Julia said.

'I wasn't up the hill with her today.' Kay paused for a

moment, staring at the kettle, as if wondering exactly why it was she hadn't been on the walk. Then she remembered. 'My knee's giving me trouble, you know. So I didn't go. I wasn't there.'

Walter put a cup of hot sweet tea in front of her and said, ineffectually, 'There there, Mrs Davies. Why don't you sit down.'

Instead, she flung herself into his arms, saying over and over again, 'I wasn't there... I wasn't there.'

5

The lunchtime crowd at the Buttered Scone was an even mix of locals and out-of-towners. The tourist season was picking up, and there were some lovely warm days forecast, which explained the prevalence of cameras, day packs, sensible shoes and exotic accents. As well as the popularity of the more expensive menu items.

Julia knew most of the others. Berrywick wasn't a very big village, and just about everyone in it wound up at the Buttered Scone every now and then. Unlike the visitors, who were eating the hand-caught artisanal smoked trout salad, and the organic lamb with home-grown vegetables, the locals were mostly eating Flo's renowned scones, which were roughly the size of a human head, but fluffy and buttery, or her home-made pies and toasties. Nothing wrong with Flo's toasties. In fact, Julia thought she might have just that herself.

Julia greeted the locals that she knew as she made her way through the busy restaurant to an empty table towards the back. The mood was rather subdued, and, unsurprisingly, the talk of the day was the terrible accident that had claimed the life of the local vet.

'Sad day, isn't it, Julia?' said local builder and handyman, Johnny Blunt, turning around in his chair at the table next to hers, so as to face her. 'Poor Dr Eve. She was lovely to my old Percy. I've had to take him in to see her many a time this last year or so, what with his hips and all.' Johnny had an ancient terrier who had looked to be on his last legs since Julia had arrived in Berrywick, but was still staggering gamely around the paths and fields two years later. She'd begun to wonder if he was in fact immortal.

'Lovely to my Jake, too,' said Julia. 'He hurt his tail by over-wagging, if you can believe that.'

Old Johnny Blunt gave a forceful cackle, but stopped abruptly, out of respect to the sad circumstances, tugged the sides of the blue knitted cap that he wore pulled down to his bushy eyebrows, whatever the weather, and said solemnly. 'She'll be greatly missed, will Dr Eve.'

'That's no lie,' said Flo, who had arrived behind Julia in her silent plimsolls, making her jump. 'And by her poor mum most of all. Just a year or so she's been living with her daughter. And losing her in this awful accident. Imagine how it must have been for Eve. The feeling of falling, waiting to hit the ground. And then, nothing. Kay will be haunted by it, that's a fact.'

Flo shuddered, and whipped the pen from its place clipped onto her apron, saying, 'Horrible, thing, horrible. We've carrot cake today. What'll you be having, Julia?'

Flo had a way of running her social commentary and her order-taking into each other in a seamless way that sometimes came out rather strange.

'Cheese and tomato toastie, please, Flo. I'm jolly peckish. I had a busy morning at Second Chances. Seems the visitors are back all of a sudden.'

'Right you are. It's been busy in here too, run off my feet I am. Not that I'm complaining. Happy for the business. And to drink?'

'Apple juice, please.'

'Coming up.'

'And a refill on the coffee if I may, Flo?'

Flo nodded to Johnny, and moved silently away to surprise some other patron. It wasn't more than a few minutes before Johnny turned around in his chair to speak to Julia some more. 'I'd better go and visit her, poor Kay.' Julia noticed that he was speaking at regular volume, which presumably meant he had his hearing aids in. Without them, he bellowed alarmingly. 'She'll need a friend. I was at school with her, you know? A year or so above me, she was, but I knew her quite well.'

Julia moved her own chair to avoid craning her neck.

'No, I don't think I knew that you were at school together.'

'We were. And her people lived down the road from where I grew up. Didn't see much of her once she moved away to Cheltenham, of course.'

One of the many things that had surprised and amused Julia about village life, was the way people spoke about relatively nearby places as if they were on another continent. Cheltenham was perhaps ten miles away, but the way Johnny Blunt talked about it, it might as well have been Johannesburg.

'We've connected again though, now she's back in Berrywick.'

'I saw the two of you having lunch together the other day,' said Flo, startling Julia for a second time. She leaned over and put a glass of apple juice on the table. She held the coffee pot in her other hand. 'I was wondering if it was perhaps a date you know. Johnny and Kay. Kay and Johnny.'

Johnny Blunt blushed an alarming purple and stuttered, 'Now, Flo, why would you say a thing like that?'

Julia noticed that he hadn't actually denied the relationship, but rather deflected the whole subject.

'Ah, you know me, Johnny. I'm a soppy old romantic at heart.'

There was a touch of sadness to Flo's smile, and Julia wondered if she was thinking about her own Albert, who was in prison, and would be for some years to come. It made Julia sad too, thinking of what he'd done, the lives he'd ended, and the lives he'd devastated, all in some hopeless quest to keep an ancient secret. Everybody had wondered if Flo might leave the village when he went away, but she was made of stronger stuff than that.

'Here you go then, Johnny,' Flo said, topping up Johnny's cup. 'Enjoy.'

Johnny sipped his hot coffee. Julia sipped her apple juice.

'I'm sure Kay Davies would appreciate your company, Johnny. I was there when the police told her, and she seemed so frail, so terribly sad.'

The old woman's rather eerie calm had quickly dissolved the previous afternoon, and she had wept into Walter's chest, leaving his blue shirt damp with her tears. Walter had looked over Kay's frail shoulder and the soft grey hair of her head, to meet Julia's eyes, his own filling with tears of sympathy.

'I'll go over there this afternoon.' From the way he said it, it was clear that Johnny Blunt didn't relish the prospect, but he was a kind man for all his gruffness, and he wasn't a coward. He would do the right thing and support his friend.

'You're a good friend.'

'She was in fine spirits when I saw her for lunch the other day. Better than she'd been in a while. I know she loved Evie, but it wasn't easy, moving in with her. A grown daughter. Not that Kay is one to complain.'

'It wouldn't have been a simple matter, you're right. Not for Eve either, I imagine. Having your mum live with you.'

'My impression...' Johnny hesitated, and continued carefully. 'My impression is that it was somewhat forced, you might say, by circumstances.'

Unlike many of the regulars of the Buttered Scone, Johnny Blunt did not talk freely, and he was certainly not a gossip. He lowered his voice and spoke tentatively – a first, in Julia's experience of Johnny Blunt. 'Financial circumstances, was my impression. Kay lost her money somehow, is my impression. That's why she came to live with Eve. Anyway, Kay said she and Eve had their issues. Eve worried a lot, she said. It wasn't easy. But last week, she said that she'd found a solution to the troubles, and that things would be much better in future. It's all in the past now of course, whatever it was, poor things. A right shame.'

This time, they heard Flo coming – she was talking to another customer on her way over. Johnny turned back to his cooling coffee. Julia awaited her lunch, tummy growling in anticipation.

'Toastie for you. This should keep you going till supper,' Flo said, and put down the golden slab of toasted sourdough bread oozing yellow cheese onto the plate. A slice of tomato and a single leaf of lettuce was a nod to decoration, vitamins and roughage. Julia felt momentarily guilty for ordering the toastie instead of something healthier, like a salad, or a bowl of tomato soup. Then a whiff of melted butter and cheese reached her, and she had no regrets.

'Yum, thanks, Flo. It'll more than keep me going. I will have to take Jake for a good long walk after this. He'll be mad for a walk anyway. He was home alone while I was working at the shop.'

'A dear chap, is our Jake. I'll see if there's not a bit of sausage for him.'

'Ah, Flo, you do spoil him.'

'Well, he's a good boy, mostly. And even when he's not he's a dear.'

There can be no one alive who doesn't love to hear their

children praised or their dogs complimented. Certainly, Julia felt a little glow of pleasure at Flo's words. And an additional glow of heat from the large, rich sandwich. It would all have been most pleasant were it not for her mind running through the events of the previous day, and through what Johnny Blunt had said about Kay having found a solution to her troubles with her daughter.

What could she have meant by that? What troubles was she referring to? And what kind of solution had she found? Julia Bird's mind was unsettled, to say the least.

6

Detective Inspector Hayley Gibson popped her head round the door that led from the reception area to the offices beyond. She caught Julia's eye and made a small 'this way' gesture with her head. Hayley's movements were efficient and precise, as if she was loath to waste any energy while accomplishing the task at hand. Her wardrobe was similarly motivated by efficiency and the absence of fuss.

Julia got up from her chair – one of a row of uncomfortable moulded plastic chairs along the wall – and walked past Cherise, the desk sergeant, who was being regaled by a very determined woman with what seemed to Julia to be an unnecessarily convoluted and acrimonious story about a plum tree. She heard the desk sergeant say apologetically, 'Yes, I understand it's spring, and the blossoms... and the bees... but even so I'm afraid you can't lay a charge...' and then Hayley closed the door behind them. Julia was a little sad to leave the mystery unresolved.

. . .

It was always something of a shock to see Hayley's office, so at odds with her precise and efficient habits and manner, with its maelstrom of papers, sticky notes and tottering piles of files. 'Tea? I could wash a mug,' Hayley offered, not very encouragingly. Julia was rather in the mood for a cuppa, but when she looked at the three used tea mugs lined up on the far edge of the desk, each with a soggy tea bag languishing at the bottom inside a ring of elderly tea stain, she decided it wasn't such an appealing prospect after all.

'No tea for me, thanks. Why did you want to see me? What can I do for you?'

'Thank you for coming in. It's about Eve Davies.'

Julia nodded. This was hardly a surprise.

'The forensic report has come in, and there are some questions, or rather, anomalies.'

Julia nodded again, and waited.

Hayley picked up a folder and opened it to reveal a sheaf of papers and a stack of photographs – the old-fashioned kind, printed out, not glowing on a phone screen. She picked up the top photograph and frowned, then tossed it onto the desk in front of Julia.

'You recognise this.'

Julia did, of course. In fact, it gave her a little chill. 'That's the path at the top of the hill. That's where I was when I saw the body. That's where Eve fell from.'

'Right. It seems to me, though, that it's not such an easy thing, slipping off that path. I mean, look. It's a good three feet from the path to the edge.'

'That's true. In fact, I only saw her body because of the dog, Fergus. He was on the cliff side of the path and wouldn't move, so I walked over and bent down to pick him up. Maybe that's how Eve fell. Maybe she followed the dog, and then went over to the edge.'

'Possible, possible,' Hayley said. 'So she walked over, and then what?'

'I suppose she lost her footing.'

'The ground is flat and quite even. It hadn't been raining, so it wasn't slippery or muddy or wet. There are a few rocks around, but it's certainly not tricky terrain, and Eve was quite an experienced hiker, and generally quite athletic, what with the yoga and Pilates and Padel. Not one to fall over her own feet on a flat surface. It wasn't even windy.' Julia noted how Hayley had already found out quite a lot about Eve Davies.

'Maybe she tripped over something else? Perhaps she tripped over the dog.' Julia almost added that she quite frequently tripped over Jake, but didn't want Hayley to think she was some doddering old woman.

'Tripped over the dog, right at the edge of the cliff, and fell to her death? It seems so... unusual.' Hayley frowned.

'I suppose that's what an accident is. A brief moment in time when someone loses concentration, or there's some disruption, or distraction, or mishap, and the unexpected happens, and the consequences are inexplicably dire.'

Hayley sighed, and fanned the pictures out in her hand, as if she was playing poker. She snapped them closed, tapped the edge of the pile against the table, and put them down.

'How well do you know Dr Davies?'

'Not well, as I said. She's Jake's vet. We would chat when I brought him in, you know how it is, exchange pleasantries, and a bit of news. But mostly she liked to talk about dogs. She was mad about dogs. I've seen her at village events, and meetings. And we would chat occasionally when we met on the path, the same path she fell from. I like her. Liked her. She was smart, good with her human and animal patients.'

'Did she seem to be in good mental health?'

'Yes. She seemed, I don't know... principled, engaged. She cared about the world.'

'Cared in a worried sort of way? Was she depressed?'

'She was a bit upset when I saw her last,' admitted Julia. 'But I got the impression that she'd got involved in something distressing, and that was what had got her into a stew. She didn't know how to handle something, and was questioning if she could make a difference.'

'Got herself involved in something distressing?' Hayley's eyebrows seemed to be nudging her hairline. 'Questioning if she could make a difference?'

'She was always on this or that mission, this or that committee. She often had a petition going at the front desk, some local drama or animal-related controversy. I got the feeling it was something like that. She said she was worried that something terrible was going to happen.' Julia sighed. Something terrible had, indeed, happened, although she doubted very much that this was what Eve had meant.

'That sounds a bit like she might have been feeling depressed?'

Julia was quiet for a moment. 'Yes, I think she was down about the hopelessness of it,' she admitted. 'The thing that was worrying her.'

Hayley took a moment to digest this, then carried on with her questions.

'What do you know about her private life?'

'Oh, there would be better people than me to tell you about that.'

'Yes there are, and I'll ask them too. But what do you know? Did she have a boyfriend? Girlfriend?'

'Not as far as I know.'

'Have you heard anything else? No gossip from the Buttered Scone?'

Hayley said this with an ironic lift of the eyebrows that acknowledged Julia's fondness for the place that was well known to be Busybody Central.

'Oh, actually yes. Not really gossip, but I bumped into Johnny Blunt there yesterday. He mentioned that Eve's mum had been living with her for about a year – financial reasons, was his understanding – and that it wasn't entirely a peaceful transition. Apparently there was some friction there. It's not easy, having your mum move in with you as an adult.'

Hayley frowned again. 'Well, *that* doesn't sound like something worth throwing yourself off a cliff for.'

It took a moment for Hayley's words to sink in.

'Hayley, you don't honestly think that she...'

'From what I've heard about Eve, it would surprise me, but it's a possibility I have to consider, based on the forensics. The path is set well back from the edge, and even if she'd walked over, it's hard to imagine how she could have slipped, or tripped. I think it's possible that she jumped, to be honest. Maybe she felt too hopeless. Maybe the local drama was too much for her this time.' Hayley gave a sigh, as if *this* was something that she could relate to.

Julia was surprised by the strength of her visceral reaction to this theory of Hayley's. She wouldn't even consider it. She *knew* it wasn't true. She *knew* Eve wouldn't take her own life. Yes, she had been a bit down the last time they spoke, but Eve wasn't the type of person who gave up. She was a fighter.

She breathed deeply and slowly to calm herself, and told Hayley as much: 'I know you have to consider all the options, Hayley, but I'm almost one hundred per cent convinced that you're on the wrong track here. There's nothing in her behaviour or circumstance that makes this make sense.'

'Yet. We still have to interview her friends and family.'

'Right, of course. I don't know what will turn up, but whatever it is, I don't believe Eve jumped.'

'Why are you so sure?'

Julia thought about this. Why was she so sure?

'For a start, she had the old dog with her. She would never

do that to Fergus. Leave him alone up on the hill, with no guarantee that anyone would find him.'

'Suicidal people are generally past the point of thinking about other people. Or other dogs,' countered Hayley. 'But I suppose your logic makes a fair amount of sense in this particular case.'

'Besides, Hayley, if she wanted to end it, it's such a risky way to go about it. Remember what the paramedic said? She said it was only by chance that she broke her neck and died.'

'True. She said Eve landed badly when she fell. It was more likely she would have lived with a horrible injury.'

'And she's a vet, remember. She had access to all sorts of medications. She could have found a much easier way to take her own life, if that's what she really wanted to do.'

'You make some strong arguments, Julia. If she wanted to take her life, she could have done it easily and painlessly. This risky method doesn't make sense, not unless it was completely on the spur of the moment. Which it could have been. I'll get Walter to do some more digging, interview her mother and her colleagues and friends, but...' Hayley looked momentarily defeated, but perked up somewhat at a thought. 'Maybe there is still a chance it was just a terrible accident after all.'

'Or...' The word that came out of Julia's mouth surprised her almost more than it surprised Hayley. 'Or could she have been pushed?'

7

It's a strange fact of life that even in the most terrible circumstances, life persists in going about its business. The earth turns. Day follows night follows day. Dinner follows lunch follows breakfast.

And the daily tasks are always with us. Dogs must be fed. Eggs collected. Clothes washed and hung out to dry. Julia had been out for hours, and she knew that she would have to do all of these and more on her return from the police station. And she still had to make something nice to take to her book club that evening. Lemon cake would be nice, she thought. She was eager to get home and get started, but Hayley wasn't finished with her.

'Take me through the walk,' Hayley said. 'Try and remember everyone you saw that day.'

'Okay, well, Aunt Edna was there in the car park, for sure.' Hayley rolled her eyes to the ceiling, not in an unkind way, simply acknowledging the fact that Aunt Edna, being away with the fairies, was about the worst possible source of information of all the citizens of Berrywick. She tried anyway. 'What did Edna say?'

'Honestly? Nothing that made any sense. She spoke to Jake a bit, as I recall. She does enjoy a good chat with Jake. But she said nothing that would be of any use.'

'Who else?'

'Nicky Moore. Sebastian was with her. They were on their way back to the village. She'd left something in the town hall. A bag maybe? Or was it an item of clothing?'

'I'll get Walter to talk to her.'

Or listen to her, knowing Nicky – Julia thought, but didn't say.

DI Walter Farmer arrived as if in response to his name. He knocked, and poked his head round the door. 'You need me?'

Hayley beckoned him in and said brusquely, 'Yes. I want you to interview people who were on the path when Eve died. In case it wasn't an accident.'

'Not an accident?' Walter's eyes were wide with astonishment. 'But surely...'

'Just investigating all possibilities, Walter. She might have jumped, or, as Julia would like us to consider, been pushed. Make a list. There's Aunt Edna, Nicky Moore, who else, Julia?'

Julia, flustered by the idea that Eve's death might not have been an accident, drew something of a blank. 'Those are the only two I can name, but there were others. Let me think. There was a jogger, a woman. I noticed how fast and fit she looked.'

'Description?' Hayley said.

'Fast and fit? That's all I remember about her. Sorry. And she didn't have a dog, which is a bit unusual. I usually remember the dogs. In fact, if I think about the dogs, maybe I'll remember the other people who were on the path. Yes! The huskies were there on Tuesday. There's a guy who has two huskies on those very long leads. Their names are Aurora and Comet.'

'His name?'

'Oh, I don't know his name. Because the dogs don't call him.'

It was quite a good joke in a mild sort of way, but it didn't get more than a flicker of the eyes from Hayley. Perhaps now wasn't the time for such wit.

'Anyone else?'

'There was a woman with one of those designer dogs.'

Hayley looked at her blankly.

'You know, those special crosses everyone has these days. Like Labradoodles are a cross between Labradors and poodles? Well, there are all these other sorts of hybrids. I stopped to ask her, and hers was a Schnoodle – a cross between a poodle and a schnauzer.'

'Do you know the name?' Walter asked. And added, for clarity. 'Of the woman.'

Julia shook her head apologetically. She knew neither the human's name nor the dog's name.

'Right, Walter, I think you've got enough to get started. Ask around and see if you can identify these people. And anyone else whose names we got on the day. You will need to ask them where they were, where they were going, if they know Dr Eve Davies, and if they saw her. Where she was at what time, who she was with – if anyone – and if they could ascertain anything about her state of mind or mood.'

Hayley turned to Julia. 'Maybe someone saw something that will give us more clarity. If she jumped, she might have stood there for a while, thinking. Someone you saw might have seen that.'

'Or if she was pushed, I might have seen the person who did it. It's a horrible thought. He – or she, I suppose, might have been on his way down when I was on my way up the hill.' Julia suppressed a small shudder.

Hayley frowned slightly. 'Don't go jumping ahead, Julia. There's no evidence that anyone pushed her. Walter, when you speak to these people, ask them who else they saw on the walk, then find them and interview them too – you know the drill.'

'I know the drill,' he said flatly, as if not relishing the task. 'Best I get onto it then. Make the most of the afternoon.' He stood up.

'Thanks, Walter. Keep me in the loop.'

'Will do, boss. Bye, Julia.'

Leaving the police station, she saw DC Walter Farmer driving away. His lanky frame was hunched over the steering wheel and she thought she could make out a little frown of concentration or concern on this forehead. He had a busy day or two ahead of him. As did Hayley Gibson. She had taken the other interviewing task – that of speaking to Eve's friends and family. It was the more delicate task of the two, and Julia didn't envy her having to do it. Right now, Eve's death was a tragic accident, a momentary lapse of concentration or a misstep or a loose rock. When a detective started snooping around asking questions, it would be a matter of hours before word was out that this accident might not have been quite so accidental.

Julia looked at her watch and did a quick calculation. It was already nearly three o'clock. Book club was at six. There wasn't time to make the lemon cake she'd intended to make to accompany the chocolate brownies she'd made the day before, and have it cool and iced in time to take it that evening. It would have to be scones. In the time she'd been at Berrywick, she had raised her baking game (admittedly from an extremely low base, as in, her baking skills were non-existent). Now, she had quite the repertoire, and could whip up a batch of perfectly fluffy, buttery scones in a matter of minutes. She didn't even need the recipe, although she always checked it, just to be on the safe side. Julia Bird was a cautious woman.

Luckily she had all the ingredients at home, as well as the

necessary toppings. Julia was a traditionalist, as far as scones were concerned. She had rich farm butter, her own homemade strawberry jam – excellent, if she did say so herself – and the thick clotted cream she bought from a local dairy farmer. Her mouth watered at the thought, and she hurried home from the police station to get started.

8

Jake lifted his head, ears cocked. Moments later, Julia heard Sean's car pull up outside the house, and the car door slam. And then again.

Jake was on his feet. He might not be the very cleverest dog in the world – he was not at all like that border collie on YouTube with a hundred-word vocabulary – but when it came to food and friends, he was genius level. He must have heard Leo's paws on the pathway after the second slam of the door, because moments later he was turning circles at the front door and whining.

Julia opened the door. She and Sean instinctively stepped back to avoid being knocked over by the ecstatic canines, who were a blur of tails and happy faces.

'Out you go, dogs, you can play outside,' Julia said, nudging Jake to the door with her foot. 'Come in for a moment while I get my coat.' She took Sean's hand, pulled him into the house, and shut the door. He hugged her hello, and nuzzled her neck.

'Hmmm. You smell good.'

'That's the scones you're smelling,' she said with a laugh. 'I made scones for book club. And chocolate brownies.'

'Oh no, it's definitely you.' He gave her a naughty, flirty smile, and leaned in for a quick kiss. 'But the scones smell nice too.'

The scones presided over the kitchen table. They were arranged on a plate in concentric circles, and each one its own circle of scone, cream, then jam. She'd made extras, which were in a cake tin in the pantry, awaiting their chance to brighten up a breakfast or teatime over the next few days. The brownies were in a tin, easy to carry.

'We'll have to get going pretty much immediately,' Julia said, looking at her watch.

'Pity,' he said. The mischievous glint in his blue eyes made her heart pound. Julia had imagined she might be done with romance when she'd got divorced at sixty. She felt, if not delighted at the prospect, at least resolved. She'd have friends and interests and a dog and a garden. If she didn't have a partner, well, that was okay.

And now here she was with her heart racing and a silly smile tugging at her lips.

'Penny for them?' Sean asked.

'Oh, they're worth much more than that,' she said. 'Come on then. I'll take the brownies. You bring the plate, let's go.'

The reading area was at the front of the library, next to a large window from which one might watch the comings and goings of the village – which were minimal at six o'clock on a Thursday evening, but still, it was a nice view. The cobbles glowed softly in the last of the day's light, and the trees rustled gently in the breeze.

The space was set up with comfortable chairs and a table with an urn of hot water, cups and saucers, teabags, milk and sugar. Julia put down the plate of scones which she had held carefully on her lap while Sean had driven them the short distance into the village. She opened the tin of brownies, and placed them next to the scones. There was already a fine-looking carrot cake on the table, presumably the work of Jane, who was talking to Tabitha, the librarian, at the counter, their voices bright and the conversation tinged with laughter and exclamations.

'Julia, Sean, welcome.' Tabitha beckoned them over, setting her baubles and bangles clinking and jangling. 'Jane was just telling me her wonderful news.'

'I'm a grandmother!' Jane said. 'Hannah had a little boy yesterday.'

'Oh how lovely!' Julia went over to give her a hug. Jane was a few years younger than Julia, and had a youthful manner. Her steel-grey hair was cropped into a funky style, and she radiated warmth and curiosity and good cheer. 'What a blessing.'

'It is, it really is. They're calling him Tom, after my dad.'

'And they're so lucky that you live nearby,' said Tabitha.

'I couldn't be happier.'

The door opened and two more members came in together. It was a punctual group. There was Diane, Julia's colleague from the charity shop. There was Dylan, the... what to call him? Boyfriend? Holiday fling? Friend? Whatever – the romantic interest of Julia's daughter, Jess, who was studying in Hong Kong, and had spent a month in Berrywick in the autumn. Julia tried on the thought of Dylan and Jess living nearby, and having a little baby called Tom. Although Julia's father's name was Norman, and she couldn't really imagine Jess going for that.

She shook the crazy thoughts out of her head – there was no grandchild in her near future, called Norman or anything else, and neither did she want one. Not yet. It felt as if she was in her second youth, romantically, at least.

'Julia?'

She turned to greet Pippa, the puppy wrangler. 'Isn't it the saddest news about poor Eve Davies? She was the vet for all my guide dog puppies. She was wonderful with the pups, and always made sure we got a special rate on the dog food. She did discounted work for the Guide Dogs association. It's the most terrible loss.'

'So very sad, Pippa.'

'And I heard that you found her, Julia.'

'I did. I happened to look off down from the ridge where she'd fallen.'

'I was there too, An hour or two before you found her, I think. Strangely, I saw her mother. I forget her name...'

'Kay.'

'That's it, Kay. I saw her when I was parking for my walk. She was getting into a taxi. Awful to imagine that when she was getting into Lewis's taxi to go off to the shops or home or wherever, her poor daughter might have slipped off that path. It must have been at around that time.'

Diane came over and joined them. 'Are you talking about Poor Eve?' Julia noted that Eve's name had been transformed. She was now universally referred to not as Eve, but as Poor Eve, with a capital P.

'Isn't it just awful?' Diane said. 'And her poor mother. My husband's mother knows her, and she says she's—'

Whatever Diane's husband's mother's revelation was, it was interrupted by Tabitha's call over the heads of the assembled book clubbers.

'Shall we get started?' she called forcefully, expressing it as more of an instruction than a question. Much as everyone loved books, it was sometimes quite a job to tear them away from the more general chatting, especially if there was an important subject to be teased out, examined, and discussed. They moved slowly into place, arranging themselves on the comfortable seating. Sean and Julia shared a small sofa. Immediately, Tabitha Too, the library cat, jumped up and sat between them like a chaperone, making sure their legs didn't touch.

Julia stroked the warm fur and enjoyed the rumbling rattle of the cat's purring, the rise and fall of its ribcage under her hand. Tabitha Too had been simply Tabitha, until Tabitha the Human was appointed librarian. The cat was now called Too, for short. Seeing as she was a very independent cat, and didn't come when called either Tabitha or Too or *pusspusspuss*, or respond to any sound but the opening of the small fridge where the milk and cat food was kept, it seemed like a reasonable solution to change her name rather than the librarian's.

The book clubbers read broadly and deeply, and were a lively lot with plenty to say about the books and about life in general. The format was quite fluid – mostly, people gave short reviews of books they had read and liked, and people borrowed them or didn't. Sometimes there was a theme, but mostly not. When the hour was up, Julia had three books – one police procedural, one late life uplit (this was now a thriving category, it seemed), and one encouragingly slim Commonwealth Prize short-lister. It was a selection which, she thought, covered all the bases, and all her likely reading moods.

When the book chat part of the evening was over, there was a restrained rush for the tea table. Julia couldn't help but watch a tad nervously to determine the relative popularity of her scones and brownies, and Jane's carrot cake, hoping for a good showing. Most people had all three. A good solution all round.

She found herself next to Diane as they left the minor crush around the urn.

'What were you about to say about Eve's mum?' asked Julia casually.

'Oh, yes. My mum-in-law knows her from Cheltenham. They lived on the same road and went to the same bingo game on a Thursday. Until Kay moved here to Berrywick last year, of course.'

'She moved to live with Eve, and now Eve's gone,' Julia said. It really was terribly sad.

'It won't be easy for her,' said Diane. 'My mum-in-law said she had to move. Financial reasons. Kay couldn't afford to live on her own in Cheltenham anymore, poor thing. Had to move in with her daughter. Eve was supporting her, from what I can gather. I wonder what will happen now?'

No wonder there was tension between mother and daughter. It sounded as if the living situation was forced on them by circumstance, rather than by choice. Likely neither of them was too happy. Julia remembered what Eve had said about finding her mother's lack of worry slightly annoying.

The room emptied quickly after tea, the members heading out into the cool night with their tote bags bulging with books, or piles of books tucked under their arms. As the others left, Sean straightened the furniture, while Julia helped Tabitha clear the cups and plates. When it was just the two of them in the little kitchen, Tabitha turned to her friend and said in an oddly tentative manner, 'Well, I've got some news.'

Julia was about to make a joke: 'Pregnant, are you?' or something along those lines, but she saw the shy smile on the librarian's face and just said, 'Tell!'

'I've had a poem accepted for publication in a poetry magazine. I finally got the courage to send one off, and they want to publish it in the next issue.'

'Oh that's wonderful! Well done,' Julia enclosed her friend in a huge warm hug. 'You are such a good writer. I always said so. And look! First time, a win!'

'Ah well, thank you, Julia. I'm very pleased, I must say.'

'This is just the beginning for you, Tabitha,' said Julia warmly. 'Booker Prize, here you come.' Julia knew that Tabitha had always wanted to write a novel – and in fact, was working on one. But so far, she hadn't had the courage to share her work – not even with Julia. Hopefully the success with this poem would convince her that she had a real talent. Julia felt genuinely excited for what the future might hold for her friend.

The library was soon back to normal, and Julia and Sean were in the car on the way back to her house.

'Thank you for driving me home,' she said, as they pulled up in front of the house. She released her seat-belt buckle, and when she turned back he was sitting still, his hands on the wheel.

'There's something I've been wanting to say to you, Julia.'

His voice was soft, and solemn. Whatever he had to say, it was something important. But it was unclear whether it was good important or bad important. She felt the blood rushing around her body, and thrumming in her ears. He cleared his throat. He seemed awkward. A horrible thought struck her. Surely he wasn't breaking up with her. Was he? Things were going so well. Or so she thought.

'Julia, I wanted to say that I love...'

The L word! She almost laughed with happiness. It had been a small niggling worry to her – one that she barely admitted to herself, it seemed so embarrassingly teenage – that neither of them had actually said 'I love you' to the other. But here it was. She looked at him sitting in the driver's seat, unusually awkward, and she was taken over by a soft feeling, a feeling of fondness, and gratitude and, yes, love.

Sean cleared his throat and continued. '... I wanted to tell you that I, um, I love... I love the time we have together, and how well we get along together, and I...and I wanted to thank you for that.'

'Oh.'

He looked surprised by her answer, and then concerned. Julia felt a flush creep over her face, as she scrabbled for an appropriate response.

'Oh, yes, Sean. Of course. Thank you. I love our time together too.'

It came out stiffly. She gave him a smile, equally stiff.

'Best get back to the dogs,' she said, opening the door and getting quickly out to hide her face, hot with embarrassment and shame and disappointment. 'I'll bring Leo out. Goodnight.'

9

Julia opened the door to the chicken coop, and rattled the bucket of grain.

'Chicky, chicky, chicks. Good morning. Out you come, girls,' she called. 'It's your playtime.'

Henny Penny led the way. She was the hen at the top of the pecking order, large and glossy, with a bossy, confident sort of bustle to her stride.

Julia had Jake on a lead. He didn't chase the chickens, and would never harm them, but she couldn't entirely trust him not to play over-enthusiastically with them when they were out in the garden, foraging, and give one of the more timid ones a fright. Henny Penny treated him like a harmless old friend. She walked determinedly over to him. He lay down, so they were more or less on eye level, and looked lovingly at her. The two of them had a special relationship of mutual adoration, with Jake being perhaps the more adoring. Henny Penny pecked something from the grass right next to him. He sighed with admiration. Henny Penny walked on, looking for the next titbit.

Julia's thoughts turned to her own relationship with Sean. Was she Jake in this scenario? The more adoring one who hung about waiting? Was Sean the more casual and carefree Henny Penny? Would he be walking on, looking for the next titbit? What even was a titbit, come to think of it? What a strange word. And what did it mean in the analogy?

She had a stern – if silent – word with herself. She was being very silly. She and Sean were grown-up humans with years of experience in relationships, a marriage each in fact, not to mention their respective training as doctor and social worker. Also, they were of the same species. A significant difference. And neither of them ate worms.

The other hens had exited the coop nervously and were now touring the border of the lawn, where it met the flowerbeds – a rich source of bugs and worms. They moved as a loose flock, staying together for comfort and protection, keeping a beady eye on Jake and giving him a generously wide berth, just in case. Their heads bobbed up and down jerkily in a way that always reminded Julia of puppets.

Part of her reaction to last night's interaction with Sean was simply embarrassment. She'd misinterpreted what he was going to say, and she felt sheepish about it. The deeper issue – of what the relationship meant to each of them, and where it was going, and if that was what they both wanted, in equal measure – was the more difficult one to deal with. To Julia's mind, their relationship struck just the right balance between intimacy and independence. They were close, and loving, and found each other attractive, and enjoyed each other's company. But they each had their own homes, interests and friends. It was about as perfect as you could get.

And yet...

Love. The word meant something. Or many subtly different things. 'I love being with you' or 'I love your company' was different from 'I love you'. Full stop. Did she want the 'I love you'? Why did it matter?

She sighed.

Yes. Yes she did.

She went inside, taking Jake with her, and leaving the hens to their scratching and pecking. Enough of this teenage behaviour. She would have tea and a scone over the morning crossword puzzle. Give her brain something more useful to do.

Julia put on the kettle and opened the cake tin, taking out one of the scones. She eyed the others with suspicion. The way they just sat there, temptingly, calling for lashings of butter and jam and cream, spelled trouble. She could feel them lurking, beckoning, eroding her 'only one' resolve. She needed to get them out of the house. Or eat them all right now, so that they couldn't tempt her – but that rather defeated the point. What she should really do was give them to someone, someone who needed a bit of a lift.

Kay.

The thought came to her in a flash.

She would give them to Kay. If anyone needed a bit of comfort, it was her. A couple of buttery scones wouldn't go amiss. Poor Kay.

Julia held the grieving mother in mind as she shepherded the chickens back into their coop (a more difficult manoeuvre than luring them out, but she had learned from Jake that animals responded well to the simple inducement of treats).

As she shepherded the chickens, she remembered what Pippa had said the night before. That she'd seen Kay in the parking area of the hill walk on the day her daughter died. At the very time, in fact. Odd, now that Julia thought about it. What was she doing in the parking area? And why had she called a taxi? Had she started the walk with her daughter and then abandoned it? A blister, perhaps? But then why hadn't she mentioned it? Julia cast her mind back to the conversations with Kay immediately after Eve's death. The implication had certainly been that Kay was alone in the house while Eve walked. What had she said? That she didn't go because of a sore knee. But then why was she in the car park?

The questions niggled at Julia, but she wouldn't find an answer unless Hayley Gibson decided to share information. Julia could hardly question the grieving mother herself.

Unless... Julia felt the familiar prickle of excitement that came with a good idea. Lewis Band. Pippa had said she'd seen Kay getting into Lewis's taxi. Lewis was a local chap who was based in Berrywick and mostly did short runs around and between the surrounding villages. The older folks liked to use his services, because they knew him and trusted him. He was old enough to be trustworthy, but young enough to be on the ball behind the wheel. Some of the much older folks remembered his dad, who was the village milkman. This was considered a plus – Lewis was the second generation of Bands to be driving professionally, one delivering milk bottles, the other, passengers. You couldn't go wrong with that kind of heritage. 'And at least you know Lewis isn't going to bonk you on the head for your pension money,' was a not uncommon refrain, despite a complete absence of anyone, ever, in the history of Berrywick having met this fate in any taxi.

Lewis arrived to fetch Julia, rather to the bewilderment of Jake. He sat with his head cocked to one side, trying to work it all out. What car was that? And who was in the car? Julia was getting in! Where was she off to? And why wasn't he invited?

'I won't be long, Jakey, don't worry,' she called to him from the car window, her cake tin on her lap. She turned her attention to the driver: 'Thank you, Lewis. I'm going to Kay Davies' house in Timber Lane.'

'Ah yes, I know it.'

'Of course, you brought Kay home the other day, I think.'

'I did. A sad day. A very sad day.'

'It must have been hard for you. I heard that you picked her up from the parking area at the hill on that very day her daughter died.'

Julia was deliberately playing it cool, as if she was just chatting, not scoping for information. She needn't have bothered with subtlety. Lewis was most willing – in fact, eager – to share his recent brush with death.

'Very horrible feeling, it was. I took the older Mrs Davies into Edgeley on an errand, and meanwhile her daughter – lovely girl, Eve – was falling to her death.'

'Did you wait there for her?'

'Oh yes, she wasn't gone more than five minutes. I managed to find a parking spot, which is like finding a hen's tooth around there in the Main Road, I can tell you. Goodness, it's like London, some days.'

Julia, who had lived in London for many years, and had once been stuck in a traffic jam near Buckingham Palace for a whole morning, doubted the comparison, but she didn't make anything of it. Lewis continued. 'Luckily, someone came out of a parking spot right there by the betting shop, as if they were waiting for me. I parked at the door and Kay just ran in. She was out in a jiffy, and we were on our way home. Of course, her luck changed after that.' He shook his head solemnly. 'Ah, there's no good news there. Poor Eve.'

'Why did you pick her up at the little car park, and not her home, d'you know?' Julia tried to make this sound casual. Had Kay been fleeing the scene?

'She quite often makes me get her there,' said Lewis. 'Says she doesn't want the neighbours talking. Never been clear what she thinks they're going to say.'

They sat in silence for the remainder of the short drive, Julia watching the trees and hedges slip by her window. She held the tin of scones lightly on her lap and let her mind go blank, the countryside passing blurry and unseen.

The car slowed.

'Here we are then. You give my best to Mrs Davies, now.'

'I will do, thank you, Lewis.'

For the second time that week, Julia entered Kay Davies' front door and stood in the little hallway amongst the coats. Fergus sniffed enthusiastically at her shoes, no doubt smelling Jake and Leo and chickens and the wide world.

'I hope you don't mind me coming unannounced. I wanted to check up on you and bring you a few scones for your tea.' Julia proffered her tin of scones to Kay.

'Oh that's very nice of you. I love scones. Do come in.'

Julia lingered in the hallway. 'I won't stay long, Kay. I don't want to be a bother.'

The older lady sighed. 'To be honest, I could use the company.'

'If you're sure...'

'I am. It's lonely without Eve around. I've been busy with the police, and the funeral home, and all that. But no one to have a cup of tea with. Come on, I'll put the kettle on.'

Kay pottered around the kitchen, filling the kettle, taking out cups. As she did so, she talked.

'Eve was at work all day, of course. But there was someone to talk to at breakfast or in the evenings, if she wasn't off on some committee or a walk or at the Padel place. It's a long day on your own, isn't it?'

Julia nodded in sympathy rather than agreement. She had, in fact, been surprised to find how easily she filled the days in Berrywick when she moved here. What with Jake and the chickens and the garden and her volunteer work at Second Chances and her various errands around the village and a few new friends, her days were quite full. But she said, 'It can be, but it's early days, you know. And you've had a terrible shock. It takes months to get back any sense of normality, so don't be too hard on yourself.'

Kay handed Julia two plates which she put on the kitchen table, then reached into another cupboard for a pot of jam.

'I suppose you're right.'

The kettle whistled. Kay walked over to the stove. 'Could you get the milk out?' she asked Julia. 'There's a little jug in the fridge.'

Julia reached for the fridge handle and stopped, taken aback by a picture of Kay and Eve stuck to the door of the fridge, a recent one by the looks of things. They were at a wooden table by a river, swans in the background.

'The last photo I have of her,' Kay said, following her gaze. 'At the Topsy Turvy Inn. I asked a chap at the next table to take it. It was just two weeks before she...'

'It's a lovely picture, Kay.'

Julia scanned the photograph for evidence, of what she hardly knew. Affection, closeness, or its absence. A premonition of things to come. It gave her nothing, of course. It was just a moment in time, two women with the rather fixed smile of people waiting for the photo to be taken. She reached for the handle again, but again she stopped, her attention on a piece of paper next to the photo, attached to the fridge with a magnet in the shape of a corgi. On it were printed numbers, which she couldn't make out clearly without her glasses. She might not be able to make sense of the content, but she recognised the logo.

'The milk?'

Julia opened the fridge and took out the jug. She handed it to Kay, and they both sat down at the kitchen table.

'It's nice of you to pop in. I only moved here from Cheltenham a year ago, and although everyone's friendly, and people have been very kind, I don't have many friends around here, except for my old school friend, Johnny.'

'Well, we could walk together some time if you would like. I know you used to walk with Eve.'

'I did. We enjoyed our afternoon walks. Although of course she was much fitter and younger than me. Not that it did her any good in the end. I can't help thinking, if I'd been there with her on the path that day it might not have happened. Everything would have been different, you know? She might not have fallen.'

'Oh, Kay. That's such a sad thought. Of course, you couldn't have known.'

Kay, who Julia had thought rather cold, was suddenly weeping.

'I should have been there with her,' she sniffed.

'It's not your fault.'

'Oh, you say so, but you can't know.' Kay couldn't speak properly for the tears.

'Where were you, when...' Julia asked in the mildest tone she could manage, without judgement or accusation.

Kay looked up at her, suddenly contained. She patted her eyes with her sleeve.

'I was here,' she said decisively. 'Right here at home.'

But Julia knew that she wasn't.

10

Hayley and Julia had only just settled into their chairs in Hayley's office when they were interrupted by a *ratatat* on the door frame. DC Walter Farmer was in the open door, bearing a folder of papers and an eager smile.

'Come in, Walter.'

'Hello, Mrs Bird. Julia.'

'Hello, Walter. How are things going? Have you been interviewing the walkers?'

Walter looked at Hayley. This was, after all, a police matter, and Julia was, after all, a retired social worker of no official standing. He wasn't giving out any information without the permission of the boss. Hayley nodded, indicating he should go on.

'Go on, Walter. What did the walkers see on the path?'

'Well, I spoke to...' he rifled through the papers. 'Seven people. Seven people who actually saw Eve. There were a whole lot who didn't see Eve and didn't know what I was talking about,' he said with a sigh, like he couldn't imagine such wilful ignorance. 'There was Aunt Edna.' He paused, silently acknowledging the uselessness of that interview. 'Nicky and

Sebastian. They led me to Pippa. I found the jogging lady, the one without the dogs, whose name is Gabi Harfield. And the man with the huskies – Karl Inger, his name is. And another fellow, who was...' Walter consulted his notes. 'Who was foraging for stinging nettles, apparently. To eat them. Takes all types. And a bird watcher, who was on the same bench for the whole time. Takes all types, as I said.'

'Did you find out anything useful?' asked Hayley, always one to cut to the chase.

Walter looked dejected. 'I'm afraid not. They all saw Eve alone on the path. Well, she was alone with the dog. She seemed fine, no sign of distress or anything out of the ordinary. Normal, as far as anyone could tell.'

'Did anyone speak to her?'

'Only Nicky, in passing. She said...' Walter flicked through his notes. 'She said they had a brief chat about Nicky's cat, who has arthritis, apparently, but has responded well to treatment. I'm afraid I got a bit confused about how much of what Nicky told me was what she said to Eve, and how much was just *her* telling *me* about the cat. Sorry I can't be more helpful, boss.'

'That's okay, Walter. You did your job. It's all useful. Dotting the i's and crossing the t's, you know.'

'Right. So do you think that she just slipped and fell?'

'From what you say, Walter, there's no evidence to suggest anything different. But I'm not ready to rule out the alternative.'

'That she took her own life,' Walter said, shaking his head.

'Or... what if she was pushed...?' Julia chipped in. 'If she was pushed, she'd look completely fine and normal – until she wasn't. And whoever pushed her is hardly likely to admit it.'

'No disrespect, Mrs Bird, but I think your unfortunate brushes with murder might have given you the wrong idea about the dangers of life in the Cotswolds,' said Walter.

'You're probably right, Walter. I hope you are. It's just that...'

'What?' asked Hayley.

'Well, the reason I popped in was to tell you something...' She rifled through her brain, and discarded the word 'suspicious', opting instead for the less accusatory, 'Something odd.'

The two police looked at her expectantly.

'Kay Davies was in the parking area the day Eve died. She took a taxi from there to Edgeley.'

'She did?' Hayley asked in astonishment. 'She didn't tell me that.'

'She didn't tell me either, Hayley. I happened to hear about it from the taxi driver, Lewis Band.'

'Actually, the jogger lady and that dog training woman saw her too,' said Walter, glancing at his notes. 'Kay Davies was in the parking area when she arrived.'

'Oh for goodness' sake, Walter, why didn't you mention that?' snapped Hayley.

'You asked if people saw Eve on the path,' said Walter. He sounded like a petulant child caught out being naughty. 'You didn't ask about Kay in the car park.'

Hayley briefly held the bridge of her nose and took a deep breath.

'I have spoken to you about being too literal,' she eventually said, through clenched teeth. 'This is a very good example of that. A very good example indeed.'

Hayley gathered herself, frowning thoughtfully and tapping a pencil against her desk. She opened her mouth to speak. Then closed it. Then opened it again to say curtly, 'So you questioned the driver, Julia? Lewis?'

It was clear that Hayley's irritation was in danger of transferring itself from Walter to Julia.

'Well, I didn't *question* him, no. But he drove me to Kay's, with the scones I had for her.'

'Is your car in the garage? Broken down, is it?' Sarcasm wasn't Hayley's usual style and she wasn't very good at it.

'My car is fine. I felt like a walk, except that it's quite a walk with a tin of scones, so I thought I'd get a lift one way and then walk home. Which is what I did. And we got talking, in the taxi, Lewis and me. Anyway, my point is...'

'I get your point. Kay Davies was at the parking area, and she failed to mention it.'

'Well, no. I mean, yes, but it gets even more strange. We got to talking about Eve's death, and when I asked her where she was when Eve died, she said, "I was here. Right here at home." But I knew for a fact that she wasn't at home. Because I knew she was in a taxi to Edgeley.'

'Doing what, I wonder.'

Julia couldn't help feeling a tiny spark of pride in herself for being able to provide the answer: 'Gambling. Lewis waited for her outside the betting shop. There was a piece of paper on Kay's fridge. I recognised the logo. I'm pretty sure it was a betting slip.'

'Well then, that answers that.'

'But why is she lying about where she was?' asked Julia. 'What is she trying to hide?'

Hayley shrugged. 'Who knows? Perhaps a chat to Mrs Davies will clarify matters.'

She reached for her phone. Julia and Walter watched her quick fingers tapping the screen. She put the phone to her ear. 'Mrs Davies? I'd like to just go over a few last details, if I may. Do you think you could come down to the station? Four would be fine, thank you.'

She turned to Walter. 'Find out about the will.'

'The will?'

Hayley sighed. Julia imagined her counting slowly to three in her head before she answered: 'Eve Davies' will, Walter. I want to know who benefited from her death.'

. . .

Julia left the detectives to their business. She was suddenly tired. It had been a long and emotionally draining week. A long day, too, what with trooping around Berrywick with scones and bits of information. She'd have a quiet night in, alone, and a quiet weekend. She had her summer vegetable seeds to put in, that's what she'd do. Her mind turned to planning. The tomatoes in the big pots at the kitchen door, where they get full morning sun, and she could keep a close eye out for snails. The salad greens in a mixed bed, also close by for snipping. The artichoke plants could go in the flowerbed opposite, they were so pretty with their silver-grey leaves. She'd have to clear a bit—

'Hey!'

A cyclist yelled as she veered, unthinkingly, into the road. She leapt back, knocking into a fellow pedestrian.

'Watch where you're going,' he shouted angrily.

She stumbled to right herself. Someone grabbed her arm.

'Julia! Are you okay?'

It was Diane, who she worked with at Second Chances, and who was in her book club.

'I'm fine. Sorry, did I knock into you? I was lost in thought.'

'Just a tap. Come, sit a minute. Catch your breath.'

Diane led her to the bench at the bus stop. Julia sat down gratefully. She felt quite shaken by the near miss with the cyclist.

Diane took a roll of fruit pastilles from her handbag, held them out towards Julia, and loosened the top one with her thumb.

'Sugar.'

Julia took one and popped it into her mouth. The crunch of the sugar that coated the outside, and the deep blackberry flavour of the pastille itself, took her back, soothingly, to childhood.

'Thank you. I should have been concentrating better. It is the busy time of day, after all.'

'Those cyclists come out of nowhere,' Diane said loyally, even though they both knew it was entirely Julia's fault. 'Honestly, between the cyclists and the tourists in their rental cars, driving top-speed on our small roads, it's a disgrace. Someone needs to do something.'

A bus arrived and stopped, opening the doors to let them in. Diane waved it off cheerfully, shouting, 'Just sitting for a moment, thanks!'

'I'm embarrassed to admit I was thinking about my garden.'

'Well, I'm surprised I wasn't run over myself, the last day or so.'

Julia thought Diane pretty much immune to running over. She was quite startlingly noticeable, with her height, and her long red hair that she usually wore loose, like a fiery cape well below her shoulders.

'I'm reading that book Dylan recommended at book club. I can't put it down. And I think about it when I'm out and about.'

'That's the best feeling, isn't it? When you can't wait to get back to a book.'

'It is. I love that book club. Such good recommendations. And the chatter, of course.'

'Oh, that reminds me. You mentioned that Mark's mother knows Kay. You were going to say something, I think, but you didn't finish the story.'

'Ah, well, I don't like to gossip.'

'Of course, not at all...'

Julia paused. She knew that Diane would fill the gap soon enough, and so she did.

'But anyway, yes, like I said, Mark's mum, my mum-in-law, knows Kay. Lovely woman, according to my mum-in-law, but she got into a tight spot with money, and that's why she moved in with Eve.'

'Yes, so I heard. Poor thing, it's hard coming out on a fixed income, or a pension.'

'Yes, it must be hard.' She wasn't a gossip, Diane, and Julia could see she was holding something back. After a minute's silence, Diane said, 'Anyway, I was thinking that it's lucky that they had that time together, given how things worked out.'

'Yes. It's not an easy thing, taking in a parent, but as you say, as things worked out...'

'I don't think Eve was delighted to take her mum in, at first, though.'

'So I heard.'

'But they worked it out. The thing is, Kay had a weakness for gambling. All sorts. Even the bingo. But horses, mostly. And it didn't always go in her favour – never does, does it? She got herself in a spot of bother, owing a bookie money. Not break your knees stuff, but not pleasant. Anyway, Eve paid her debt, and took her in, on the condition that she gave it up. And she did. She got on top of her addiction, and they had that last lovely year together, at least, before Poor Eve died. Strange how life works out, isn't it, Julia?'

'Very strange. Very strange indeed.'

11

It wasn't fair, not fair at all, but Julia was very cross with Jake. His tail, which had been healing nicely, was now worse, thanks to a particularly wild early morning walk. Jake had been walking so calmly on his lead that she let him off to sniff around a bit. No sooner had he slipped the noose than he proceeded to go completely bonkers. He chased a swan, fell in love with a cockerpoo, discovered an abandoned half-biscuit, swam in the river and attempted to climb a tree after a squirrel. Each adventure was accompanied by bounding delight and a blur of a wagging tail.

By the time Julia had wrangled him back on the lead, his tail hung limply at a sad angle, and he seemed to wince whenever he moved it. When she touched it, he whimpered.

The painkillers Dr Eve had given them were finished. It wasn't even a week ago that she had taken the chocolate rascal to the vet. So much had happened, and the world had changed so dramatically that it felt longer.

Julia allowed herself a brief sigh and rang the number, still saved as Dr Eve Davies, on her phone and explained the situation to Olga, the receptionist.

'Poor Jake. I'm sure we can give you a repeat on the painkillers. Dr Ryan will be in soon, I'll check with him. Come on by in an hour.'

So much for Julia's lovely quiet Saturday in the garden. Oh well, she needed to get Jake's favourite dog treats, anyway. She used them for training. Lord knows what they put into the Good-Dog-Go Fair Trade Organic Beef and Barley Treats, but he would literally hop on one leg singing if there was one of those treats at the other end of it.

An hour later, Julia was at Dr Eve Davies' rooms, with no Eve. Julia hadn't seen Olga Gilbert since Eve's death, and was shocked to see how thin and shaky she looked. Her hair could do with a wash.

'Oh, Olga, I'm so terribly sorry about Eve. It must be awful to come to work without her.'

'Awful. I can't stop thinking about the accident. What she felt when she went over. And at the bottom...' She shuddered.

'We can only take comfort from the fact that it was likely very quick,' said Julia, remembering the angle of the neck, the residual warmth of the body. 'She didn't suffer.'

'And now there's this horrible gossip in the village, people saying she took her own life.'

The consulting room door opened, and Dr Ryan came out. Julia had seen him before, but only in passing, when buying dog food. They had never consulted him. Jake, of course, thought he was just lovely and, with his tail out of action, expressed his affection by nudging him with his big brown head and slobbering on his neat khaki trousers and his shiny leather loafers.

'Took her own life?' he said. 'What absolute nonsense! Eve was the last person to do that. She had so much to live for. And so many responsibilities. Just a week ago she accepted a position on the board of the British Dog Society, the charity. On top of all the other volunteer work she did for animals. She had been put on the committee at the Padel club just the month before. I even teased her about being such a head girl.'

'She was the sort of person anyone would welcome on a committee or in an organisation,' said Julia.

'She was,' Olga agreed. 'Clever, caring, organised.'

'I'm also involved in the British Dog Society,' said Dr Ryan, 'and I can tell you, she took her responsibilities seriously. No way would she abandon those dogs. And on that topic, there is absolutely no way she would have done anything that would leave poor old Fergus alone on the hills. There is no way that she jumped.'

'That's why it's so painful to hear...'

'People talk, but they soon get tired of talking. I know it's painful, but try not to listen, Olga,' Julia said. 'It will just make you sad and angry.'

'Good advice,' said Dr Ryan. 'Anyone who knew Eve knows it's not true. It's a horrible rumour that'll blow over. Eve's death was just a tragic accident. Now, let's see about that tail.'

Julia left a few minutes later with another five days of pills for Jake, and a stern warning for both of them to 'look after that tail'.

As soon as she got into the car, Julia fished her phone out of her bag. Jake sat upright in the back seat, regarding her in the rear-view mirror, wondering where they were going next, and when.

'Just a minute, Jakey, I need to phone Hayley Gibson before we go.'

Hayley picked up on the first ring. 'Hello.'

Jake sighed loudly and slumped down in the seat to wait out the conversation.

'Hayley, it's Julia.'

'I know. Your name comes up.'

'Right, well, I thought I should tell you, I was at the vet to see about Jake's tail and I've just seen Eve's colleagues. Olga the receptionist, and Dr Ryan, the other vet. They are absolutely certain that she was in good mental health. Busy. Lots to live for.'

'Julia, you know as well as I do that suicide is a complicated business. You never know what's going on with someone under the surface. I'm not sure we'll ever be able to rule out suicide, but for the sake of her mother, and based on the available evidence, I am persuaded that she slipped.'

'You don't think someone might have pushed her?'

'Julia, she was alone on that path. All the witnesses say so. And everybody liked her. Why would anyone want to kill a vet?'

'What about her mum? What did you find out about the will?'

'I spoke to Kay Davies,' Hayley said. 'She gets Eve's house, and half the cash. The rest goes to the dogs. Literally. Charities.'

'Hayley, I found out that Kay was supposed to have stopped gambling. She promised Eve. She'd got into debt before, and she might have been in trouble again. And she lied about her where-abouts on the afternoon Eve died. And now she's inherited enough money to get her out of any new debt she might have. And Eve was worried that something terrible would happen. I know it sounds crazy, but Kay was on the scene and she had a motive. Do you think it could be her?'

'No,' Hayley cut in quickly. 'I don't think. She admitted to the lie, straight off the bat. She lied because she is a gambling addict and she promised Eve she would quit. Then she fell off the wagon. She didn't want her daughter to know, so she dashed off to the betting shop while Eve was out walking. She took the taxi from the car park because she didn't want the neighbours telling Eve.'

This tied in with what Diane had told Julia – that the condition of Kay's staying with Eve was that her gambling was all in the past. It also tied in with what Lewis had said.

'And, Julia, again. Eve was alone on the path. Nobody saw Kay with Eve. In fact, we *know* she went to the betting shop at the relevant time. It totally rules her out.'

A strapping fellow walked past Julia's car with a brace of sausage dogs and entered the door to the vet. Jake sat up straight to peer out of the window at them. She could tell from the tension in his body that he was readying himself for a bark. Julia put her hand over the phone and said, 'No, Jake,' in a quiet but mildly threatening voice.

'Julia, Kay didn't kill Eve,' Hayley continued. 'It all checked out. That betting slip you saw on the fridge? It was bought at two thirty on Tuesday afternoon. And Walter checked the time of the taxi trip with Lewis, the driver. Everything is logged these days, down to the mile and the minute. It all adds up, Julia. Kay lied to Eve, but she didn't kill her. The timing just doesn't work at all.'

Julia thought about it carefully. Hayley was right; there was no logical way that Kay could have been on the path, pushed Eve, raced back down, caught a taxi to the betting shop and been back in time to hear the bad news. Kay was not the murderer.

'Well, I'm glad Kay didn't kill Eve.'

Insofar as there was any good news in this horrible death, this was a relief to Julia. She had hated the thought of a mother pushing a daughter off a cliff path in order to take her money.

'So if it wasn't Kay, who was it?' Julia said this more to herself than Hayley.

'No one, Julia. Eve wasn't murdered. I've seen the forensics, Walter has spoken to everyone we could find on the path that day, we've looked into it. Nobody saw anything suspicious. Eve was alone. There's nothing to suggest she was murdered. There's always still the chance that it was suicide, and we might never know. But the one thing that I'm sure of is that it wasn't murder. Now you need to let the matter rest.'

Julia sighed. Unlike Hayley, she was absolutely sure that it wasn't suicide. It made no sense. Eve wasn't the least bit suicidal and, had she been, there were far easier ways for a vet to end their life than throwing themselves off a frankly rather pathetic cliff. And as for the theory that she fell; it just didn't sit right. Like most people who walk the same route every day, Eve would have been unlikely to venture off the path to the edge of the cliff. And even less likely to slip, had she done so. It wasn't exactly the most complicated terrain. Still, there was little evidence to support her conviction that Eve was murdered. And Hayley sounded fed up with her. She decided to stop arguing.

'Okay, Hayley. You're probably right.'

'I'm sure of it. Bye, Julia.'

Julia sat for a moment, then reached for the key in the ignition. 'Home time, Mr Jake. It's nearly time for your supper.'

As she turned the key, she remembered something, and turned it off again. 'That reminds me, Jake, I was so busy with your tail and the talking that I didn't get your treats! Goodness, my brain. Hang on.'

The three sausage dogs came out of the door just as Julia was about to come in. Their strapping owner followed. Tripping along on their twelve stubby little legs, they looked rather like a centipede. A centipede dragging a giant. He nodded and held the door open for her awkwardly. She heard the phone ring, and Olga answer chirpily, 'Cotswolds Veterinary Care, good afternoon.' Now Julia stood back and held the door, letting the man go past. It was all rather tricky with the three leads and twelve dog legs and two people. She was pleased when the little group went on their way, amidst barks and snuffles and muttered apologies. But she could still hear Olga's voice carrying over the sounds.

'Of course, it's a terrible pity it ended like this. But now that Eve's gone, my job is safe,' Julia heard Olga say. Julia shrank back against the wall to listen to what came next: 'I think we can both agree that this outcome is best for both of us.'

12

Julia leaned against the wall, reeling from what she'd just heard. It sounded like Olga was actually relieved that Eve was dead. That made no sense. And what did she mean about her job being safe? Who on earth was she speaking to? Was it possible that Olga knew something about what had happened to Eve?

And if that was the case, what should Julia do about it? Should she just come out and ask her? Should she go back to Hayley, who would no doubt be furious that Julia was still snooping, and still suspecting foul play?

The swirling questions were interrupted by a man's voice.

'All done, and she didn't feel a thing, did you, Moxy?'

The voice was familiar, but it took her a moment to place it. Jim McEnroe, that's who it was. She moved through the doorway into the vet's waiting room to confirm her identification. Yes, there he was, the journalist from the *Southern Times*, rather rumpled in his end-of-day jeans and button-down white shirt, with a bundle of shiny black fluff in his arms.

'Julia!' he said, apparently delighted to see her. 'Fancy meeting you here.'

'I have come and gone and come back right this second – I

forgot the Good-Dog-Go Fair Trade treats,' she said, her voice slightly raised, addressing a point between Jim and Olga. She wondered if she sounded just a little bit crazy, but she didn't want Olga to know what she had overheard.

Jim didn't appear to notice anything strange in Julia's manner. 'I brought my new puppy for her vaccinations. This is Moxy. She's a, *ahem*, Schnoodle.' He had the grace to cough embarrassedly at the word, and added, for clarity, 'That's a cross between a poodle and a schnauzer.'

'She's adorable.' Julia stroked the little dog in his arms. Her fur was as soft as spun silk.

'She is. I'm a bit nervous, I've never owned a dog – well, not since I was a kid, and my parents did most of the work. But I'm working remotely from home so much these days, I thought now's the time. I might just get her a toy while I'm here,' Jim said, surveying a rack with a bizarre array of rubbery items designed for the entertainment of dogs. On her own visits to the vet, Julia had often examined the same selection with mild astonishment. There were your regular balls and bones and sturdy knotted ropes, of course, and then there was the squeaky plastic mallard duck. The glow-in-the-dark hamburger. A horribly lifelike squirrel.

'What do you think, Julia?' Jim said, holding up a ball with an upper and lower row of white teeth on it. He held it to Moxy's mouth, as if seeing whether it matched her colouring. Moxy was a dear little thing with shiny mahogany eyes and a nose so black it disappeared into her glistening black fur. The lurid ball stood out shockingly against her blackness, she looked as if she was grinning a horrible toothy grin.

'Nope.'

'Okay then. This?' He reached for a rather garish yellow ball instead.

Dr Ryan came through from the consulting room and

handed a file to Olga. 'Just the standard vaccination charge,' he said.

'Thank you, Dr Ryan,' said Jim. He turned to Olga. 'And thank you, Olga, for helping me find little Moxy. I'm so pleased with her.'

'Oh nothing, nothing, no worries, it wasn't, not, well, nothing to do with me, absolutely not, absolutely not me,' said Olga, cutting him off rather rudely. She sounded flustered, for reasons Julia couldn't fathom. 'Let's get the invoice sorted out then. There's the vaccination, and that'll be fifteen pounds for the ball.' Julia reckoned the pup would have been just as happy with a plain old tennis ball for a tenth of the price, but didn't say so. 'And if you give me just a minute, Julia, I'll help you with the treats.'

Dr Ryan looked mildly perplexed by her odd manner, and disappeared to the safety of his consulting room. While Jim paid his bill, Julia thought about what she'd overheard earlier. It sounded suspicious, as if Eve's death had somehow benefited Olga. That her job was safe because of it. Was Olga in some kind of trouble at work, she wondered? She looked at Olga, who had been processing Jim's credit card, and who now handed it back to him with a tight smile. She was a bit of an odd bod, highly strung, but she couldn't imagine why her job would be in danger. She always seemed most efficient when Julia came into the vet. But if her job *was* in danger, was that something she might kill for?

But Julia could also not imagine her as a cold-blooded killer. An image flashed into her mind's eye. Olga's two hands flat against Eve's back. The shove between the shoulders. Eve scrabbling, arms flailing, her face, briefly shocked and terrified. And then the fall over the edge of the cliff. The tumbling. Eve hitting the ground. The sickening thud, the crunch of bone. And Olga with her hands on her hips, looking triumphantly down on the body from the top of the hill.

The image was not impossible. Eve was not a heavy woman. And she knew Olga well, she wouldn't have suspected her of murderous intent, so there wouldn't have been a struggle. Olga could have approached her quite naturally, and just given her a push. But surely there was no way it could have happened like that. Olga was surely incapable of such violence. Besides, Julia thought with relief, Olga would have been right there behind the desk at the vet when Eve died, manning the phones as she was every day. She couldn't have also been up on the path, pushing people. It might be that Olga was for some reason relieved that Eve was dead – but if she had been sitting at her desk, she was no murderer.

Julia was brought back into the moment by Olga calling her name. 'Here you go, two packets of Good-Dog-Go Fair Trade Organic Beef and Barley Treats. That'll be ten pounds, please.'

Julia took out her purse and handed over a note. She took the treats, noting that good behaviour did not come cheap.

As she and Jim turned to go, a woman arrived with a large bird in a cage. Julia didn't like birds in cages. They rather gave her the creeps, and it seemed cruel, somehow, but the bird was a beauty.

'Hello, Polly,' Olga said.

'Hello,' said the woman and the bird in unison. Were they both called Polly? Surely not. 'Here for Dr Ryan,' the woman continued, the bird presumably near the end of its vocabulary. 'Glad to see you're back, Olga. Are you feeling better?'

'Oh yes, fine thank you.' Olga sounded surprised.

'I spoke to Dr Ryan on Tuesday, when you weren't here.'

'Ah, yes. I could hardly get out of bed on Tuesday. Flu. I went to Dr Naidoo that afternoon, and she said there was a lot of it about, and I'd be better in a day or two, and she was right. Right as rain.'

'Good to hear. Dr Ryan gave me an appointment for today. I hope he put it in the book.'

'Yes, he did. Here you are: two p.m. Dr Ryan will be out in a mo.'

Julia felt as if a bucket of cold water had been poured over her head. She hoped she didn't look as shocked as she felt.

Because from what she had just heard, Olga was *not* at her desk on Tuesday. And if Olga was not at her desk, then who was to say where she really was. She could quite easily have been pushing Eve off a cliff after all. She had no choice but to tell Hayley everything that she had heard.

Having now concluded her business – both planned and not – Julia left, with Jim and Moxy right behind her. Outside the vet's rooms, Julia stopped and stroked the little dog's head, and played with her ears, which were deliciously soft and floppy. 'She really is a dear little thing, Jim.'

'She is. Olga put me in touch with the breeder, actually. But it's a bit daunting, having a pet. I need to start getting her to puppy socialisation and training classes.'

'Well, you can bring her round to play with Jake sometime if you like. And you can join our walks if she's had all her injections. Jake would love the company and he's very gentle for a big old galumph.'

They both looked at Jake, who was peering eagerly at them through the car window. She'd left it open for air, and heard his excited whine.

'That would be cool, thank you. I'll give you a ring and make a plan to get together.'

'Do. She can meet the chickens too – it's a good thing for country dogs to be used to livestock. And you can give me the inside scoop on all the drama and scandal of life in the Cotswolds.'

Jim laughed. 'Knowing you, Julia, *you* could probably fill *me* in.'

Julia smiled. She probably could.

13

'Honestly, Julia, you need to drop this,' Hayley said. She had sounded brisk and tetchy when Julia phoned, and Julia had misgivings about sharing what she'd learned, especially first thing on a Monday morning. She should perhaps have waited until eleven, when the tray of tea and biscuits came round the Berrywick police station, improving moods as it went. But it was too late for that kind of brilliant strategic thinking now. She'd phoned at nine on the dot, and put forward her theory, which Hayley had roundly rejected, and now Hayley sounded properly cross. 'I don't want to hear any more about Eve Davies' death. And I certainly don't want to hear accusations about her receptionist. That Olga Gilbert is no one's murderer.'

'But, Hayley, there's something odd. She was worried about her job... And then, she was off sick. She even said that it was for the best that Eve was dead!'

'Julia, please.' Now Hayley sounded sick and tired, rather than brisk and tetchy, which was actually somewhat worse. 'I've got a peeping Tom going round Edgeley and Hayfield, sneaking around, looking in people's windows. Three reports in the last few days. I do not have time to investigate imaginary murders.'

'A peeping Tom?' Julia was momentarily distracted from her theories about Olga. She had heard nothing of this, which was unusual, although she had not in the past few days been to the Buttered Scone, where such news would have efficiently changed hands, table to table, like some novel virus. After her Saturday plans had been disrupted by Jake's tail, she had spent a leisurely Sunday gardening with Sean and Jake and Leo.

'Yes, the victims are upset, as you can imagine,' Hayley said. 'Last night he climbed up a ladder outside some poor old lady's upstairs window. She got such a fright, she collapsed. Her husband had to call an ambulance.'

'Goodness, that's horrible. Is she all right?'

'She's fine, but the locals are in a tizz and the brass isn't happy. And it's only a matter of minutes till the press gets hold of it. They do love a peeping Tom headline.'

It occurred to Julia that she hadn't heard the term peeping Tom in years. It did seem like a crime whose time had come and gone. They were probably doing their peeping on the Internet these days.

'You're right, it's bound to get out. I hope you catch him soon. But, Hayley, as far as Olga goes—'

The detective cut her short. 'No. I don't want to hear any more about Olga Gilbert, Julia. We questioned everyone we could find who was on the path that day. They all mentioned seeing each other, and not one of them mentioned seeing Olga Gilbert. She was not on the path that day. She did not kill Eve Davies. Nobody killed Eve Davies, Julia. And I don't want to hear another word about it.'

Julia knew when to stop. She was annoying Hayley, which was the last thing that she wanted to do. She had no intention of turning into one of those mad old bats who pester people who have a bit of power. She'd known enough of those in her time as a social worker. Whatever Julia herself might think, it was time for her to leave Hayley alone.

'I understand, Hayley. I'm sure that you're right and I've let my imagination get carried away. Good luck with the peeping Tom.'

Julia put the phone down. Despite what she had said to Hayley, she was not at all convinced that Olga had been ruled out. It was quite unlike Hayley to not even follow up on a lead like this, and it made Julia deeply uncomfortable to just step away, as she had implied to Hayley she would do. They might be letting a murderer get away with it, after all.

It struck Julia that it would be very simple to confirm Olga's innocence, if not her guilt. All she had to do was determine whether she had, indeed, been to see Dr Naidoo on that Tuesday afternoon. Was she really sick and seeing the doctor? Or was she out and about, pushing her boss off a cliff? She took a sip of her tea, which was unpleasantly cool. She considered making another cuppa, but didn't move from her seat at the little desk in the sitting room where she paid her bills, wrote her letters, answered her emails and made her calls.

'Dr Naidoo...' she said musingly to herself. If you lived in Berrywick, and needed a doctor, you went to Dr Sean O'Connor, or Dr Priya Naidoo, or you went further afield to one of the other villages, or to the bigger towns if you needed a specialist.

'How do I find out if she really was at Dr Naidoo's?'

A plan began to form in her mind, but she put it aside almost immediately. It was too risky. Too scary. What if she got busted?

The plan was not to be dissuaded though. No sooner had she pushed it away, than it crept back in.

She would make that cup of tea after all. Get away from the plan.

She stood up, but somehow, instead of going to the kitchen, she went to the little carved wooden bowl on the dressing table where she kept her keys. She took her car keys in her hand, and before she knew it, she was out of the front door.

.   .   .

Dr Naidoo's reception area was so calm and pretty that Julia felt momentarily tempted to sit down, put her feet up on the pale wooden coffee table and lean her head back against the deep, comfortable sofa. It would be lovely and peaceful to just stay there, amongst the framed pastoral landscapes on the cool cream walls, amongst the potted ferns, and the hanging hen-and-chicken plants, with the air conditioner set at the perfect temperature, and a water cooler glistening with condensation, a tray of sparkling glasses alongside. But she didn't sit. With her heart fluttering in her throat, she walked up to the reception desk, where a pleasant-faced woman greeted her warmly and offered her help.

'I hope you can help me. My friend was here last week Tuesday, and she thinks she might have left her reading glasses. I live close by so I said I'd pop in and ask.'

The woman searched the area around her at the desk, and her pleasant face clouded over. 'Oh, I am sorry, I don't see anything here. Tuesday, you say? I wasn't here on Tuesday, so I can't say... Maybe the person on duty would know.'

'I think it was Tuesday. Olga Gilbert is the patient's name.'

'I'll check the book, and see which one of my colleagues would have been here.'

She checked the book – which wasn't in fact a book, but a scheduling programme on her computer.

'Ah, Anna was working on Tuesday. I'll give her a ring. If she found the glasses she might have put them aside in a safe place. What time? Olga Gilbert you say? Now that's funny. She is a patient here, but she doesn't appear to be in the book. Are you sure it was Tuesday?'

'You know, now that you mention it, I'm not sure. Was it Wednesday? Or even last week? Goodness, I'm so embarrassed. I'll check in with her and see.'

'Not to worry, let me see what else I can find...' The pleasant woman was determined to help her, peering at the computer screen, the phone in her hand in preparation for a call to Anna. This was exactly why Julia avoided this kind of under-cover snooping. You got stuck in a trap of your own making.

'Please don't worry, I'll phone once I have my facts right.'

They would have gone on telling each other not to worry for quite some while longer, possibly until the end of time, but for the arrival of a harassed-looking young mum with two very small children, twins by the look of them, both shrieking their little blonde heads off.

Julia took the opportunity to step away from the desk, making 'after you' gestures to the young mum and 'thanks and goodbye, and sorry to be a bother' gestures to the pleasant woman. The receptionist turned her attention to the little patients and their mum, and Julia bolted for the door, carrying with her the knowledge that Olga Gilbert had not been to the doctor on Tuesday afternoon, no matter who she told otherwise.

Julia's nerves had been quite jangled by her morning adventures. She was a good snooper but a poor fibber, she realised. She wouldn't be doing that again, it was much too stressful. After lunch – a tossed-together salad of fresh garden greens combined with the last five olives in a jar and some left-over bits of cheese – she took to the sofa with her iPad. She subscribed to a few magazines, which she tended to neglect. Now she would rectify that. But first, a bit of light stalking.

Before she looked into what she could find about Olga – which was, after all, her main aim – she allowed herself to look at Jess's social media accounts. She tried not to follow Jess too obsessively, but it was hard. Instagram Jess was familiar, but also strange. A shinier, more groomed, less complicated person than her human counterpart. There she was on a boat in the bay, the hills and towers of Hong Kong behind her. At night in a street market, one side of her face lit up by a mauve neon light. In a bar somewhere. With three other girls at what looked to be a birthday brunch. Her daughter, living her life.

Dylan was active on her profile, liking and hearting. He made occasional comments. 'Love' was one. What did that mean? Was it 'Love the pic', 'Love you', 'I love you', 'I'm *in* love with you'? It was maddeningly nuanced, this love word. She flushed with embarrassment and hurt at her recent misunderstanding with Sean. She realised she'd been so concerned with his intended meaning that she hadn't considered her own. Did she love him? It was an interesting question. She let her mind float around with it for a while without trying to answer it.

She closed Instagram and opened Facebook, where she had a modest scattering of friends, and followed a few accounts, but seldom posted.

Disconcertingly, the app opened to a picture of Dr Eve Davies, and a lovely little tribute to her on the 'I Love Berrywick' page. Julia scrolled quickly through the many, many comments expressing sadness and shock, and appreciation of her work with animals.

One of the comments on the post was from the Berrywick Padel Fiends, a page presumably devoted to local Padel. Julia clicked on that page, and on a whim, followed it. Then she scrolled through the posts, not sure what she was looking for, but with that buzzy feeling that she got when she was on the track of something.

And there it was. A post featuring the unmistakable features of Olga Gilbert. She was dressed, rather incongruously, in athletic wear and was in a group shot with three other women, all holding rackets. 'It was a hard-fought friendly against Hayfield. And we won!' was the caption. The pic had been posted on the page by Padel Unlimited, the local centre with six courts on the other side of Berrywick from Julia. She wouldn't have thought Olga one for competitive ball games, but how would she know? She was tall, so maybe she had good reach. It was useful in tennis, so presumably in Padel, too.

Of much more interest, though, was the timing of the post. The post featuring Olga was dated Tuesday night. Had Olga been playing the game on Tuesday afternoon, having faked a sickie from work? That would explain where she was. And, if Olga had been at Padel, she hadn't been murdering Eve, and Julia could stop worrying about her lies. But although the picture was posted on Tuesday night, it wasn't clear when the match had taken place.

Thinking about tennis, Julia had experienced a powerful physical memory – the satisfying feeling of the ball connecting with the strings of the racket, knowing it landed solidly in the centre, and hitting it hard and true across the net. She felt a sudden longing for that precise feeling. It had been years since she'd played. She and Tabitha had first bonded over tennis, in fact. They played socially at uni, long evenings on the court in summer, followed by drinks at the university tennis club. It was there that she first met her ex-husband, Peter, too, although they didn't start going out until a year or two after uni.

So long ago, so very long ago. A gentle melancholy settled on her, the sort of quiet sadness that came from the recognition of time passing. Those girls, that boy, those tennis games. They were gone forever.

Unless, of course, she and Tabitha were to take up this new sport.

And if perhaps they were to find some answers while they were there, well, that would just be sheer luck, wouldn't it?

14

Tabitha and Julia looked at each other and started chuckling in unison.

'Oh heavens, look at us!' Tabitha said, patting down her T-shirt and her long cotton shorts. Her hair was tied back in a bandana. The only nod to her habitual stylishness was an unusually modest pair of stud earrings with a yellow stone.

'I look like I'm in my pyjamas.' Julia looked down at her own outfit, which consisted of an elderly pair of leggings that had done good service when she did online yoga during the pandemic, and a T-shirt Jess had given her with a picture of a chocolate Labrador on it and the words 'Who's a Good Boy?' About the only positive thing to be said for her outfit was that the shirt was as good as new, but that was only because it was so ridiculous that Julia had never worn it.

'If we like this game, we'll go and get some proper clothes,' Tabitha said. 'In the meantime, let's hope we don't see anyone we know.'

'Tabitha!' came a voice from across the car park. 'Fancy seeing you here.'

'So much for your wishes,' Julia muttered to her friend. 'Now we're busted.'

'Oh heck.' Tabitha straightened the bandana, as if that would help.

'And Julia! Hello!' It was Pippa. 'I didn't know you gals played.'

'We don't, at least not yet. We thought we'd give it a try, and the website said there's an introductory session on Tuesdays, so we decided to come along.'

Julia was only telling half the truth. They were trying out the sport, yes, but she was also on a fact-finding mission. She thought she might get more information about Olga's match at the Padel centre itself, or from Sandy, who was going to be giving them the introductory lesson.

'Oh it's marvellous, you'll love it! Shall I show you where to go?' said Pippa.

They followed Pippa to the little office with a large banner reading *Padel Unlimited*, and underneath, *The world's fastest growing sport!!!* A shiny young person in short shorts and a crop top was bustling about with an iPad, taking names and details from another pair – a man and a woman who seemed to be a couple.

When she'd finished inputting their details, she turned to the two women and asked brightly, 'Are you here for the intro session?'

'Yes we are,' Tabitha answered. 'I phoned yesterday. It's Tabitha and Julia.'

'Lovely. I see you're on the list. Susan and Trevor will be joining too. Okay? I'm Sandy, and I'll give you a short intro and you can have a bit of a game. Okay? There are four of you today, so that'll work out nicely.'

'Sounds good,' Julia said, in what she hoped was the sort of enthusiastic tone of voice employed by players of 'The world's fastest growing sport!!!'

They learned that Padel is like a cross between tennis and squash, always played in doubles.

While Sandy spoke, Julia took the opportunity to surreptitiously examine the noticeboard for clues. There was a lot of bumf about rules and regulations and booking procedure, which seemed unlikely to prove useful. There was an update on the expansion of the club – there was a legal hold-up, apparently, something to do with zoning and planning permission. This was not at all unusual in the Cotswolds – almost any development in the area had someone desperate to go ahead with it, and someone equally desperate to block it. There was a notice about an AGM meeting, which was briefly interesting – on the off-chance that Olga might have gone to that – but it turned out that it was only the following week.

'Oh!' Julia started at the sight of a photograph of Eve Davies. Her pretty, wholesome face with its constellation of freckles, and her hair in shining golden-brown curls to her shoulders. The little smile on her face seemed so poignant. Of course, she had no idea she'd be dead before long. But then, we all proceed in denial on this matter, don't we? thought Julia, rather grimly. She was dressed in her sports gear, holding a racket. The picture was taken right here at the courts, and recently by the looks of things.

The flyer on the noticeboard announced her sad passing, and expressed the regret of the management and the committee.

'I'm sorry, did you know Eve?' asked Sandy, who had reached the end of her lesson and noticed Julia looking at the flyer.

'Yes, she was my dog's vet.' Julia wasn't going to offer her other connection, as the finder of Eve's body.

'Yes, my kitty's too. She was very good with animals. And good at Padel.'

'I'm sure. She seemed very athletic. Was she competitive?'

'Oh yes, she didn't like to lose on the court or off it,' Sandy said, and made a brief, awkward noise somewhere between a laugh and a cough and a harrumph.

It wasn't quite what Julia had meant, but she was intrigued. She looked at Sandy and waited.

'Oh, you know how people can be...' Sandy said, blushing.

Julia waited some more.

'Club politics. There's always something. Eve was a person who stood her ground, is all. She had principles about things. And she didn't mind telling you. I appreciated that about her, but not everyone likes that kind of approach.'

'You're right about that.'

Fully briefed on the workings of Padel, they headed for the court. Even on a Tuesday at eleven, the courts were full of happy young foursomes bounding athletically around. Only one court was free, and it was booked for the newbies. She paired up with Tabitha, facing the couple who were somewhat younger, but didn't give the impression of being alarmingly fit. They started slow, everyone feeling their way, hitting easy shots, giving each other a chance. Sandy had told them that the ball was allowed to bounce off the walls, which seemed rather an unpredictable arrangement, with significant potential for disaster. But Julia was prepared to give it a go. She smacked the ball across to their opponents' side of the court, where it hit the wall and bounced surprisingly quickly back to hit Trevor on the head.

'Hey!' he yelled, more in anger than in pain. He glowered at Julia.

'Sorry!' she called.

'Be more careful,' he muttered, which she thought was rather unreasonable. It wasn't as if she had that level of control over the ball. And he should have stepped back and hit it instead of standing there like a twit.

Trevor stepped in front of his wife to take the serve, looking straight at Julia as he slammed the ball over the net as hard as he could. She stepped to the side, and it narrowly missed hitting her. It clipped Tabitha, who was behind her, but didn't connect hard enough to cause injury.

'In Padel, there's really no need to hit the ball too hard,' Sandy said from the sidelines, addressing them all with a message clearly intended for Trevor. 'It's more about where you place the ball.'

Trevor was quietly fuming, his face pale and his cheeks blotched with red, his mouth a thin line of rage.

'Let's all try and stay in position,' said Sandy gamely.

He appeared to be deaf to her instructions, poaching shots that were clearly in Susan's territory, and smacking the ball around as if it was his worst enemy. Julia caught Tabitha's eye and they made a silent agreement not to let him get away with this nonsense. They channelled their nineteen-year-old tennis-playing selves, and hit the ball back firmly and steadily. Julia was surprised at the precision and control they managed to achieve on occasion, their forty-year-old skills honed by their intense irritation with the bullying Trevor.

With the two of them successfully batting the ball about and not reacting to his bluster, he turned his attention to his partner, shouting, 'Yours!' as the ball flew past them both. 'Concentrate, Susan,' he muttered bitterly under his breath after poaching and fluffing a shot in her corner.

'Let's have some fun! It's just a friendly introduction, and we're all learning,' said poor Sandy, who was probably re-evaluating her career choice at this point.

Julia hit the next ball firmly and precisely to Susan, to give her the chance of a satisfying return (and, it must be said, to annoy Trevor). Susan drew back her racket in preparation, her expression one of quiet concentration. She stepped forward and Trevor appeared in front of her swatting at the ball. His racket connected poorly, sending the ball skittering over the net at a peculiar angle. It hit Julia's shoulder, not hard, but she got a fright and stepped awkwardly away. She fell, turning her ankle and losing her balance. As she went down, she put her hand down to stop herself crashing too heavily to the ground. It all happened so quickly she was quite surprised to find herself lying there on the court at an awkward angle.

Tabitha came running over. 'Oh, Julia, are you all right?'

Sandy followed, looking anxious. Trevor and Susan came after her.

Julia was more in shock than in pain. She did a quick scan of her body. No broken hip, which is always a good thing. A twinge in the foot, but the ankle was fine. Her left wrist was sore and her hand felt bruised where she had landed.

'Let me help you up,' said Trevor, pushing forward and reaching out a hand.

'I've got it, thank you,' said Sandy curtly, turning her back to him. Julia held out her good hand, and Sandy gently helped Julia to her feet.

Tabitha rubbed her shoulder. 'Can you walk okay?'

'I think so,' said Julia, feeling up and down her arm, pressing to see where it hurt. 'My ankle is fine, but I've sprained my wrist, I think.'

They settled her on the bench by the court. Susan brought an energy drink out of her bag, and offered it. 'Sugar. Good for the shock.'

'Thank you.' Julia took a long swig of the drink. It was a lurid blue colour, but tasted, rather disconcertingly, of raspberry.

Sandy ran to fetch an ice pack from the little office, which she wrapped in a towel and laid gently on the wrist.

The three women gathered round, with Trevor lurking a few steps outside the circle.

'Can I get you a bandage? Or something to eat?' he called meekly from behind Tabitha.

Julia shook her head, and took another sip.

'Anything else I can do for you?' he was clearly trying to weasel back into everyone's good books after behaving like a complete prat.

'An apology might be a good start.' Tabitha was good at conflict, Julia always thought. She was very direct, and spoke in a calm and even tone without a hint of aggression. It was disarming.

It certainly worked with Trevor. 'Yes, you're right. I'm sorry. I am terribly competitive, and it was absolutely inappropriate today. I behaved badly. If there's anything I can do, I would like to be helpful.'

Susan's jaw literally fell open. This is something you read about, but imagine it to be a metaphor until you see it in real life. She couldn't have looked more surprised if Trevor had been suddenly covered in gold scales and started singing 'God Save the Queen'. It was obvious that apologising wasn't Trevor's strong suit. They had all witnessed a rare event.

'I think I'll just sit here for a moment. It'll probably settle down. Tabitha can drive us home.' He nodded. She relented, slightly, and threw him a bone: 'Perhaps you could bring our things to the car,' she said, indicating their bags. He nodded gratefully. Susan closed her mouth. The two of them gathered up the rackets and bags and jerseys.

'I'll have to file an incident report,' said Sandy. 'It's a rule.'

'All right then. What do you need?'

'Personal details, which I have from your forms, and your statement of what happened and the nature of the injury.'

'Happy to do that, if that's what you need.' Julia was only too familiar with the world of forms and health and safety rules from her previous career as a social worker. Come Armageddon, some poor soul would be filling in a form about it.

'I'll get the form,' Sandy said.

She came back with her iPad in hand. Julia took it, and typed slowly. 'I went for a ball, tripped and twisted my wrist.'

Under the heading 'Medical treatment required' she wrote 'None'.

'Are you sure about that?' asked Sandy, who was watching Julia write. 'Shouldn't you have someone look at it?'

'It's fine,' said Julia, who felt that she had lived enough years and hurt enough things to know a sprain from a break.

'Her boyfriend's a doctor, he can look if she's worried,' added Tabitha, making Julia blush at the word 'boyfriend'. It still felt strange to have one.

Julia handed the form back, knowing it would be one more drop in the great sea of completely useless paperwork that flowed more strongly by the day, and was of absolutely no benefit to anyone, ever.

'Thank you,' Sandy said with a smile. 'I'm sorry about the wrist, I hope it's not too sore.'

'Oh, it's going to be all right, I'm sure. I'll take an anti-inflammatory before I go to bed, and it'll likely be as good as new in a day or two. I might even come back and play again. I enjoyed it.'

'Really? Well, you'd be welcome. I give private lessons, too. A couple of lessons is helpful to get you started.'

'I will definitely come for a few lessons if I decide to take up the sport.'

'Good. Give me a call. And don't worry if you can't make up a foursome, there are always people looking to link up. It's a friendly crowd. Competitive, but friendly. You'll get to know people soon enough.'

Julia knew an opportunity when she saw one, and this was an opportunity for a bit of information gathering.

'I probably know a few of the players already. If I'm not mistaken Olga Gilbert plays here, doesn't she?'

Tabitha shot her a look of wry amusement, tinged with admiration at the sheer opportunism of her best friend.

Sandy had no idea that she was being pumped for information, and answered happily. 'You're right, she does! She's very keen, and quite a good player.'

'I heard so. Didn't she win a tournament or something just last week? I think I saw a photo...'

Sandy smiled. 'Well, not a tournament, but there's a friendly competition with the other local clubs. She and her partner won Tuesday's game.'

'Ah yes, that's what it was. So they play on weekdays, do they?'

'Yes, different groups play at various times, of course, but the friendly matches amongst the clubs in this area are on Tuesday afternoons. Most of the people who are in the friendly league are not working full-time, or they are flexible in their hours. Some take the afternoon off, like Olga. You might like it. First Tuesday of the month. From two to four p.m.'

It hadn't been an altogether successful visit – she would have hoped to complete her investigations without physical injury – but it had been useful in one way, at least.

Olga Gilbert might have lied to her boss about her whereabouts that Tuesday, and might have been worried about it – but she'd been playing Padel when Eve fell from the path. She was off the list of suspects for Eve Davies' death.

15

Having a bandage and sling on your wrist was rather like having a new puppy, Julia discovered. It attracted attention from passers-by, and caused people to speak to you in unusually high-pitched tones.

'*Oh poor you!* What did you do to yourself?' asked Wilma, who was, for once, on time to open up Second Chances, the charity shop where Julia worked once a week, generally on a Wednesday.

Julia explained about the fall.

'Padel?' Wilma said, not even trying to hide her astonishment that the injury was sports-related. 'Goodness, I wouldn't have thought *that* would be your scene.'

Julia was mildly irritated at her tone. After all, it wasn't as if Julia was a complete sloth. She walked the dog every day, and on occasion – well, once or twice since she had moved to the Cotswolds – did yoga videos on YouTube. The implication was that Wilma herself held the monopoly on physical activity, and it was true, she was extremely energetic. As a rule she dressed in a sort of hybrid active/leisure wear, as if she might at any moment take the opportunity to do a few stretches, or perhaps take a little jog round the block.

Wilma continued, in a patronising tone, 'You must be careful when you start something new. Start slow. You're not thirty anymore you know! The balance isn't what it once was.'

'Oh, it wasn't a balance issue. My balance is excellent.' Julia heard the defensiveness in her own voice, and wished she'd managed a more chilled response.

'Is the arm fractured?'

'No, just a sprain. Sean gave me a sling, though. He said it's best to keep it immobile for a day or two.'

'Handy having a doctor for a boyfriend,' said Diane. 'Patch up all your scrapes. Or even *meeeend a browowow-ken heart...*' She sang that last phrase in a truly terrible imitation of the Bee Gees who had made the song of that name famous. Julia and Wilma laughed. The little awkwardness between them dissipated, along with Julia's irritation. It never lasted long.

'You should take the front counter today, Julia,' Wilma said in a kindly tone. 'It'll be easiest with your wrist. I'll get going with unpacking and sorting that big donation of books that came in last week.'

They all looked at the three boxes, blocking the way at the edge of the storeroom, awaiting attention.

'I can give you a hand with the books, Wilma,' said Diane. 'I'll get a pencil and write the prices on the inside covers. Will you be able to operate the till, Julia?'

'I'm sure I can manage the till and the change. It's really not a bad injury. As long as I keep it quite still, it doesn't hurt at all.'

'Well, that sounds like a good plan for the morning,' said Wilma, pleased.

'Yes, it does. Now, shall we start with tea?' There was enthusiastic agreement to Diane's suggestion. She went into the back room to put the kettle on.

. . .

They had just finished the first cuppa – the first of three, if this day followed the usual pattern – when the tinkling of the doorbell signalled the arrival of a customer. Julia recognised her at once, although she hadn't seen her for a year or more. The young woman had the distinguishing factor of being the owner of the most improbably long and thick false eyelashes ever seen in Berrywick. They swooped upwards almost to her eyebrows and fanned out dramatically. Julia had first seen her at the reception desk at the property company her father owned in the village, and Julia had been reminded of Petunia, her grandmother's prize Jersey cow who likewise had a marvellous set of eyelashes, although hers were natural, of course.

'*Oh poor you!* Hurt your arm, did you?' the girl said, by way of greeting.

'It's just a sprain. I had a fall.'

'Got to be careful, especially in the wet weather. Easy to lose your footing.' Was everyone going to be so very patronising about her injury? Clearly, the young woman thought she was talking to a doddery elder.

'Oh no, not that kind of fall. I didn't trip. It's a *sports* injury. Padel.'

'Ah gosh, yes. My dad plays.'

'Your dad is Will Adamson, isn't he?'

'Yes. How did you know?' The young woman sounded slightly defensive.

'I was at his office a while ago. I recognised you. You were on reception, right?'

'Yes, that's right. Hi, I'm Kimberley.'

'Pleased to meet you, I'm Julia Bird.'

'Do you know my dad from Padel? Have you ever played Padel with him?' The tone of Kimberley's questions reminded Julia, rather incongruently, of a young mother asking if their child had made a new friend at playschool.

'No. I'm new to the game, I haven't really played with anyone other than the people in a trial session. If I sign up, I plan to get a couple of lessons to get me started.'

'Maybe you can play with him,' said Kimberley, smiling.

Julia remembered Kimberley's father well. He was a tall, handsome man, in good shape. But there was something rough about him. A steely streak. She imagined he'd be quite the terror on the court. She had a sling to remind her of the dangers of hyper-competitive blokes on the Padel court. Besides, she doubted that she'd be in Will Adamson's league, no matter how many lessons she had. 'Maybe,' she agreed.

'Well, everyone who plays seems to love it,' said Kimberley.

'It seems like a nice club. I imagine the members are quite friendly.'

'I don't know. I don't play sports.' Kimberley seemed to find the very idea distasteful. 'But if you want to talk to someone about it, speak to my dad. He'll tell you all about it. But bottom line, he loves it, even with all the drama that goes on with the teams and all. Gosh. It's like secondary school, from what I hear,' she said patronisingly, although she looked to be no more than five years out of secondary school herself. 'The fallings out and the break-ups. The friends and enemies. In fact he's looking for a new partner. There was an accident... I mean she...' She stopped, blushing.

'Oh dear, was his partner Eve Davies?'

'Yes. How did you know?'

'You mentioned an accident. And I know that Eve played Padel. I put two and two together.'

'It was so tragic. Poor woman, just shocking. Although of course she and dad had already had a row, so they probably wouldn't have been partners anymore anyway. Not that he's not...' The girl was terribly flustered at the turn the conversation had taken, and everything she said made it worse. 'He's very... I mean, it's awful, of course... He's upset, even though they fought.' She closed her eyes for a long moment, presenting Julia with the unnerving sight of her eyelids smeared in iridescent blue eyeshadow, fringed by the massive lashes. She took a long breath, opened her eyes – thank goodness – and changed the subject. 'Anyway, I'm looking for something for a fancy dress. It's a speakeasy theme, you know, like flappers, that sort of thing. Do you have anything like that?'

'Have a look at the more formal wear over there,' Julia said, pointing with her good arm to the rack on the far wall. 'There might be something that works for the theme. There's a pretty red shift, it is kind of flapper-ish.'

'That sounds good, and I do like red. I'll take a look.' She wandered off in the direction of the dresses.

'And there's lots of lovely costume jewellery,' Diane called over from the storeroom doorway, where she was taking piles of books from a box and sorting them into categories – fiction, history, and cooking, mostly. The perennial favourite donations of the Berrywick reading community. 'And we have some other accessories that might be fun. Feather boas. A headband. That kind of thing.'

'Cool, thank you.'

Julia felt uneasy about what Kimberley had told her. Will Adamson, on her brief acquaintance of him, had not been a man that you would want to get on the wrong side of, but it seemed that Eve had somehow found herself there. On his wrong side.

She wondered what might have been the cause of the fight between Eve and Will. She imagined that Will might be the competitive sort and maybe he thought Eve wasn't good enough. Although Sandy had mentioned how competitive Eve was, so it could be the other way around. Or maybe it had nothing to do with their Padel skills. Maybe there was something else that made them fall out?

'*Oh poor you!* What did you do to your arm?' This time, the question came from Pippa, who had come in with a large bag, eliciting another tinkle of the bell which had roused Julia from her pondering about Eve and Will.

'Just a sprain.' Julia said brusquely, trying to nip the conversation in the bud. She did not want to hear *Oh poor you!* one more time, and she especially didn't want to hear people's annoying assumptions about her balance. She wasn't ninety, for heaven's sake. She could stay upright on her own two feet quite fine, thank you.

'Clothes,' Pippa said, hoisting the bag onto the counter. 'I hope Jake wasn't to blame for your sprain. They do tend to get underfoot, dogs. I nearly broke my neck falling over one of my current lot of guide dog puppies just yesterday. I only just managed to steady myself by grabbing the table. Managed to knock over a vase of gladioli. What a mess, but no injury, at least.'

Julia felt bad for being irritated in anticipation of remarks that did not come. 'Glad you're okay, Pippa. A fall is scary, even a near miss. There was no canine involvement in this incident. I fell on the Padel court on my first game. I got quite a fright, but the injury isn't bad at all.' She waved her arm about a bit to demonstrate.

As she did this, she saw that Kimberley had approached the counter and Wilma was ringing up her purchases. She sighed in frustration, but Pippa didn't notice Julia's distraction.

'Of course, I saw you there with two fully functional arms. Gosh, an injury on your first outing,' said Pippa. 'I hope it hasn't put you off. All the young people are playing. Soon everybody and their cousin will be joining in.'

'It's certainly a very popular sport,' agreed Julia, wondering if she was included in the group known as 'everybody and their cousin'.

'Poor dear Eve was a good Padel player, you know.' Pippa said this in a hushed voice, as if Eve's spirit might take offence at the revelation.

'Yes, I knew that she played.'

'She told me that she was on the committee, even. Who'd have thought you needed a committee for a social sport? Not me, but there was a lot to talk about apparently, or more like argue about, by the sound of it. They'll miss her there, I'm sure. Don't know how she had the time for it all, what with her veterinary practice, and the dog charities, and then saving this, that and the other thing. Newts, I think. And moles. Or voles. Frogs? Bats? All that, and the Padel committee, too. Amazing woman, such a loss.'

As Pippa said this, Julia heard the little ping that indicated the door of the shop had opened or closed, and saw Kimberley disappearing down the street. She would have to find another way to learn what had happened between Eve Davies and Will Adamson.

16

'Goodness, Sean, bubbles on a Wednesday night! What's the occasion?' Tabitha accepted the cold bottle of champagne that he offered, along with a hug.

'We're celebrating,' he said, wiping his feet on the doormat and stepping into her cottage after Julia.

'Are we? What? Oh my word, are you two...? You're getting...' Tabitha looked back and forth from one to the other, her expression moving from confusion to delight, and was veering back to confusion when Julia spoke: 'Oh, heavens, Tabitha, no...' She felt a rush of embarrassment and horror, which was reflected back in her friend's face. They blushed.

Sean stepped in and saved them all from further awkwardness. 'We are celebrating the success of our soon-to-be published poet!'

'Ah, get on, Sean.' Tabitha looked bashful and pleased in equal measure. 'It's one little poem.'

'In a top poetry journal! We're so proud of you, Tabitha,' Julia said. 'It's wonderful news.'

'I really am pleased, thank you. Maybe I'll get up the courage to start that novel. Again.'

'Now we're talking!' Sean said, punctuating his sentence with the pop of the cork leaving the bottle. He poured the bubbles into three champagne flutes that Tabitha had taken from the sideboard in the sitting room.

'To love, life and poetry.' He tapped his glass against Tabitha's, and then Julia's, holding her gaze a beat longer. 'And to healing.'

He surprised her, still. He had the no-nonsense approach of a country doctor, kind and empathetic, but reserved. He tended towards the gruff rather than the effusive. And then he came out with a surprise bottle of celebratory champagne, and the line, 'To love, life and poetry.'

Julia sipped the champagne – it tasted like weddings – and sat on the wingback chair by the window. Tabitha seemed in good spirits. She had a youthful, lively air about her, moving briskly and gracefully between the kitchen and the little sitting room. She came in with a small bowl of almonds and another of olives. Her greying curls were soft and pretty, and her golden eyes were warm with interest in the world and its citizens.

Tabitha sat on the sofa, Sean having claimed the other one of the pair of wingbacks. She looked graceful and beautiful against the backdrop of a large hand-woven kente cloth, patterned in geometric shapes in rich green, gold and red, that took up most of the wall behind her. The cloth was a nod to her Ghanaian heritage. Tabitha somehow made the kente-in-the-Cotswolds-cottage style seem effortlessly just right.

'Has Callum decided to stay on in Vietnam?' she asked Sean, referring to his younger son who had been teaching English there for the past two years. His contract was soon to come to an end, so he had a decision to make.

'It looks like it. He thinks the school will renew the contract. He likes the work and has a girlfriend there, Cam, her name is. I think she's the big drawcard.'

'Gosh, well that's news. I hope she's as lovely as he is.'

Tabitha, unlike Julia, had met Sean's sons before they left the Cotswolds. It sometimes felt strange to Julia that Tabitha had known Sean longer, and in some ways – like this – better, than she did.

'She seems very nice, and clever too. I met her when I went over last year, but only briefly and the relationship was new. Remember, I was only there a week, that was all the leave he had, and it's hard for me to leave the practice for too long. We've had a couple of Zoom calls since, the three of us. Not my favourite, I always feel rather self-conscious, seeing myself on the screen. But better than nothing.'

'It must be hard, even with the tech.' Tabitha looked sympathetic.

'It is,' said Julia, thinking of her own relationship with Jess. 'But it's wonderful how the young get about. I wish I'd done more of it myself. But it's not easy to keep the relationships close with them away for so long, and in different time zones. Good heavens, it's impossible to work out when to call Jess in Hong Kong. Thank goodness for the iPhone with its world clock, or I'd be waking her up at three in the morning.' She kept her tone light, but she felt a sharp stab of longing for Jess. How she'd like to give her darling daughter a hug and have a good old natter over a cup of tea.

'I know you miss Jess terribly, too,' said Tabitha, patting her knee. Julia sometimes wondered if she was a mind reader, but knew that she was just a sensitive person and a good friend.

'I do. But I was lucky to have her for those weeks over Peter and Christopher's wedding. And hopefully Sean will see Callum before long. He is talking of coming for a visit when the school breaks for the long holidays.'

'I hope he'll come back for a good few weeks, possibly with Cam. It seems quite serious, and he did mention the possibility of bringing her over with him. And, of course I'm very eager for him and Julia to meet.' He gave her a quick smile when he said it, and looked away.

Gosh, but Sean was full of surprises, today. This was the first time Sean had so publicly and definitely articulated this wish to introduce them all to each other. It did seem quite 'official', meeting each other's children – if not nearly as official as Tabitha's earlier assumption that there might be a wedding. She blushed anew at the memory.

'Well, I'm looking forward to meeting them too, Sean. We should try and firm up the dates, and perhaps offer to take them on a little trip. He might like to show Cam a bit of the country.'

'That's a good idea. I'll suggest it.'

Thinking of the four of them motoring down to Bath on a jaunt, Julia felt the acute absence of Sean's other son, Jono, in the conversation. Jono lived much closer to Berrywick than Callum did. He was in London – as far as anyone knew – but he was every bit as absent as his brother on the other side of the world.

When Sean and Julia had first met, he'd told her that his older son was studying music. There seemed to be a pair of invisible quote marks around the words – 'studying music' – as if there was some uncertainty about the endeavour. In the past year or so, the word 'studying' had disappeared altogether. Jono was now described, when he was mentioned at all, as 'making music'. If he was, he certainly hadn't shared it with his father. She knew that Sean was deeply sad and worried about his son. He was gutted that the young man was so at sea in his life, and so reluctant to keep in contact with his father. Jono didn't visit, for various dubious reasons: he 'didn't like the country' or he was 'busy writing a new song' or he 'couldn't afford the train ticket right now' (Sean had of course offered to pay). Sean was at a loss as to how to help him find his way, or how to rekindle the relationship that had been worn threadbare to the point of breaking. It was deeply painful for him. If only she could help. Perhaps they could include Jono in the family outing, and persuade him to come too.

Tabitha's voice broke through Julia's pondering, but she noticed just in time to hear the final phrase, '... do you think?'

'Sorry, my mind wandered for a moment. What was the question?'

'Shall we go to the table?'

'Yes, let's. It smells wonderful. Am I hallucinating or is that peanuts I'm smelling?'

'Of course. Peanut soup, my mum's family recipe. Your favourite.'

'Yum. You are the best, Tabitha. Thank you.'

Friendship, champagne and peanut soup left Julia feeling deeply content and a little sleepy. She watched the dark trees slip by the car window to her left. To her right, the handsome profile of Sean O'Connor, her boyfriend, or partner, or significant other, or whatever it was you called your fella when it was the 2020s and you were both in your sixties. The awkwardness of Tabitha's misinterpretation had dissipated. Julia knew that she didn't want marriage. She had done that, and happily, but would not do it again. And she realised that neither did she require official declarations of anything. She'd made an issue in her head when there wasn't one in the relationship. Sean was a good man, who showed his love through his behaviour – his kindness and thoughtfulness, his presence and attention. If he didn't say, 'I love you', that was fine. She loved him, and he loved her, and they both knew it.

'Hang on a minute, look there...' Sean pulled the car to the side of the road and pointed in the direction of the house alongside them.

'What are you looking at?' she said. On the other side of a low stone wall a house was partially visible through the trees. It seemed to be shut up for the night, dark except for one golden square upstairs, presumably indicating the inhabitant's bedroom.

'I thought I saw someone. There, over by the rhododendron bushes. Isn't that a person?'

It was indeed. It was a beautiful moonlit evening, light enough to see a black-clad figure edge towards the house, hugging the overgrown perimeter. He – she presumed it was a man – stopped and looked up at the lighted window. A cap was pulled down low over his face. His behaviour could only be described as 'skulking'.

'The peeping Tom!'

'What?'

'Sean, Hayley told me there was a peeping Tom out and about. It must be him. What is the name of this road?'

She reached into her phone for her bag.

'Alexandra Close.'

She was already dialling.

'Hayley! I think I've spotted your peeping Tom on Alexandra Close. There's someone creeping about. It's number...' she looked about.

'Twelve,' Sean said, having spotted the house number.

'Number twelve. Sean's with me. We were driving home. Shall we apprehend the man?'

'Absolutely not,' said the detective inspector. Julia could hear Hayley's footsteps and the clink of her car keys. She barked into the phone, 'Julia, stay in your car. Do NOT get out. I'm on my way.'

It was excruciating not being able to do anything but watch the man creep around the garden, looking up at the window. Two bats flitted about the eaves, briefly stark against the full moon. It was beautiful, if it weren't for the prickle of fear Julia felt. What if he tried to break in? Fortunately, he seemed to have no such intent. He simply skulked around, looking up. The curtains were closed and the angle was such that she doubted he'd see anything anyway. Not unless whoever was in there came right up to the window.

Headlights reflected in the rear-view mirror, coming up fast behind them. The lights were turned off before the car stopped – presumably so as not to alert the peeping Tom. Hayley Gibson jumped out and headed over to the car.

'Where?' she asked brusquely.

'There,' Julia said, pointing.

But the man had disappeared.

17

At the far end of the main street, the shops were fewer and less fancy, and increasingly interspersed with offices offering useful, if not glamorous, services. There was a laundromat, a tax consultant, a physiotherapist... And William Adamson Property Company. Through the frosted glass door, Julia saw the outline of a person she recognised as Kimberley. She pushed the door open and stepped inside.

'Oh, hello,' Kimberley said with a slight frown of recognition that quickly cleared. 'From the charity shop!'

'That's right. Julia. I was passing, and I thought, well, I'll take your advice and ask your dad about the Padel club.'

'Right, sure. He's on a call, but why don't you take a seat, and you can go through when he's done.'

Julia sat down in the little reception area. What Kimberley had said about a falling out between Will and Eve had woken Julia up at 3 a.m., and she hadn't been able to get back to sleep. She knew that Hayley would be furious if she came to her with yet another theory about Eve's possible murder, but at the same time, she could not let it alone. Eve hadn't jumped. And Julia really struggled to see how she could possibly have fallen. And now she knew that Will Adamson had fallen out with Eve, and from the sounds of things, just before her death. 'But nobody saw him on the path,' she could hear Hayley telling her, in her head. And she couldn't argue with imaginary Hayley's point. It was a good point. But still, finding out just a little bit more might help her sleep at night.

However, now that she was here, she was a little uncertain as to the wisdom of her plan. She remembered Will Adamson as rather a scary individual. But, she reminded herself, she wasn't there to confront him, or accuse him, just to chat about the club and see if she could find out anything more about Eve. To soothe her nerves, she looked around the waiting room. A big aerial photograph of Berrywick occupied most of the opposite wall. It was odd to see the village like that, the roofs, with the little squares of the chimneys. The roads and the river. The round blobs of the trees.

On a display table, next to the map, was a perfectly preserved manual typewriter, with a little plaque next to it. Julia went over and bent down to read the plaque: *Property of William Adamson, snr. Founder.*

'That was my granddad's,' said Kimberley. 'He started the business at his kitchen table with nothing but that typewriter. My dad keeps it as a memento. When he's feeling really sentimental, like maybe on my birthday or something, he even uses it to type a note.'

'That's really sweet,' said Julia. 'A special family heirloom.'

'Would you like a coffee?' Kimberley asked. 'It's good coffee. Cappuccino, if you like. We've got a machine.'

'A cappuccino sounds delicious, thank you.'

Julia moved closer to the aerial photograph, looking for her own house. She followed the river and found the nearby bridge and the crossroads, and her lane, and there it was. Her home. She peered in, hoping to see the chicken coop, or perhaps Jake lazing on the lawn, but at that distance it was blurs and dots.

Besides, it was probably taken before she, Jake and the chickens had taken up residence.

'It's rather fascinating, isn't it? Seeing it all from up above like a great big raptor.'

She turned to see Will Adamson, who had emerged from his office and was watching her like some great big raptor himself.

'Hello, Mr Adamson, I'm not sure if you remember me. I came in a few months ago. I was looking for an apartment for my daughter...' Julia blushed slightly. The last time they had met, she pretended to be looking for an apartment for Jess. The reality was, she'd suspected Will Adamson of committing a murder at the time. And here she was, back again.

'Of course. Come into my office and tell me what I can do for you.'

Julia followed him into his office, where they sat on either side of a large desk. On the wall behind her were framed certificates of his diplomas, degrees, awards and achievements.

'It's about the Padel club. I'm considering joining, but I'd heard it was rather, shall I say fractious?' He frowned and raised an ironic eyebrow at the odd choice of word. 'Kimberley said that you played there, and said I should pop in and ask you about it. I was passing, so here I am.'

'Fractious, you say? Well, it's a sport you know. Not a knitting club. Although I suppose a knitting club could be fractious too. You would know better than me.' Will laughed, like he had said something hilarious.

Julia would *not* know, being entirely deficient in the skills required to deploy any kind of needle or thread for any purpose at all. Her mother had been a wonderfully competent sewer, and made all Julia's childhood frocks, and whipped up curtains, and mended things like actual magic, but the talent had skipped a generation. Perhaps two, because Jess showed no sign of turning into a keen seamstress.

'Vicious, no doubt, those knitters. *Not* that I would know,' said Julia.

'Well, with sports, there's always going to be some tension. Competition, you know. All that sweat and testosterone. The will to win. The court is not a place for ninnies.'

'But there are friendlies, aren't there? There was a lovely one last Tuesday, apparently, did you play?'

'Two coffees!' Kimberley came in with the tray just as he was about to answer. She put it down and stood next to her father, beaming as if she'd laid an egg.

'Thank you, my darling,' he said warmly to his daughter, and then, to Julia, 'Oh yes, Tuesday, the social game. I played. Very nice, it was. Good fun.'

Will Adamson was an odd man. One minute he was making harsh comments about testosterone and the knitting club, but when his daughter walked in, he was suddenly a kitten.

'Pleasure, Dad. Enjoy.' Kimberley patted him on the shoulder and left.

The steam coming off the foam-topped cups smelled rich and delicious. Julia often thought that the smell of coffee was better than the taste, and the real reason for its enduring popularity.

'Ah – so you must have seen Olga Gilbert there too.'

Will frowned. 'Where?' he said.

'At the social game. On Tuesday.'

'Ah yes, quite. Indeed, Olga was there. Lovely lass.'

Lass was not entirely the word that Julia would have chosen to describe Olga.

'And you partnered with Eve, am I right?'

'Well, not on Tuesday,' said Will hastily. 'That was the day that she died. Terrible loss. Terrible. If only she had been at Padel, not slipping around on the hill.'

'But you played with her usually?' Julia knew she was in danger of becoming too pushy.

'Yes, yes. Well, sometimes. It doesn't do to get too attached to a partner, does it. Like I said, this is no knitting club.' He laughed again. He obviously found knitting a particularly amusing occupation.

'Hmm, yes. So, all in all, would you say it's a friendly club to join? For me, that is?' said Julia, remembering her cover story.

Will looked her up and down. 'I'm sure you'll be fine,' he said. 'Just don't get pushy. Like some people.'

Julia wondered if this was a veiled reference to Eve, but thought she better let sleeping dogs lie at this point.

'Well, thank you, Mr—'

The ringing of the phone interrupted her farewell. Will answered without so much as a polite nod of acknowledgement in Julia's direction.

'Will Adamson. Ah, Brian, what can I do for you? I see... Right... Yes... No...'

He leaned back in his big leather chair and looked straight over Julia's head while he spoke. It was as if she was invisible. 'I promise you, Brian, if there's a square foot of land in this county for sale for such a thing, I'd know about it. No one knows this place like I do. I make it my business to know every inch of Berrywick, every building, every tree and every path.'

Julia recalled the big aerial photograph of Berrywick and its surrounds, and imagined a tiny square foot of it, marked out on it with a yellow highlighter wielded by Will Adamson.

He was still talking into the phone in a loud and authoritative manner. 'I hear you. It's the problem all over, Brian. It's a complete nightmare for all the developers – no one knows that better than you. Getting the permissions from the council, from residents, what have you. It's impossible. Everyone wants to be able to park their car, but no one wants a car park. Same with shops. Same with Padel courts. Same with everything. And heaven help you if some damn hedgehog lives in the field you're wanting to dig up. Or some bloody daisy grows in the useless bog. Then the eco warriors are all over you like a rash. This property game, I tell you. It's a bugger.'

He looked at Julia when he uttered the word, and gave her a nod somewhere between an apology and an acknowledgement. She wasn't invisible, then. Good to know.

'As I said, Brian. Difficult business. But I've got a few tricks up my sleeve yet. Let me put my feelers out, make some calls, see if I can sort something. I know a chap... you never know. I'll be in touch.'

Julia thanked him as soon as the phone was put down, and stood up. Will was back on the phone before she was out of the door.

'Thanks for the coffee, it was really good,' she said to Kimberley.

'How was it? Was Dad helpful?'

'Oh, yes, he likes the club. You're right.'

'Maybe you could play with him sometime.' Kimberley sounded wistful.

Julia smiled. 'I doubt he'd want to play with a beginner like me.' Or with an older woman, she thought but didn't say.

Kimberley looked sad, batting her ridiculous eyelashes as if she might be holding back tears. 'He *didn't* play on Tuesday,' she said in a low voice. 'I know, because I can see his diary. It's shared. He actually cancelled the diary entry for the game. I think he didn't play because he hasn't got a partner to play with. After the falling out with Eve, he must have gotten a reputation for being difficult. He's got no one to play with him now, and Padel is his passion. He knows that I worry about him since Mum died. I think he lied to you because I came into the office. He didn't want me to know. He didn't want me to worry about him, that's why he lied. But now I'm even more worried. Poor lonely Dad.'

'Yes, poor Will. What actually happened with him and Eve?'

'I'm not even sure, that's the worst of it. I heard him on the phone to her saying that she's never open to change, so I think that maybe she wasn't taking his suggestions about her game well. Dad can be a bit... bossy. But then when I asked him, he said everything was fine. He always tries to protect me. Like lying about where he was on Tuesday.'

It could be that, thought Julia. He could be lying to save his daughter's feelings, and his own self-esteem.

Or...

Or, he could have been somewhere else last Tuesday afternoon. Like on the hill path. Taking his revenge on his ex-Padel partner. He'd talked about people being pushy. Maybe he was the one who had done the pushing.

18

Julia's suspicions about Will began to dissipate as she drove home. Not because she thought Will Adamson was a kind-hearted, peace-loving fellow. Rather, because she realised that there was a great big hole in her theory. She was basing it on Kimberley's belief that her father was lying, that he wasn't at the social game. But for all she knew, he *was* playing on Tuesday. Kimberley didn't necessarily know everything about him. And his diary might not have been updated. She needed to get corroboration one way or another before she went to Hayley Gibson with yet another half-baked theory.

Fortunately, there was one way to find out – she could phone Olga Gilbert. She couldn't quite work out how to go about ascertaining whether Will Adamson had indeed played at the friendly tournament on Tuesday, other than ask, 'Did Will Adamson play at the friendly tournament on Tuesday?' which seemed rather too direct, especially given that Olga had lied about where *she* was that afternoon. Julia hoped that if she introduced the man more generally, a good idea would come to her, or Olga would drop a useful piece of information. She'd have a think about how to approach it before she spoke to Olga.

Jake was delighted to see her after their long and traumatic separation of an hour and a half. He was a lunatic, granted, but who wouldn't love to be treated to a one-dog welcoming parade, a chocolate-brown blur with a lolling pink tongue, running victory laps around the garden, sending chickens and clods of earth and bits of grass flying in all directions, then turning multiple tight circles, and bouncing up and down, before finally collapsing at her feet for a pat, and perhaps a little treat, if she happened to have one handy.

Julia found him a rather crusty-looking bit of cheese. It had gone hard, but he wasn't fussy when it came to cheese. He swallowed it in a single gulp and looked around hopefully, wondering if there were seconds.

'You should have chewed it,' she said, giving him an ear scratch. 'You know you always regret it when you swallow the snack whole.'

With Jake greeted and treated, it was time to phone Olga. After the preliminary niceties, she said, 'I wanted to let you know that you've inspired me, Olga. I've decided to join the Padel club. I'm a bit nervous, to be honest. Maybe you can give me some tips.'

Before she could elaborate about the nature of the tips she was hoping to elicit, Olga launched into a detailed description of what one should look for when purchasing shoes, which wasn't very helpful, seeing as Julia had already decided to play in her plimsolls until she was sure she liked it. When there was a brief lull in the explanation of soles and grip, she jumped in. 'That's very helpful. I was more concerned about the social aspect. Finding people to play with, and a partner and so on. I heard the club could be a bit cliquey. How do I go about getting involved?'

'Oh, that's easy. There are always newcomers looking to play. It's a good idea to find a few regulars though, or at least a partner.'

'Tabitha is probably going to join too, but I was wondering about a mixed doubles partner. Someone mentioned Will Adamson was looking for a partner.'

'Gosh yes, he used to play with Eve, you know.'

'Yes, very sad.'

There was a respectful pause.

'Do you know Will Adamson at all?'

'I know him.' It wasn't exactly an enthusiastic endorsement.

'And? Do you think I should ask him?'

'I don't know... He's a reasonable player. Maybe a bit too good to be a good partner for a beginner.'

'That's what I thought.'

'Honestly, I don't think he'd be a good fit, Julia. He's very competitive. I'd say aggressive.'

'Oh, well thank you for your honesty. That doesn't sound like a good fit for me.'

'Really, it doesn't. He was going to come to play in the most recent friendly, but he cancelled at the last minute and I must say, I was quite relieved. Friendly isn't really his thing.'

'The friendlies on Tuesday?' said Julia, hoping that Olga didn't remember that Julia had overheard her lie about being at the doctor that day.

'Yes,' said Olga, sounding slightly surprised. 'There are friendly matches most Tuesdays. And you don't work, do you? You'll probably be able to play more than *I* ever can.'

Julia put the phone down feeling a sense of pride, even triumph. She had cleverly confirmed that Will was lying about his whereabouts on Tuesday afternoon. He *had* cancelled Padel, just as Kimberley thought – was it because he had no one to play with, as his daughter assumed, or was that because he found out Eve was going to be on that walk? Or had he lured her there, arranged to meet?

'Julia Bird, super-sleuth,' she said to Jake. He looked at her adoringly and thumped his tail heavily on the ground. He thought she was just the cleverest human in the world.

Julia made herself a cup of tea, and sat down to think about exactly what it was she could now tell Hayley. She wanted to be sure that Hayley would listen with an open mind, not get irritated and send Julia away with another reprimand. As she mentally laid out the pieces, it gradually dawned on her that she hadn't made as much progress as she'd thought. She had caught Will out in a lie, granted, but that was a long way from proving or disproving his involvement in Eve's death. For a start, his motive was weak – it was hard to imagine anyone killing someone for breaking up a Padel partnership. Unless there was something else between them, something romantic, perhaps? Could they have been in a relationship that went sour? She tried to picture the two of them together. Aside from their athleticism and drive, they seemed to have little in common. Their interests, their personalities, their values... It seemed unlikely, but you never could tell, could you? And whatever else you said about him, Will Adamson was objectively a good-looking man.

The trouble with that theory was that there was not even a sniff of a rumour about a romantic involvement, and Berrywick was a village where romantic secrets were hard to keep, and rumours abounded.

And there was a bigger problem. No one had seen Will Adamson on the path on the day Eve died. DC Walter Farmer had interviewed everyone who had been there that afternoon, and followed up all the reported sightings of joggers and amblers and dog walkers. They had all been mentioned by each other, but no one had mentioned him. Will Adamson was a distinctive fellow, tall and strapping, with a powerful physical presence. It seemed likely that if he'd been there, and someone had seen him, they would have remembered him.

Detective Inspector Hayley Gibson would raise exactly that

point, of course. An aggressive manner doth not a murderer make. And as for his lie about where he saw that afternoon, well, that could be explained away. He hadn't been seen on the path. That's what it all kept coming back to.

It looked as if Will was off the table as a suspect. Murder was perhaps off the table too. But Julia still couldn't buy it. A strong, fit woman like Eve slipping on a perfectly safe edge. It didn't make sense. And as for the suicide theory – well, that was clearly ridiculous.

Assuming someone did push Eve, whether Will or someone else, why did no one see them? Was there some other way to get to the top of the hill, without passing anyone on the path? Julia didn't think that the police had looked into that as an idea at all, and now that she thought about it, it seemed perfectly possible. The Cotswolds was hardly the Amazon rainforest, filled with unpassable vegetation and dangerous animals to bar one's path. Maybe the killer came up some other path, or scrambled up avoiding the path altogether.

She thought of the big map of Berrywick and surrounds that dominated Will Adamson's office. And his boastful claim to know Berrywick better than anyone else. If anybody could find out about an alternative route on that well-loved walk, it would be Will Adamson. And it wasn't impossible to imagine another access point, another path.

Julia reached for her phone and called up Google Earth. She had investigated Berrywick from above three years ago, when she decided to buy a home there. She'd checked out the paths and roads, the walks, the river. Measured the distance to the shops, and to Tabitha's house. Now she was looking for another way for someone – Will Adamson? – to reach the top of the hill, unseen. And push a woman to her death.

The screen filled with a bird's-eye view of Berrywick, not dissimilar to the photograph on Will's wall. The difference being, she could zoom in, spreading and pinching her fingers until she found the access road, and the parking area. The path that she usually took, the one that Eve and all the other walkers had taken that fateful day, was clearly visible. She followed it, but it was surprisingly difficult to work out where she was on the map, with all the usual visual clues flattened by the top-down perspective. She managed, after a bit of effort, to find exactly the spot from which Eve had fallen. And above the main path on her map – but below it in real life – was the place where she had landed. It all looked so innocuous, just trees and bushes and grass. But not even a fortnight ago, there was a dead body there.

Julia zoomed in to the very spot at the top of the hill where Eve must have been standing. It was a little way off the main path. She could make out the flattened, earthy area where she had stood and peered over. To the right, a stand of thick bushes and young trees. There was something dark and long. She remembered a fallen tree, a big oak. She was in the right place, at least. Behind the trunk of the fallen oak was a clearer patch, and leading from it, a faint, curved line. She zoomed the map out a bit.

Yes. There was no mistaking it.

There was another path.

19

'Goodness, Julia. I can't believe you found that little side path.' Hayley sounded genuinely impressed, with a hint of self-recrimination.

'It just came to me. I had this strange hunch that there was another access point.'

'More to the point, I can't believe we didn't see it.' Hayley ran her fingers through her hair in a familiar gesture of frustration that, Julia knew, would cause the short hair to spike up angrily, and gradually return to its usual position over the next few minutes.

'It was Will Adamson's aerial photograph that gave me the idea to look at the area on Google Earth. That's the only reason I found the little path.'

'Still, damn shoddy police work.' The Detective Inspector leaned her elbows on her desk and let her head hang for a moment.

Julia found herself in the unusual position of comforting Hayley Gibson in the face of failure.

'You really can't see it from the ground. I've walked the path a million times and I've never seen that little branch of the path.

It's just not visible. That's why I think Will, with his knowledge of the area, and his maps and so on, he might be who you're looking for.' Julia was polite enough not to point out that Hayley had not, in fact, been looking for anybody.

Hayley cut her off. 'Julia, people do not kill each other over amateur ball games. It's a crazy notion. She broke up a tennis partnership.'

'Padel.'

'Whatever. He's not going to push her off a cliff because of that.'

'He's very touchy. And it might have been a spur of the moment thing. In the heat of an argument.'

'If it was a heat of the moment shove, he wouldn't have taken the hidden path to get there,' Hayley pointed out. It was a fair point, one that Julia had not thought of, and had no answer for.

'Julia, I know you don't like the guy – a quite reasonable position, I must say – but being a jerk doesn't put him at the top of the suspect list. Now can we drop it?'

'Dropped,' Julia said, lifting her right arm and flicking open her hand, as if dropping a ball.

Hayley nodded, and moved on. 'It was getting dark when you phoned yesterday. Walter went to the site early this morning, with the forensic team. They're going to comb the path. I doubt there will be anything to find. It's been ten days since Eve died. If there was ever anyone on that path, then you can forget about footprints. In fact, it's unlikely they'll find anything of any use. But still.'

It was true. It was highly improbable that there would be evidence to link Will to the place – unless they found a great big signet ring, or perhaps a cotton handkerchief with the initials *WA* engraved or embroidered on them. But things like that only happen in books.

'Not that I'm at all convinced that this makes a difference.

Just because there's a path doesn't mean that anyone used it.'
Hayley paused, as if weighing up whether she believed her own
words. Julia wouldn't labour the point, but she thought it was
incredibly unlikely that the hidden path coming out at exactly
the point that Eve fell could be a coincidence.

'And *if* she was pushed, I'm actively *un*convinced that Will
Adamson had anything to do with it,' said Hayley, who sometimes gave the impression of reading one's mind. 'You know I
respect your instincts about human nature, Julia, but this time, I
think you're wrong.'

'I could well be. I hope I am.'

'Well, let's see if Walter and the forensic team come up
with anything useful. I'd like to be able to put this case to rest.
And let Eve Davies rest peacefully, too.'

Julia nodded, and changed the subject. 'Any progress on our
good friend Tom?'

'Tom who?' Hayley frowned. She was smart, but she had a
rather earnest, focused, approach to the world, which meant
that small attempts at humour often passed her by.

'Peeping Tom. Your case...'

'Oh, him. We haven't had a reported sighting since you
spotted him and we lost him. Maybe he got a fright and has
mended his ways.' Hayley made a disbelieving grunt as she said
it, at the exact same moment that Julia said '*Hmmmfff.*' They
smiled at each other, a wry smile that acknowledged that they
had both been out in the world enough to know that the
mending of ways – while possible – was not easily come by.

Their brief moment of contemplation of human nature was
interrupted by Walter, who burst into the office.

'Got some evidence for you!' he said triumphantly, dropping a bag on Hayley's desk. Two bags, in fact. There was the
familiar evidence bag with its labels and seals, and inside it,
another bag, also familiar to Julia. She opened her mouth to
speak, but thought better of it. Let Walter finish his story first.

'Forensics have dusted for prints, we should have results by the end of the day.'

'Good work, Walter.'

'Thanks, boss. Conditions weren't optimal, I have to say. Rain, dust, and so on. And after ten days...' He shook his head sadly.

'Yup. Well, let's see. Describe the scene for me, Walter. I'll go there later, when I've gotten a handle on all this paperwork.'

Hayley stared mournfully about her desk, which was, as always, an alpine mountain range, the peaks and valleys of which were created by teetering stacks of papers on the shifting tectonic plates of ancient files. This was not something you could 'get a handle on' of a morning. This was the work of a lifetime. Maybe two.

After a moment's silence for the state of the desk, Walter continued. 'It's not visible from the main path. You can't see the entrance, a huge oak has fallen right across it, you'd never know the path was there, unless you'd known it before the tree fell. It's very overgrown, and there were no signs of regular use. No one seems to know about it.'

'Other than, potentially, Eve's killer,' said Julia. Hayley frowned at her, but Walter smiled.

'Yes. Hard to tell if anyone had been up there recently though. No footprints, or obvious damage to the undergrowth. Only this bag of dog treats. It's a clue, at least. It could lead us to a suspect.'

Hayley sighed. 'It might be a clue, Walter. Although this is the Cotswolds. I think there are more dogs here than there are people. You're considered rather suspect if you *don't* have a pocket full of dog treats. Sometimes a bag of treats is just a bag of treats. Loads of people must be carrying those exact same treats.'

'Myself included. I recognise those dog treats, and have a good idea where they came from,' said Julia.

'Go on.'

'Good-Dog-Go Fair Trade Organic Beef and Barley Treats. Dr Eve used to sell them. They are like crack cocaine for dogs. They cost a fortune, but I buy them from her occasionally to help with Jake's training. Jake will do anything for them. It is quite bizarre. I reckon if I had enough patience, and a hundred thousand pounds to spend on those treats, that boy could write a sonnet.'

Hayley snorted, the kind of snort that passed for a laugh when you are discussing death, and asked. 'So you think Eve Davies might have dropped them?'

'Could be, although what would she be doing on that little path?'

Hayley shrugged. 'What would anyone have been doing on that little path?'

'But she was seen by everyone on the main path,' pointed out Julia. 'If someone dropped treats on the hidden path, it was someone that could have climbed the hill with nobody seeing a thing.'

'Fair point, Julia,' said Hayley, with a nod of concession. She turned to Walter, all business, rattling off thoughts and instructions.

'Walter, you can take that back to the evidence room, and please keep on top of forensics. Brief me as soon as there's anything. For all we know, those treats have been lying there since before the oak fell down. They were most likely dropped when the path was still in regular use.'

'Right you are, boss.'

'I think they're quite new on the market, Hayley,' said Julia, trying not to sound like she was contradicting the other woman. 'And that oak must have fallen a long time ago.'

'I'm just saying let's not jump to conclusions, Julia. Again.'

'Fair enough.'

But Julia couldn't help feeling a slight shiver of recognition. Whatever Hayley might say, those treats were important.

20

As Julia approached the Padel courts, the traffic slowed almost to a standstill. There was some sort of hold-up in the road.

'Are they doing roadworks?' Tabitha craned her neck to get a better look.

'I don't know. We're very early though, we've got plenty of time before our lesson.'

Julia edged the car forward. 'There's someone with a sign. It looks like a one-man protest.'

A small and unprepossessing fellow was holding a sign with what appeared to be a picture of a large spotted frog on it. Being sixty-ish, neither of them could make out the wording at that distance.

'A three-man protest. Or three-person, more like,' said Tabitha, as they drew up in line with them. As well as the small fellow, there were two women. Julia could read the signs now. The frog sign read: *Protect our habitat. CROOOAAAK!* The others said: *No more development* and *Nature for nature.* That last was rather confusing, but Julia got the idea.

'It must be to do with the proposed expansion. The plan to build more courts,' said Tabitha.

'Will Adamson was complaining about how every development is stopped by something like this,' said Julia.

Tabitha shook her head at Julia. 'We agreed that you'd be focused on the Padel this morning.'

Julia laughed. 'I am, I am.'

As Julia turned the car into the driveway leading to the club, she found herself feeling unaccountably guilty, as if she was personally kicking frogs out of their comfy, damp homes.

Sandy was waiting for them, dressed, as before, in minimal amounts of bright Lycra, racket in hand. 'Glad you made it into the club okay, what with the protest outside.' She said this as if they had braved hundreds of violent protesters to reach their destination.

'It was all quite peaceful. The cars were slowing down to look, but we had no trouble getting in. Who are the protesters?' asked Julia.

'It's mainly a chap called Hamilton Cunningham-Smythe. He's a nature boff. He had a show a while back.'

'I remember!' said Tabitha. 'It was a quirky sort of nature programme all about those little animals that you get in the woods and fields and hedgerows, frogs and rats and voles and so on. What was it called now?'

'*Cunningham's Cunning Critters*, it was called,' said Julia. 'Jess used to like it when she was about eight. She called him the Frog Dude.'

'That's him. He's the main force behind the protest,' said Sandy.

'Jess'll be tickled when I tell her that we had a sighting of Frog Dude in the wild. She absolutely adored him. So he's trying to stop the expansion of the courts, is he?'

'Yes. The owners are trying to get permission to build more courts and some other facilities on the adjacent field, and he wants to stop them. It's a tough one.' Sandy sighed. 'Look, I love the game, and it's my livelihood, so I get it. People want to play, and there's more demand than there are courts. If they build more courts, the players will get bookings more easily. The owners will make more money. But it is a nice bit of country-side, I must say. And the wildlife has to live somewhere, doesn't it?'

'It does. You can't have the whole countryside full of car parks and Padel courts,' agreed Tabitha, who was known to get particularly annoyed about the spread of car parks. Julia thought again of Will Adamson's telephone conversation but kept the thought to herself.

Sandy nodded. 'That was Eve's point, too. Not a popular one amongst the committee members, as you can imagine.'

'They are all pro the expansion?' asked Julia.

'They are. As far as I know, Eve was about the only one on the committee who opposed it. But oppose it she did – and she wasn't going to let the development go ahead on her watch. Voted against it and got other members of the committee to vote her way too, although nobody felt as strongly. Because of the animals. She loved the game, but she loved animals more. Being a vet and all. She thought it was more important to have a place for the birds and the frogs than to have more courts. She said – and she's right, I suppose – that when a piece of the countryside goes, it stays gone. That's the problem with all this develop-ment. An acre or two here and there adds up, and soon there's nowhere for the frogs and mice and bats and so on.' Sandy sighed again. 'I dare say without Eve there's very little standing in the committee's way. Now. Shall we get started?'

She handed them each a racket. They had decided to have a couple of lessons and make sure they liked it before they spent the money on getting their own kit.

'How's the wrist?' asked Sandy, gently touching Julia's injured wrist.

Julia's injury had recovered quickly, and she was confi-dent that she could play Padel with it. She swung her arm and made a few gentle practice strokes with the racket, testing the strength. 'It's fine. I think I'll be all right to play. Let's do it!'

As they played, Sandy gave them tips on how to hold the racket, adjust the grip, where to stand, how to move. Sandy's instructions were very helpful. It was always surprising what a difference a bit of insider info from an experienced person could make. Tabitha was getting the hang of it too, and while neither of them could be described as the Roger Federer of Cotswold Padel, they had fun, and got up a bit of puff. There were a few twinges in Julia's wrist if she hit the ball hard – not something that happened very often, it must be said – but her arm held up well.

On her daily walks with Jake, Julia often found that she fell into a meditative state, and her mind wandered in interesting and useful ways. A problem that had been bothering her might be solved, or a creative insight emerge, almost from her unconscious. Granted, some of the creative insights were things like, 'I could make a lovely tart out of all those tomatoes in the garden,' but occasionally they were significantly more profound or useful.

Padel was rather more exerting and required too much of her attention for these free-floating good ideas to come out, but as the three women hit their last couple of shots, and walked towards the exit, an idea came flying into her head with the force of a hard serve over a net.

'Sandy,' she asked, keeping her voice casual. 'Is Will Adamson on the Padel committee?'

'Yes, he is.' Sandy's tone was neutral, but her face wasn't. It bore a look of distaste, the lips drawn thinly together.

Bam! The ball landed, just where it needed to be.

'Will was in favour of the development, I suppose. Being in the property development business.'

'He is in favour, yes. More than in favour. He's actively

championing the building of those courts. He's an investor and stands to make a lot of money if it goes ahead.'

Tabitha and Julia exchanged meaningful glances. Julia had told her friend about her suspicions about Will.

'So he must be cross to have opposition, first from Eve, and now from the frog squad,' Tabitha said, nodding her head in their general direction. She gave Julia a small smile, proud of her own sleuthing.

'I'm sure he is,' said Sandy, packing her racket into a sports bag. 'He is no fan of Mr Cunningham-Smythe. Nor of Eve, for that matter. Although I'm sure he feels bad for being so aggressive towards her now that she's gone.'

Julia was less sure, frankly. Will Adamson did not seem to be a man who was burdened by excessive self-reflection or remorse. She pulled on a zip-up fleece. It was chilly, now that they were off the court and cooling down.

'Thanks, Sandy. That lesson really helped me get the hang of things.'

'Me too,' said Tabitha. 'I think we should play a few games, and then perhaps another lesson. Just to get us the edge we need for the top leagues, you know.'

'You give me a ring when you're ready to polish up your brilliant skills, ladies,' Sandy said with a laugh. They watched her go.

'I was thinking,' Julia said.

'Always a dangerous occupation.'

'Not this time, Tabitha. I was thinking I might ask Frog Dude for a photo with the two of us, to send to Jess. She'd get a kick out of it.'

Tabitha raised her eyebrows. 'And if he happened to let slip any information about the development, or Will or Eve...'

'Serendipity, Tabitha. Pure serendipity.'

Hamilton Cunningham-Smythe huffed and puffed, flattered and embarrassed by Julia's request. As soon as he spoke,

Julia remembered how her and Jess had laughed at his strange speech patterns that made him sound like someone far older than his years. 'I suppose that a photograph would be eminently agreeable. Providing that it is acceptable for me to hold the sign up. The message must prevail, you know. All hands on deck and all that. Tally ho.'

'Oh, definitely with the sign. She will want to see the frog. Because of you, she loves frogs,' Julia said, not quite sure what to make of the sudden naval imagery.

'Frogs are extraordinary chaps,' Hamilton said, looking pleased. 'Amphibians are particularly vulnerable to habitat degradation, you know, which is why we can't have this sort of development. Absolutely caddish behaviour. Other animals are at risk too, of course. Water rats, and others that live in a riverine environment. Birds too. And bats. Extraordinary chaps, bats. I'm doing a survey of bats in the area and I am going to share with you that I am extremely concerned. Extremely.' He dropped his voice for the last part, as though imparting a great secret.

Julia was nodding solemnly, but had a sense that Hamilton would not stop talking if she didn't interrupt his flow. 'Come on, Tabitha,' she said. 'Let's get our picture. You stand on the other side of Hamilton.'

They stood on either side of him. Julia held her phone at arm's length, trying to get a good angle for a selfie. She had never cracked the selfie. Someone was always cut off, and she herself always looked anxious. Which she was, because she was no good at taking a selfie. She moved the phone a bit to the left, so she had the whole of Tabitha, but she hadn't got the hang of which little button to press, so she fumbled it when she tried to actually take the photo.

'Just a minute,' she said, repositioning the silly thing. Now her arm took up half the screen.

'Could one of your colleagues perhaps take the picture?' Tabitha asked. 'It might be better.'

Frog Dude looked as if he was sorry he'd agreed to this foolishness, but he called out to a woman in Wellington boots and a long, shapeless jersey the same colour as the frog on Hamilton's sign. 'Regina?'

Regina stomped over in her wellies, put down her sign and took the phone from Julia.

'Smile,' she said grimly.

'Thank you, Regina. How kind, what fun, Jess will be delighted. Hamilton, you really influenced her love of animals and nature,' she said.

He looked pleased and bashful. 'That's good to hear.'

'Good luck with your cause. I knew Eve Davies, the vet. Sadly no longer with us, as I'm sure you know. I believe she was on your side on this one.'

'Oh she was. Wonderful chap, dear Dr Eve. A great supporter. She will be greatly missed. Our mission will be much more treacherous without her, I think I can share that. She was the voice of reason when others showed themselves to be positively dastardly. The cad who is the ringleader, he's even more determined to get the additional courts built now. And with Eve dead, he might just get his way. That's why it's imperative that we fight. And I happen to know that this chap's plans don't stop there. He wants to have a tearoom, and a shop, and there will be more parking.' He almost spat the last word. 'It's a disgrace.'

Hamilton paused and caught his breath. 'He's the sort of cad who will stop at nothing,' he said, his voice sad. 'I think we might be fighting a losing battle on this one.'

The words 'stop at nothing' rang in Julia's ears.

Did that include murder?

21

'Oh my lord! Mum! That picture...' Jess dissolved into giggles on the other end of the phone. She flung her head back, and Julia admired her merry manner and the straight white teeth that had cost her parents many hundreds of pounds at the Harley Street orthodontist that everyone said was the best. Mother and daughter were on a video call, Julia's phone propped in a little holder on her knees. 'You and Tabitha are absolutely hilarious. You look like two batty old ladies.'

'At least you said "look like", instead of "are". I knew you'd love it. That's why I phoned as soon as I woke up.'

The time difference was a continual challenge, but they'd finally got the hang of adding or subtracting eight hours quite efficiently. It was 8 a.m. in Berrywick, but 4 p.m. in Hong Kong. Julia had sent the photo the previous evening, her time, when Jess was asleep.

'I can't believe you met Hamilton Cunningham-Smythe in person. Frog Dude! My childhood hero!'

'He was protesting outside the Padel courts when we went to have our lesson. You would have gone mad for him, Jess. He's a bit older, obviously, aren't we all? But he looked the same as he did on those old shows you used to watch. That rather charming dishevelled thing he had going. And that voice! It's unmistakable, I'd recognise it anywhere. His odd turn of phrase. He kept calling people "cads" and "chaps".'

'Actually, I think I recognise that cap he's wearing in your picture. It's either the same one he wore on the programme, or he's had a succession of similar ones. Same with the jacket.'

'It's probably a standard uniform he's worn since he was fifteen. Good idea, come to think of it. Think of the time you'd save – you could just rotate three or four different but same items, and there you go. Anyway, he was pleased to hear he had made an impact on you when you were little, and he was very sweet about having the photograph taken.'

'What exactly were you doing there?'

Julia explained about her new sport, and the development and the fields and the protest. She didn't mention dead Eve Davies. Jess's visit to Berrywick had been marked by another death, and she didn't want her to get the impression that the little village was a dangerous hotbed of murder and mayhem.

'Oh I miss you, Mum. And Jake and Tabitha and...' Jess stopped speaking.

'Dylan?'

There was a pause in Hong Kong. Julia waited in Berrywick. 'Yes. I do miss him. He's a good guy. We really like each other. We had something... nice. We *have* something nice, a connection. We do speak, and message each other every day. But we're not an item. We've agreed we're not going to try and do a long-distance thing.'

'It's hard, when you like someone and the circumstances aren't in your favour. But you'll work it out, love. If you want to. And if not, you'll be okay.'

'I know. I'm just focusing on my degree. Getting that finished. Doing the very best I can on that score. And then I'll make the next decision.'

Not for the first time, Julia marvelled at the good sense her daughter displayed. They chatted some more – an exhibition of ceramics that Jess had seen, a trip to the beach with friends, and Julia's more mundane news, the charity shop, her vegetable garden, and so on. Their chats had been longer and chattier since Jess's visit. They had become so close and comfortable with each other by the end of it. Also, she had got to know half of Berrywick, and was eager for updates on all the goings on of the locals.

'Mum, I'd better go. I'm meeting a friend for drinks at some hot new place by the harbour, and I have to get ready.'

'I, too, have pressing engagements. It's all go, go, go on this side. I'll be making breakfast, and then do a bit of training with Jake.'

'Show me Jake so I can say goodbye. I don't want him to forget me.'

Feeling only mildly silly, Julia held the phone to the dog who was lying at her feet, as usual. 'Your sister's on the phone.'

He looked at the phone with disinterest, but when Jess's voice came out of it, he frowned slightly. Truly, the world was mysterious.

'Bye, Jakey boy. Love you. Mum, send love to Sean. And Tabitha. And have a scone for me!'

'Sit.'

Jake sat.

'Stay.'

He stayed. As Julia walked away from him, she could almost feel his quivering excitement. Every cell in his body wanted to hurtle after her. But he stayed. She stopped and turned to face him. His eyes bored into hers as he waited for her command.

'Come in,' she said.

He bounded across the grass and skidded to a halt, and turned to sit at her side.

'Good boy, Jake. You're a very good boy.'

Julia took the packet of Good-Dog-Go from her pocket and gave him one. He swallowed it whole, as usual, and seemed surprised to find it gone, looking about hopefully as if it might be there.

'All right, one more. Because you are very good. Maybe chew it this time.'

He snapped it from her fingers and swallowed it. Whole.

'Straight down the gullet. That's about fifty p's worth right there,' she muttered. 'You could at least savour it for a moment. Only the luckiest, most privileged dogs with the most generous owners get Good-Dog-Go Free-Range Gold-Dusted Unicorn-based Truffle-Dipped Treats.'

Jake stared at her with a line of saliva hanging from the side of his mouth. He was only interested in the treats. He never got that sort of joke but still, it was disappointing to waste such good material.

Jake only got the treats for their training sessions, which she tried to do most days, but realistically managed a few times a week. They were too expensive to be doled out willy-nilly. Only the most spoilt dogs got these. It was strange, she thought, but she wouldn't have taken Will Adamson as the type to buy his dog expensive treats. Yet she was very sure that he was the one who had walked the secret path and pushed Eve off the cliff. It made so much sense: he had the motive of his Padel development that Eve was stopping, he had lied about being at Padel that day, and he was a person likely to know about the secret path. But the only physical clue that they had was the treats. And if forensics couldn't find anything – how would they link them to Will?

The treats were exclusive items, as evidenced by their ridiculous name – Good-Dog-Go Fair Trade Organic Beef and

Barley Treat – and their ridiculous price tag. You couldn't buy them just anywhere.

'Given the location, if Will bought the treats, he would probably have bought them from Dr Eve,' she said out loud. 'Especially seeing as they were friends before they fell out.' Jake looked at her as if she was the cleverest human he had ever encountered. 'Jake, we're going on a little outing. Can't have you running out of treats, can we?'

Olga was alone in the reception. 'Hello, Julia, how can I help you? How's Jake's tail?'

'Right as rain, thank you.'

Jake wagged his tail merrily, as if to illustrate its excellent health. 'We are here for more dog treats. The Good-Dog-Go Fair Trade Organic Beef and Barley Treats that he loves. I use them for his training.'

'Well, someone's been a good boy if you're restocking already! Here you go.'

She handed over the packet, and Julia handed her a note of an unreasonably large denomination. 'Olga, can a person buy these Good-Dog-Go anywhere else in Berrywick?'

'No, only here. They aren't available at regular supermarkets, only at vets and pet supply shops. And they like to keep it to just one or two distributors in each village. So you'll have to come here for them.' Olga sounded slightly offended, and Julia was quick to reassure her.

'Oh, we don't mind coming here for them. It's not that. It's...'

Julia hesitated. As far as Olga was concerned, Eve's death was a tragic accident. If she started asking questions, Julia would alarm her, and cause her stress and pain. But Olga was the only one who might be able to tell her if Will bought the treats.

'A packet of these was found near where Eve fell. Someone

must have dropped them. Would Eve have been carrying them, perhaps?'

'No.' Olga sounded very sure of herself. 'She didn't give Fergus treats. He tends to be a bit weighty, being an older dog.'

'So they must have belonged to someone else.'

'Why are you asking? I thought the police had already spoken to all the people they knew about who were on the path that day.'

'They have, yes. But the treats were...' Julia paused. She wasn't sure that she wanted to tell Olga about the hidden path, or her suspicions about Will specifically. 'They were off the path itself. I just thought perhaps there was someone else up there. You know, someone that the police didn't take into account.'

The light of recognition flooded Olga's face. 'You don't think... You don't think someone hid and pushed her?'

'No, no, not that,' lied Julia. 'But maybe someone saw something. I don't understand how she could have slipped. I'd love to speak to anyone who could tell us more. Just to understand.'

Olga was pale-faced and flustered. And were those tears in the corners of her eyes? Julia felt terrible. Olga stammered out her answer: 'I don't know anything about that. It could have been anyone. I mean... It's just so... Gosh. I don't know.'

'I'm sorry, I didn't mean to upset you. It's probably completely immaterial, and whoever dropped them had nothing to do with Eve's death. And saw nothing. It's me and my ways. I like to know exactly what happened and how. Please don't worry, Olga. Forget I even mentioned it.'

Olga nodded glumly. She seemed a bit calmer.

'Thanks for the treats. And I'm sorry...'

'It's okay. I'm fine,' she sounded as if she was trying to convince herself of this fact, as much as she was trying to convince Julia. 'Goodbye, Julia. Bye, Jake.'

After lunch, Julia put on her gardening outfit – a motley selection of old clothes. An ancient, rather shapeless pair of trousers. A long sleeved shirt abandoned by Peter many years ago and way too big for Julia. A big straw hat. Slip-on gardening shoes made of the same waterproof stuff as Wellington boots. The outfit gave full protection against sun, thorns and dirt, as well as stylishness.

She had an afternoon of gardening planned. Spring had definitely sprung and the weeds were particularly springy. They appeared out of nowhere, seemingly overnight. She pondered, as she had often before, the fact that weeds seemed to be so healthy and hardy and bountiful, but if you wanted to grow, say, a lettuce, you had to water it and tend it and protect it from slugs and snails.

'Before you can reap you must sow,' she told Jake solemnly. 'And before you can sow, you have to clear all the weeds and the old dead stuff out of your veggie patch. Which is what I'm going to do now.' She grabbed the little weeding cushion she had to save her knees, and a special little weeding implement for extracting the weeds. It was quite satisfying work, once you got down to it.

She opened the chicken coop and called her 'chick chick chick' call, letting the chestnut-brown chickens out to stretch their legs and to forage for snacks. 'Don't hold back now, girls. Go get those snails!' she said encouragingly. They looked at her blankly. Unlike Jake, who looked like a brainless galumph, but who she sometimes thought could understand every word she said, the chickens had a certain quickness to their movements, and a brightness of eye that gave the impression of cleverness, when in fact they were terribly dim. Even Jake's bestie, the bossy Henny Penny, was no genius.

When she tired of weeding – even with a cushion for if she got uncomfortable after a while – Julia got up, picked up her secateurs, and took a tour of her garden. She liked to walk around noticing the details, and the daily or weekly changes, and snipping off spent blooms and straggly bits as she went.

Small as it was, there was a lot to see. The spring bulbs were well on their way. In a few weeks the pots by the kitchen door would be ablaze with daffodils and bluebells. The vegetables were similarly on the brink of greatness – the tomato plants were already in flower and little baby courgettes were forming. She reminded herself to fry some of the yellow courgette flowers, like the Italians did. The basil was looking healthy, and smelling like summer. In a month or so she would be making pesto.

Her old life as head of youth services had left no time for the slow delights of gardening. Nor did Peter's job as a specialist in international tax law. In fact, it was their combined hopelessness in the garden that had brought Christopher, the landscaper, into their lives. 'And here we are,' she said to Jake, with a laugh. 'Now I'm mad for gardening and Peter is married to Christopher. Funny old life, isn't it?'

Jake seemed to agree silently that life was indeed strange.

A couple of hours in the garden was about as much as she could manage, especially on a warm day. She tidied away the tools and put the hens back into their coop. Surveying her handiwork, she felt a quiet sense of achievement – she'd freed up space for another planting of lettuce seedlings – and a pleasant tiredness. She was much more relaxed than she'd been since that day two weeks ago that she'd found Eve's body. The police would soon have the forensics, and this crime – for Julia was still convinced that it was a crime – would be solved.

Her phone was vibrating on the kitchen table when she walked in. It was a number she didn't recognise, which for some reason rattled her newly acquired equanimity.

'Hello, Julia Bird,' she said, noting the wariness in her own voice.

'It's me. Olga.'

'Oh. Hello, Olga. How are you?'

'I thought about it when you left. And I think I know who dropped the treats. And I think I know what they were doing there. With Eve.'

Her voice was low, as if she feared being overheard. There was muffled talking in the background. Julia looked at her watch. It was three thirty. Olga was at the vet, presumably.

'Well, that's very helpful, Olga. Who was it?'

'I don't want to talk about it when I'm at work. We need to meet in person. Only you, no one else. Tomorrow.'

'I'll be in Berrywick, working at Second Chances. I could meet you after that...'

'No. I'll come in on my lunch break. Don't tell anyone anything. Behave like I'm just a normal customer. We can talk there.'

22

Julia looked at her watch. How was it only ten thirty? It felt as if she'd arrived at Second Chances three or four hours ago, and yet she had a good two hours to wait before she could reasonably expect to see Olga walk in, and tell her the information she longed to hear. Olga had sounded strange. Nervous.

Working at Second Chances wasn't the most demanding job in the world. There were always a few odd jobs to do – sorting, marking, cleaning, making the window display look nice – in between serving a light and steady trickle of customers. The days had a gentle rhythm to them, with plenty of breaks for tea and chats, but no one could call it utterly absorbing. This day was particularly, painfully slow. The customers were few and far between. The minutes crawled by, each following reluctantly on the heels of its predecessor in a long, slow procession towards lunchtime, and Olga's anticipated arrival.

Julia challenged herself not to look at her watch until she was sure it was at least eleven o'clock. She busied herself with the kitchenware display, wiping down the baking dishes meticulously, one by one and replacing each of them on a newly-wiped shelf. There. She looked at her watch: ten fifty-five!

Finally, *finally*, twelve thirty arrived. And then one. And then one thirty. There was no sign of Olga. Her lunch break would be well over by now. Two o'clock came. She wasn't coming. Olga must have got cold feet.

What to do, what to do? Julia knew she would go mad sitting there waiting and wondering. 'I'm going to the back for a moment, I've got a call to make,' she told Wilma, and went into the little back room where tea was made and items stored and sorted.

The phone rang and rang and rang. As Julia was about to give up, a man answered, sounding harried:

'Cotswolds Veterinary Care.'

'Oh, hello. I was hoping to speak to Olga.'

'She's not in right now. It's Dr Ryan here. How can I help you?'

'Hello, Dr Ryan. It's Julia Bird here... Jake?'

'Oh yes, chocolate Lab. How is he? Do you need an appointment?'

'Oh, Jake is fine, thank you. I was actually looking for Olga, to speak to her about a personal matter. I'll phone her on her mobile, if you wouldn't mind giving me her number.'

'She didn't answer when I phoned to find out why she was late. If she comes in I'll tell her you called.'

'Thank you.'

She heard beeping on the line, the sound of another call holding.

'I must go. It's busy here, and especially without a receptionist. And she left early yesterday for some errand. It's a bit much. She can be a bit flighty, can Olga, especially without Eve here. I must have a word.' The last bit he said grumpily, more to himself than to her, and then added, more kindly, 'I hope she's all right. If I don't hear from her, I might have to go to her house later.'

'She lives in Greenside Way, doesn't she?' Julia suddenly

remembered that Olga was in the same newish development as Kevin and Nicky.

'That's right.'

'It's not far from me. I'll be passing by there this afternoon, when I go to the shops. I can pop in and see if she needs anything.'

'I must go. Goodbye, Mrs Bird.'

A call to Nicky established that Olga lived at number 21. Julia had fretted somewhat about what she might give as an ostensible reason for asking – should she say she was delivering something? – but it turned out that subterfuge was unnecessary. She got as far as, 'I know Olga Gilbert lives in your road, but can you remind me of the number...' and Nicky was off, offering not only the pertinent bit of information, but also, as was Nicky's way, a convoluted backstory with a cast of dozens... 'Olga's place is on the left, if you're coming from the village. On the right if you're coming the other way, but you wouldn't be, I assume, living in the village yourself. You can't miss it. There's a big rhododendron outside. Just lovely, it is. She lives right opposite Hector. Do you know him? He is an actor. Or was. He was in one of those telly programmes. It took place in a newspaper office. What was it called, now? Goodness, my brain. It's childbirth that does it, I tell you. And Sebastian's five already. I can't remember the name of the programme but that blonde woman was in it. You know, the one who looks a bit like a fatter, darker, English, young Meryl Streep. Her. Anyhow, Hector, Olga's opposite neighbour, was in that show. It was on a while ago, now. Maybe five years...'

With some effort, Julia extricated herself from the extended filmography of Olga and Nicky's neighbour without being rude, and put the phone down feeling quite breathless from the deluge.

'No time like the present,' she muttered to herself, emerging from the back room to an empty shop. 'Is it okay if I get going a bit early, Wilma? I've got an errand to run. And the bakeware department is spick and span.'

Julia found Olga's house with no trouble at all – there was, as Nicky had promised, a magnificent rhododendron in full bloom, like a blazing pink beacon leading her to number 21. Even by the standards of Berrywick, which was home to many very keen gardeners and some very fine shrubbery, it was a sight to behold. It dwarfed Julia's car, which she parked next to it. She got out next to its rosy magnificence – was it cerise? Or was it fuchsia? – and found herself nodding to it respectfully as she passed.

Julia didn't know what she expected to find at Olga's house, but what she found was a perfectly nice little brick cottage in a row of similar, in a perfectly pleasant and ordinary road in Berrywick. Apart from the rhododendron, the only sign of life was a black and white cat with a rather disturbing perfectly formed black moustache and a bright red collar. It was sitting on the doormat, looking dapper and expectant.

At the sight of a visitor, the cat got to its feet and yowled angrily.

'Hello, puss puss,' Julia said, leaning over the cat to press the little gold buzzer next to the front door. She heard a ring, deep inside the house, but no other sound.

'Meeeouw...' the cat said, writhing against her legs. It had changed tack, abandoning fury and going with pitiful. It was a *sad* cat. It *needed* something. Food. Love. Everything. Why oh *why* was life so cruel?

She bent down and gave the cat a stroke. It collapsed at her feet dramatically and writhed some more.

Julia rang the doorbell again, and then shouted for Olga, suspecting that it was hopeless. She looked at the windows and noticed the curtains were closed. Olga wasn't there. She was pretty certain of that.

'Hello. Everything all right?' Julia looked around for the source of the question, which turned out to be a round head, haloed in red curls, peeking over the top of the fence. It was Olga's next-door neighbour.

'Oh, hello. I was looking for Olga, but it seems she's not here.'

'No. She must have gone to work very early. The car was out when I went out for my walk this morning.'

The car! How silly of her not to notice it wasn't there. What she did know – but didn't say – was that the car wasn't at Olga's work.

'Poor Chaplin looks like he's waiting for his tea. Olga usually leaves the kitchen window open for him when she goes out. Must have forgotten. Or perhaps it blew shut. It does that sometimes.'

Julie felt in her pocket and unearthed a loose dog treat from this morning's training.

'You're in luck, Chaplin, I've found a biscuit.' She handed it to the cat on the mat, and he fell upon it like a lion eating an impala in one of those nature documentaries that Sean enjoyed but Julia found gruesome.

'Ah, well that's good. I'm sure she'll be back soon enough. Bye then.'

The head disappeared.

Julia watched the cat crunch the biscuit, making a noise like a lion attacking the impala's femur. David Attenborough was in her head, giving the voice-over. 'And here, the magnificent feline predator, relishing the spoils of the chase...'

'I'm going nuts,' she said to the cat. The observation was its own confirmation.

Having swallowed the treat, the cat was yowling its head off, desperate for more.

'Sorry, kitty, I've got nothing,' she said, and gave the bell one last long push. As she turned to go, a glint caught her eye. The doormat had been dislodged by Chaplin's enthusiastic writhing, and something silver peeped out of the edge. Julia bent down.

It was a key.

Her hand hovered over it. She was in a state of perfectly balanced indecision. She could reposition the doormat to cover the key, or she could take the key, open the door, and open the window so the cat could get to his food.

Chaplin threw himself at her feet, mewing pitifully.

'Oh, all right,' she said. 'I'll open the kitchen window for you. Olga must have forgotten.'

With a guilty glance in the direction of the chatty neighbour, Julia opened the door. The cat shot in like a bullet from a gun, and dashed through the door. She followed him into the room, which was a kitchen and dining area. His bowl was full. He set upon it in ecstasy. Julia refilled his water bowl with fresh water, and leaned over the sink to open the window.

'There you go,' she said, but Chaplin was no longer interested in her. Too busy munching his way through the food.

Julia glanced around the kitchen. First, she went and opened the window, hoping that this was the one that Chaplin usually used. Then she looked around the room again. It was quite large for a small house, opened up in the modern way. At the far end was a table that seemed to serve as a dining table and a desk. At one end, there was a place setting, and salt and pepper grinders. At the other, a notebook, a pen, a laptop and a small nest of charger cords. On the far wall, behind it, was a bookshelf. Julia could never resist taking a look at a bookshelf. She wandered over. Olga was neat. It was alphabetised, she noticed, taking in Douglas Adams and Chimamanda Ngozi Adichie at the top left. And there was a row of Vincent Andrews's novels. Julia had a horrible flashback to the day, nearly two years ago, when she'd found the author's body between the stacks of the Berrywick Library. Olga, a childhood sweetheart, had been bereft. It made her sad to see six or seven of his books, a full set, no doubt, on Olga's bookshelf. Poor woman.

She wasn't snooping, she really wasn't, but as she turned to go, she glanced again at the notebook on the table. There was a list, and one of the names leapt out at her. Will.

She looked more closely.

Under the heading 'April' was a list of five names. And she knew two of them, Will Adamson, and Jim McEnroe. Robert Benjamin and Gina McFarlane were vague acquaintances. She didn't know the last name, Moira Walker.

She took out her phone and snapped a photograph of the list. She wasn't sure what the list meant – or why the journalist and the property chap were both on it – but her instincts told her it meant something. Something important.

On the way out, she picked up the box of cat biscuits, and shook a few more into the rapidly emptying bowl. That would keep the hungry cat going for a good long while. Who knew when Olga would be back?

'I've given you a top-up and you can get in and out of the kitchen now,' she said to the cat. 'I'll be on my way, then.'

The cat ignored her and continued his diligent eating, his head bobbing slightly as he took each mouthful.

'No need to thank me,' she said, sarcastically. She didn't know why she was addressing him out loud, she had no faith in cats' powers of comprehension. Dogs, of course, was another story. Jake understood everything she said, she was sure of it. But a cat? No.

Chaplin stopped eating and looked up at her. 'Meow,' he said politely, and gave her a nod, before returning his attention to more important matters.

23

Dusk was falling when Hayley finally returned Julia's call. Julia put down the kitchen knife she'd been using to slice onions and mushrooms, wiped her hands on her apron, and answered the phone.

'Thanks for getting back to me, Hayley.'

'Sorry it took a while. It's been a busy day. I'm leaving the station now, I'm on hands-free, so we can talk.' The detective sounded flat and tired.

'Why don't you come by? I've had a long day too. I'm busy making a spinach and mushroom omelette for supper. My hens' own eggs. I'll make you one, and we can chat in person.'

Hayley hesitated. Julia imagined her weighing up the options, as she herself would have done. On the one hand, it was tempting to go straight home – although doubtless, knowing Hayley, she would be facing a ready-made frozen meal, or a toast-based dinner, eaten alone. On the other, there was the prospect of a ready-made, free-range omelette in Julia's kitchen, and a friendly chat.

'Sure. That sounds good. I'll be there in ten.'

And there she was, nine minutes later, to be exact. They

went into the kitchen, the back door open to the cool evening air, and to let out the smell of onions and mushrooms frying in butter and oil. The eggs were beaten and seasoned, and waiting in their bowl. Julia had set the table, and set out her homemade lemonade. She might have a glass of wine herself, but she knew Hayley wouldn't if she was driving.

'Come and sit down. Help yourself to lemonade. Supper will be ready in a minute.'

Julia picked up the garden spinach that was washed and chopped and lying on a board next to the stove. She tossed it into the pan with the mushrooms, and put the lid on to let it wilt.

'So, what were you phoning about? I take it it wasn't a social call.'

'It's about Eve.'

'We're still waiting for the forensics, Julia. There's a backlog. I must say, I still think she jumped or fell. Those treats could have been on the path for ages.'

'I hear what you're saying, but some additional information has come my way.' Julia said this quickly, anticipating Hayley's reaction.

'It has, has it?' Hayley raised a sardonic eyebrow. 'Just fell into your lap?'

'It did, in fact. Tabitha and I went to play Padel, and there was a protest, right outside the gate. In my lap, as it were. It turns out, not everyone loves the fastest growing sport in the world.'

'Go on then.'

Julia explained about the proposed development, the wildlife activists, Hamilton Cunningham-Smythe, and the disagreement between the members. 'Eve was completely opposed to the idea, because of the environmental impact. It seems she was the only thing stopping the committee from voting in favour of the development. Most of them were happy to have the new courts built, and weren't very fussed about the implications. And there was one person who wasn't just in favour of the development, but had a lot to gain from it. That person is Will Adamson.'

'Julia, you are obsessed with that man!'

'I'm not obsessed, I'm just realistic. You said he wouldn't kill her over a falling out and the break-up of a tennis partnership, and I get that. But he might be tempted to kill to ensure that this development goes ahead, if he stands to make a packet.'

'A little more plausible,' Hayley admitted, with some reluctance.

'Thank you. And there's something else.'

Hayley sipped her lemonade and nodded at Julia to continue.

'Olga Gilbert, who works at the vet?'

'I know who she is. Walter Farmer interviewed her for the investigation.'

'Right, well, there's something new. I asked her about the dog treats. The ones I buy for Jake, the ones found on the hidden path... Oh heck!'

She leapt up at the smell of singed spinach and pulled the pan from the flame. 'Just in time,' she said, stirring the vegetables.

She turned off the gas and sat down. She'd finish this conversation and then get back to making the omelette.

'Olga phoned me yesterday. Yes, really, it was out of the blue. She said she'd been thinking, and she thought she knew who might have dropped the treats on the hidden path. She didn't want to talk at work, she said she'd come by Second Chances at lunchtime and talk to me. She never arrived.'

'You phoned her, I presume?'

'I did. She wasn't at work. She left work early yesterday, according to Dr Ryan, saying she had something to do. And she didn't go to work today. The really worrying thing is that she didn't phone in and tell them that she was sick or anything.'

Hayley, who had been following the story with a certain degree of scepticism, leaned forwards, her elbows on the table, and her sharp gaze fixed on Julia.

'Where is she?'

'I don't know.'

Julia took a deep breath. It was confession time. 'The vet did say she's a bit – what was it he said? – flighty. Especially without Eve around, apparently. But I was worried. I went to her house.'

'You went to her house?' Hayley's blue eyes grew round in surprise, then narrowed in anger. Before she could say anything, Julia continued. 'Yes, this morning. I went to see if she was all right, if she needed anything. But she wasn't there. Her cat was there though, and he was starving. I reckoned he hadn't been fed for a good while.'

'Cats!' Hayley grunted. 'Drama queens.'

'Turned out the kitchen window had blown shut and he couldn't get in.'

Julia had hoped to finesse the next bit, but there was no getting away from the fact that she had let herself into the house.

'There was a key.' Hayley opened her mouth, but Julia rushed on, cutting her off. 'And when I went in to feed him, I saw this list.'

She handed Hayley her phone with the picture of the list. It did the job of distracting her from the fact that Julia had entered Olga's home without permission. Julia continued. 'You see? The heading is April, and there are five names on the list. Will Adamson is one of them. Jim McEnroe another. They are both patients of Dr Eve – and I suspect the other three are too. I think this is the list of the dog treat buyers. And one of them is the murderer.'

'Whoa there,' Hayley said. 'That's a bit of a leap, isn't it?'

'Maybe,' Julia said. 'But add to it the fact that Olga is missing, and it starts to look pretty worrying.'

Hayley nodded slowly, as she did when she was thinking. Julia knew better than to interrupt her in this mood. Instead, she got up and turned on the stove. She put a heavy frying pan on the heat, and popped in a knob of butter. While it melted, she whisked the eggs a bit more with the fork. She enjoyed the rhythmic sound of the beating, which was soon punctuated by Hayley's voice.

'I agree that it's strange, but we don't know for sure that she's missing, or for how long. Did you try phoning the vet again?'

'Of course I did. I phoned at two o'clock, and then at four thirty. She hadn't been in and they hadn't reached her on the phone.'

'We know she's not home now, and not at work, but we don't know when she was last seen, or where.'

Julia poured the eggs into the bubbling butter and swirled the pan to distribute the mixture.

'I reckon she didn't go home last night at all. That cat was going mad with hunger.'

'Now, one thing I know about cats is that they are absolute drama queens. He was probably playing you for an extra meal. Successfully, as it turned out.'

'Maybe. But then where is she?'

The omelette was starting to set. Julia gently pulled the edges away from the pan, letting the liquid eggs touch the hot surface.

'At a boyfriend's house? A girlfriend's? And we don't know that she didn't sleep at home last night. She might have slept at home, and got up early this morning to, I don't know, take a train to visit her mum in Oxford.'

Julia's spatula froze. 'Does her mum live in Oxford? We could...'

Hayley looked exasperated. 'I don't know if she has a mum or where she lives, Julia. It was an example. My point is, I can think of a hundred reasons she wasn't home.'

'Right. Well maybe we should find her real mum. Or the hypothetical boyfriend.'

She got back to the job, spooning the mushroom and spinach into the centre of the golden circle of omelette. She picked up a handful of cheese from the chopping board and sprinkled it over the top. She said nothing. She was going to let Hayley speak first. She kept her eyes on the pan, folding the omelette over, and cutting it in half with the edge of the spatula.

'Supper's ready,' she said, reaching for a plate.

The two women sat down in silence. They each took a bite of the omelette and chewed in contemplative silence.

'I agree it's odd, if not necessarily ominous,' Hayley said, putting down her knife and fork between mouthfuls. 'Most of the time in this kind of situation, there's a perfectly reasonable explanation – a lost phone and a boyfriend would explain everything, in this case. But I'll ask Walter to make some calls. See if he can reach her or her known friends. For all we know she's already home, snuggled up with the allegedly starving cat. But if there's no sign of her tomorrow, and there's no word at her work, I'll take the next step.'

'Thanks, Hayley. I hope I've completely wasted your time with a mad worry about nothing.'

'Well, I hope so too. But you did the right thing by coming to me with this.' Hayley's manner had softened. 'Best to be alerted to a possible missing person sooner rather than later. I'll get the ball rolling with Walter. He can make a few calls this evening. And as I say, it could well be a misunderstanding, and it might all have blown over by tomorrow. I hope so.'

Was it Julia's imagination, or did Hayley look unconvinced?

24

Julia was in bed with a tray of tea, working her way through her online word games when she got a phone call. It was 10 a.m. She'd already been up to feed the animals, but had decided to do her morning reading and puzzling from bed. It seemed rather deliciously decadent, and when Jim McEnroe's name came up on her screen, she felt unaccountably guilty, as if she'd been caught doing something naughty.

'Hello, Jim,' she said, sitting up a little straighter.

'Hi, Julia. I hope I'm not disturbing you?'

'Oh no, just doing a bit of admin.' This was a true statement, if you counted Wordle, Quordle, Connections, Clickword and a variety of word searches and anagram finders as admin. The number of games she played had gradually crept up – she was up to seven, now – but she comforted herself with the vague hope that the daily ritual would ward off dementia. The more the better, in that case, presumably? At the very least, it would distract her from worrying about Olga, and delay the inevitable moment when she could no longer resist phoning Hayley Gibson for an update on Walter's enquiries.

'Right. Well, I don't want to interrupt your work, but I am

phoning for a favour. Remember Moxy, my new puppy? You met her at the vet when I brought her for her vaccinations?'

'Of course. How's the dear little girl?'

'She's an absolute terror! Impossible. Endless energy. Chews everything in sight.'

Julia laughed. No one knew bad puppies like she did. Jake had been a notorious terror himself.

'That's why I'm phoning,' said Jim. 'You kindly said we could join you on one of your walks with Jake. Develop her socialisation skills, get rid of a bit of excess energy. I thought an older dog might be a calming influence, and set a good example, you know.'

A good example. It amused Julia to hear Jake spoken of in such terms. He had been known in the village as 'The naughtiest dog in Berrywick' for the whole of his first year. Fortunately, in Jake's second year, Mrs Furnivall had got a Great Dane so utterly troublesome and resolutely untrainable that the denizens of the Buttered Scone agreed it must actually have some sort of condition. He took Jake's crown as Berrywick's naughtiest dog.

'Oh, we'd love that.' Another distraction sounded just what she needed. 'Jake's very sweet with puppies, and he's reasonably well behaved these days. Mostly. And when there aren't ducks around. When do you want to do it?'

'Today?' asked Jim. He really did sound desperate. 'No time like the present. And it's a slow news day. I'm working on a ground-breaking piece on the new rubbish bins in the high street, which at least three or four people believe are the wrong shade of green, as well as the inevitable land development stories – every one of which basically boils down to yes vs no to all new building or development. I could take an early lunch hour.'

'Twelve thirty?'

'That's good for me. Shall we meet at the parking area at the bottom of the hill path? There are no ducks on the hill path and it's convenient for me. I can nip home from work and fetch Moxy on the way, and work remotely in the afternoon.'

Julia nearly proposed a different route – in fact, any one of the many where she hadn't recently found a body – but decided not to. She couldn't avoid it forever.

'See you later. Bye, Jim.'

She wondered if the development story Jim was working on was to do with Padel and Will Adamson and the frogs. She could chat to him about it while they walked and wrangled dogs.

It was less upsetting than she thought, being back on the hill path, mostly because the puppy took up so much attention that she didn't have time to think about anything else. Moxy the Schnoodle was only barely trained to walk on the lead. For the first little while, she tried to ditch the collar, shaking her head, dashing off to get away from it, but finding herself still, annoyingly, attached to the lead. Jake behaved like a model hound, trotting off-lead at Julia's side. He had a look of deep concentration on his face, as if he knew that he was the senior dog, with a responsibility for setting an example to the youngster.

'He's very good,' said Jim, regarding Saint Chocolate with envy. He added wistfully, 'I hope Moxy will be like that one day.'

It was nice to have Jake's behaviour complimented. To have him *envied*.

'I'm sure she will be just lovely,' Julia said encouragingly. 'She's getting the hang of it already. She just needs practice. And treats help with the training.'

'I've tried with a bit of sausage. It certainly gets her attention.'

'Jake likes the Good-Dog-Go Fair Trade Organic Beef and Barley Treats.'

'I saw them at the vet. Didn't buy them though. Beyond the means of a humble journalist.'

They both contemplated the exorbitant cost of the treats for a quiet moment. Then Julia broke the silence.

'The police found a packet of the treats near where Eve fell. I've been wondering who might have dropped them.'

'Well, not me. I've never bought them, nor walked this path.'

Julia digested this for a moment. It didn't quite make sense.

'Are you *sure* you haven't bought them? Never?' she asked, her forehead furrowed.

Jim gave her a strange look. Quite understandable, really. 'Absolutely sure, Julia.'

This piece of information was intriguing. If Jim hadn't bought the treats, it meant that the list she found at Olga's wasn't a list of dog treat buyers. What else could those people have in common? What was their connection?

The path was quite steep at this point, and the humans didn't have enough puff for chatting. They walked on in companionable silence. Moxy had settled down and was walking calmly along next to Jim on the lead.

Without consultation, they both stopped at the top and looked out over the trees and hills, stretching towards the next village.

'This is where she fell, is it?' Jim asked, looking around.

'Yes.'

'How did you see her? You can't see the bottom of the cliff from here.'

'Eve's mum's dog was up here. Fergus. I saw that he was alone, there was no sign of Kay or Eve. It was an unusual thing. So I walked towards him...'

As she said it, she walked, just as she'd done two weeks previous. Jim walked alongside as she re-enacted the scene.

'I wanted to see if he was okay. If he was lost or injured. I got to about here...'

She stopped. It really was a marvellous lookout point. She could see the spires of the Edgeley church. The Ferris wheel of a country fair. A tractor ploughing a field, a flock of white birds following behind, swooping down for worms and bugs.

She brought her attention back to the story. 'And when I bent down to pick the dog up, I glanced down, over the edge of the hill and that's when I saw it. The body.'

'Oh my God, Julia. A body.'

Jim was as white as a sheet, peering into the abyss. The poor man seemed utterly overwhelmed, being there, at the site of Eve's death. Imagining it all.

'Yes. Eve's body. I know, Jim, it was truly horrible.'

'No...' he said, pointing. He stammered incoherently. 'Not then... Now... Julia, look!'

Julia followed his pointing figure to the base of the cliff where just a few weeks before Eve had lain in a crumpled heap.

There – she could hardly believe it – was another body.

25

Detective Inspector Hayley Gibson looked even more tired and drawn than she had when Julia had seen her two days before. Her hair was a day past due for a wash. A smudge – a badly wiped bit of food or drop of coffee – sullied the blue-and-white striped shirt under her rumpled navy jacket. She gestured to the chair with a grunt, almost as if she was too worn out to speak an actual word.

She took a deep breath, as if gathering up her meagre energy, and said, flatly, 'So you were right about Olga Gilbert. She wasn't off with a boyfriend or visiting her mum. She was in trouble. Serious trouble. I should have listened.'

'I take no pleasure in being right about this, Hayley. And I really didn't think, seriously, that she might be *dead*. It's all too awful. Olga, dead. In the same place as Eve. I couldn't believe my eyes when I saw the body. It was like a bad dream, one of those dreams where the same thing repeats again and again, in an endless loop...' Julia shook her head and sighed. 'And when I realised it was Olga...'

Hayley hesitated, thinking through what and how much to share with Julia.

'Between you and me. And I mean, absolutely confidentially...' She paused, looking to Julia for agreement.

'Of course.' Julia nodded vociferously, eager to hear what it was that Hayley was poised to reveal. She almost made the zipped-lip gesture with her thumb and forefinger, but thought better of it.

'Not a word. Not even to Jim. I know he was there, but he's a journalist... This can't get out. It could jeopardise the investigation.' Hayley looked fierce.

'I understand.'

'There was a note.'

'A note? You mean...'

'In Olga's pocket. It appears that she left a suicide note.'

'That doesn't sound right. I wouldn't have expected that at all. She wasn't the least suicidal.'

Hayley handed her a see-through evidence bag. Inside was a sheet of plain white typing paper. On it were typed the words: *I'm sorry. I can't go on. I want to follow Eve and die like she did. I'm just too sad. Goodbye.*

Hayley continued. 'She jumped exactly where Eve fell. The theory at the moment is that it's some sort of copycat thing, triggered by the loss of Eve. You knew her better than I did, Julia. Do you know if she suffered from depression? Or anything else?'

'Not as far as I know. She could be a bit odd at times, but overall she seemed like quite an ordinary, stable woman.'

'Remember, she was in love with Vincent Andrews? That was pretty far from balanced.'

Hayley was referring to the best-selling author, and local chap made good, who Olga had dated and for whom she still held a candle – okay, make that a bonfire – for decades later. Until he died in the Berrywick Library – a scene Julia would rather not remember.

'Okay, she can be a bit flaky, but, you know. Who hasn't been a bit unhinged about an old crush.'

Hayley looked at her blankly, as if she had no idea what Julia was talking about. Or, if she did, she didn't recognise the behaviour. Hayley's romantic life was something of a mystery. Julia had never seen Hayley with a significant other, and she'd never questioned her on the topic.

Julia said firmly, 'As far as I know, Olga was quite okay.'

'How did she seem to you when you last saw her?'

'She seemed fine, normal, when I saw her at the vet. But the last time we spoke, on Wednesday, she sounded...'

Julia thought back to the phone call from Olga, replayed it in her mind – Olga's hesitant manner, her low voice. 'She sounded scared, Hayley, when she called me about the treats.'

'You said that she said that she knew something. But she wouldn't say more.'

'Yes,' said Julia. 'And now she's dead.'

'So Olga was coming to see you with this apparently important and deeply confidential information. Instead of giving it to you, she decided to jump off a cliff? That makes no sense.'

'None at all.'

There was a lot about this situation that didn't make sense, as far as Julia was concerned.

'In fact, there is a lot about this situation that doesn't add up,' said Hayley, as if she had just read Julia's mind. 'For a start, why go to you instead of the police?'

Julia shrugged, opting to treat the question as a hypothetical one.

Hayley continued. 'No sign of her car, which worries me. And it's unusual for a jumper to put a note in their pocket. They usually leave the note at home, for a loved one to find.'

'Right. And it's typed, which is unusual.'

'Yes, I suppose I have seen a few typed ones, but usually from younger people. And I'm not sure they would print it out.

They would more likely post it online, or send it via WhatsApp or whatever. But most notes are handwritten. I would have thought Olga...'

A knock on the open door interrupted Hayley's observations about Olga. Detective Constable Walter Farmer was standing in the doorway. He was unusually pink in the face, and a little out of breath. He had been running.

'Post-mortem results,' he said breathlessly, waving a file. 'Coroner had the pathologist fast-track it.'

'Headlines, Farmer,' Hayley snapped.

He stepped into her office and spoke rapidly. 'Olga Gibson didn't die from a fall from a cliff. There is no evidence of that kind of trauma. No sign of broken bones. The pathologist says that Olga was suffocated and her body was placed at the scene.' He said all of this standing to attention, as if he was a soldier in the army.

Hayley threw her pencil down on the desk and leaned back in the chair.

'So Olga was murdered,' she said. She sounded like she was talking to herself rather than to Julia, and indeed, after a moment, she carried on. 'That's two bodies. Both in the same place. Both who worked together. And you' – she glanced at Julia – 'an experienced social worker, do not think that either woman was suicidal.'

'That's right,' said Julia, slightly afraid of interrupting Hayley's thoughts.

'One *could* have slipped,' said Hayley.

'But not two.' Julia couldn't help herself, finishing Hayley's thought for her. 'And not Olga, according to what Walter just said.'

'The most obvious conclusion is that they were both murdered.' Hayley sighed. 'Which I suppose is what you've been trying to tell me all along.' Another sigh.

Julia said nothing. Again, it was one of those situations

where being right held no triumph.

'And do you think they were killed for the same reason?' Julia asked Hayley, after a suitable pause.

'Or a connected one, yes. I can't see any other reasonable possibility.'

Julia paused. 'And that reason might be...'

Hayley sat up and drew a piece of paper towards her from what seemed to be a pile of notes on her desk. She turned the note over and started to write on the blank side.

'Well, let's look at that. What do they have in common?' Hayley wrote down the word 'vet' and circled it, while speaking. 'They worked together at the vet. That's their most direct and obvious link. My first guess is that the motive could be something to do with the vet practice.'

'It's hard to imagine what that might be. A client whose dog died, driven insane with grief? A dispute of some kind?'

'At this stage, I've no idea.'

'You could talk to Dr Ryan again,' said Julia. 'He works in the practice. He might have an idea.'

'What if it wasn't anything to do with the veterinary practice? There could be something else they have in common.' Hayley looked at the ceiling as if it might hold the answers.

'Well, they both played Padel.'

'True. Although it's even more unlikely that anyone would be moved to kill someone – let alone two people – over a ball game.' Still, she wrote the word 'Padel' on the paper.

'Yes, but don't forget about the frogs, Hayley.'

'The frogs?' Hayley frowned. She looked at Julia as if she'd gone mad. 'Are you feeling okay, Julia?'

'The frogs that live in the field that's going to be developed. Never mind. What I'm saying is, this could all be about the extra Padel courts and development that Will Adamson... Oh my God!'

Julia couldn't believe she hadn't thought about it!

'What?' Walter Farm asked impatiently. 'What?'

'The note! Hayley! Where's the note?'

Julia identified the evidence bag amongst the detritus on the DI's desk. She picked it up, examining the brief missive. 'Hayley, do you realise this is typed on a manual typewriter?'

'That's very unusual,' said Hayley, taking the note back and looking at it closely. 'You know, I think you're right. Now *that's* something. Who even has one of those these days? Haven't seen one for years. I wonder, did Olga own a typewriter?'

'I don't know. But I know someone who does.'

Hayley looked at her expectantly.

'You're not going to like this...'

'Go on.'

'Will Adamson. He has an old typewriter in his office.'

For once, Hayley didn't react with exasperation at the mention of his name. This time, it was incredulity.

'Are you serious? Will Adamson has a manual typewriter? How do you know?'

'I saw it in his office. It's an antique. His father's, if I remember.'

'You've always thought he was up to no good.' Hayley almost smiled. 'And good lord, it turns out you might be right. Will is a Padel player, and – more importantly – the would-be developer of the extended Padel courts.'

Walter Farmer was still in the doorway, his head swivelling from Hayley to Julia, Julia to Hayley as they spoke, bouncing off each other's thoughts, as if he was watching a tennis match – or a Padel game, perhaps.

Julia shot back. 'And his name is on the list I found on Olga's kitchen table. Whatever that list means...'

'If we are drawing the connections correctly, Will killed Eve for opposing his development, and he killed Olga because she knew too much.'

'Exactly.'

'It's not a terrible theory. Walter?' Hayley said, pushing her chair back and getting to her feet. 'We're going to visit Mr Adamson.'

26

A group of cyclists had commandeered the pavement outside the Buttered Scone, pushing the square tables together to create a rectangular table and arranging the chairs to accommodate their Lycra-clad rears. Their bicycles were clustered to one side like a pile of colourful skeletons. Their helmets cluttered the floor at their feet. Judging by the gusto with which they were engaging with their Full English, Julia wondered if they'd ridden all the way from Scotland that very morning.

Julia had the only other outside table, the one closest to the door. It was a good spot, if she was feeling sociable. She could chat to friends and acquaintances going in and out. Jake could greet his admirers and employ his charm and good looks to cadge treats from the more soft-hearted patrons. Without too much craning of her neck, she could see who was inside, and catch Flo's eye and hail a second coffee if required.

The Saturday crowd at the Buttered Scone was always heavier on tourists than the weekday crowds. The day trippers and weekenders who wandered the countryside and villages admiring the sights liked regular stops for restorative nourishment, and particularly fancied the pubs and tearooms that offered good, traditional fare. The Buttered Scone was popular for its menu of rich breakfasts, its tea and scones, and its locally sourced fresh produce. An additional drawcard was the authentic cast of Cotswold characters. Like Johnny Blunt, who was scowling under his bushy eyebrows and his blue knitted hat, slurping his tea at a table just inside the door. He looked like an extra who had been strategically placed there by central casting. 'Gruff Elderly Man', he'd be in the film credits. She smiled at the thought, and turned her attention to the menu. She knew it off by heart, but liked to go through the ritual of paging, reading and choosing.

'Ah, well, if it isn't your friend Jake!' Julia looked up from the menu to see Nicky Moore and little Sebastian standing next to the table. Sebastian fell to his knees and threw his arms round Jake's neck. 'Could you not be smooching the dog, Sebastian? I've told you about the worms, haven't I just?' She looked at Julia's face and said, 'I'm sure your Jake's fine, had all the pills and vaccinations and such, but you know, as a rule, he can't be kissing all the dogs, now, can he? No offence.'

'No. None taken.'

Nicky plonked herself down on the vacant chair. Sebastian sat on the ground, leaning into Jake and muttering quietly into his silky ears. Jake had a dreamy look.

'Terrible about poor Olga, isn't it?'

'Yes. So very sad.'

'I heard you found her body at the bottom of the hill. And so soon after you found Dr Davies.'

Julia nodded.

'Julia Bird, if I didn't know better, I'd think it was you pushing people off the hilltop path.' Nicky gave a bark of laughter, startling little Sebastian. 'I'll have to watch my back, so I will.'

'It was a very strange coincidence,' conceded Julia, with a small smile.

'So are you going to help solve the murders, then, Julia?'
Nicky's eyes shone with excitement at the thought. 'I hear you
were there, at Olga's house just the other day.'

If there were few secrets in Berrywick, there were precisely
none in Greenside Way, where the houses faced onto the little
road, and hence, into each other's front gates and each other's
windows.

'No, I'm not investigating anything. That's the job of the
police. And there's no reason to think anyone was murdered,
Nicky. Let's not jump to conclusions.' Julia herself did, indeed,
think that Olga had been murdered. But she certainly wasn't
going to be saying that to the biggest gossip in Berrywick. 'Yes, I
came to the house. I was looking for Olga. Did you see her
around much?'

'I can't say that I do. Did, I mean. She had her job at the vet,
so she was gone in the day, mostly. And she didn't have children.' Nicky said this as if the only reason a person might be
seen in the street was if they had children. Julia couldn't quite
make the link, but said agreeably, 'Different life stages.'

'She was one of those that minds their own business. Keeps
themselves to themselves.' Nicky said this with a hint of disap-
proval. In contrast to Olga, Nicky wasn't one of those annoyingly selfish people who minded their own business or kept
themselves to themselves, as evidenced by her next question:
'So what do they think happened to her, then?'

'I really don't know, Nicky. There'll be an investigation, I
suppose.'

Nicky leaned in and held up her hand, fingers spread.
'Jumped, pushed or fell,' she counted the words off on her
fingers. 'Those are the three options, right?'

Or killed elsewhere and transported there, as indeed
seemed to be the case, but Julia wasn't going to share that piece
of insider info.

Flo appeared at Julia's side, pen poised. 'The only options I can see, Nicky. You're right. What'll you have, Julia dear?'

Nicky turned to Flo, delighted to have a more communicative conversationalist on this matter. 'And isn't it strange, Flo, that she and Dr Eve Davies died the same way? On the same actual spot. Can't be a coincidence.'

'The French toast please, Flo,' Julia cut in, trying to shut down the conversation about Olga.

'Right you are, Julia, and a bit of bacon for Jake. It was no coincidence, I'm with you there, Nicky.' Flo was particularly good at multitasking, switching seamlessly between business and gossip, gossip and business, without spilling a drop of coffee. Julia realised that trying to shut the subject down now was impossible, so she sat back and let Flo continue: 'She'd been coming in quite a bit recently, had Olga. She wasn't a regular at the Buttered Scone before. She might pop in every now and then, just for a coffee once every few weeks. But the last few months she'd come in once or twice a week or so and treat herself to a proper nice lunch – she liked the trout salad, as I recall.'

'I'm glad that she was spending a bit and treating herself a bit more, at least. I noticed she had a few new outfits, too.' Nicky paused for effect and added earnestly. 'I always say, you can't take it with you.'

'You're so right, Nicky. And I always say, you never know when your time's up,' Flo added.

They both spoke with solemnity, as if they were two philosophers who had personally invented the well-known phrases. Their heads bobbed in unison and they blinked slowly at the wisdom of their words. Julia felt mildly irritated, and then immediately guilty for being so uncharitable.

The philosophers were disturbed by cyclists at the next table, who were waving to get Flo's attention. Their plates were scraped clean, the breadbasket empty and the butter and jam finished. It seemed almost impossible that the enormous break-fasts could have vanished into the slender bodies.

Flo raised her hand to acknowledge that she'd noticed them, and she was back to business. 'One French toast for you, Julia. And for you, Nicky?'

'I'm meeting my mum inside. I'll order with her. If I can get Sebastian to come along.'

'See you inside, then. Breakfast will be on its way in a mo, Julia.' Flo stepped over to the cyclists, who, unbelievably, were not hailing the bill, but ordering more coffee and croissants to charge them up for the ride home.

Sebastian was engrossed in a game. He had taken out a bag of luridly coloured plastic figurines – Julia honestly couldn't tell what they were meant to be, with their buggy eyes and their short legs and big feet. They were presumably some cartoon figure off the television, in which case, it was not surprising that they were unfamiliar to her. He had arrayed them carefully across the hilly terrain of Jake's body. He was moving the figures around from one spot to another, and describing the action to himself under his breath. Jake seemed to be quite content. In fact, he was half asleep.

'Come on, Sebastian, Nana will be here in a minute!'

He looked up, as did Jake, displacing the boy's carefully positioned tableau. Jake sat up, scattering the figurines. It reminded Julia of *Gulliver's Travels*, the big man shaking off the tiny Lilliputian townspeople.

The child started to cry, which upset Jake, who hated anyone to be unhappy, particularly children. Nicky scooped up the toys into their bag, while the boy and the dog commiserated with each other with hugs, and said their tender goodbyes.

Much as she liked Nicky, Julia found that she always came out of a conversation with her with a renewed appreciation of peace and quiet. She sat with that for a minute, enjoying the passing parade on the high street, letting it wash over her. The young couples with their pushchairs and their shopping bags. A young man with a pretty bunch of flowers – for his lover? His mother? A sick friend. An elderly couple holding hands and stepping carefully on the cobblestoned pavement.

Her phone rang. Julia didn't much like to take calls in public. She was old school in such matters, and thought it rude – even if she was alone at the table. But it was DI Hayley Gibson, so she accepted and put the phone to her ear.

'Will Adamson doesn't own a dog,' Hayley said, in place of the more traditional greeting of 'hello'.

'Oh, well, not his dog treats, then,' Julia said, after thinking for a moment. 'But he still has motive, opportunity and a typewriter.'

'Yes. But there's another thing that he has too.'

'What's that?'

'He's got an alibi for the day of Eve's death.'

'Oh.'

'Yes. I went round to his office first thing this morning for a little chat. Funny coincidence, he was actually *buying* a dog at the time. Or he was arranging to get one, I should say. That's his alibi. He had an appointment with a dog breeder over in Edgeley. Man by the name of George Mullins. Will is getting a puppy for his daughter, a girl by the name of...' There was a pause, and the sound of Hayley flicking through her notebook.

'Her name is Kimberley,' said Julia, helpfully.

'How do you know...? Never mind. Well, Kimberley is getting something called a Jackapoo for her birthday, apparently. She's turning twenty-five. The daughter, not the dog, obviously. The dog's only seven weeks old. A Jack Russell poodle cross, I'm assuming. Would be known as a mongrel, back in the day, but it's all designer dogs now, cross this and cross that. Heaven knows what that will look like, but that's not my business. Anyway, on the day of the murder, Will went to visit to choose one of the puppies. He got a female, he says.

He's picking it up in two weeks' time, on Kimberley's birthday.'

'And you confirmed his story with this George fellow?'

'I did. When I left Will's office I went round to the place myself. It's out past Edgeley, an acre or so, pens for the dogs. George's mum Debbie confirmed that Will had been at their place on Tuesday. He had arranged to come and see the puppies at three in the afternoon, and he was there on time. George was out when Will arrived – he had gone out to get the puppy food, and was delayed, apparently. They must go through a lot of it, with all those dogs. The place was alive with them. Anyway, Debbie said she showed Will around, he played with the puppies a bit, and chose one. With the travelling time there and back, there's no way he could have been on the cliff path when Eve died. He's got a solid alibi. He's off the hook.'

Flo put a plate in front of Julia. The thick golden egg-soaked slab of bread glistened with butter. Julia mouthed 'Thanks'.

Flo smiled, and moved on to the cyclists' table with the bill.

Julia was surprised at how reluctant she was to accept that Will was in the clear. It had all fitted together so seamlessly. Plus, she didn't really like Will Adamson.

When Flo was out of earshot, she said, 'What about the note? Did you see the typewriter in the office?'

'Yes. It was there on the little table, just as you said. I'm pretty sure Will's in the clear, but I typed up the words and I've got forensics checking the make and model, just in case. Have to say though, Julia, if Will has got a solid alibi for Eve's murder, I'm pretty sure the typewriter forensics will show that it wasn't typed on his machine.'

'But typewriters aren't that common,' said Julia.

'Oh, I think there are more of them around than you think, Julia,' said Hayley. 'I saw one just today.'

'If it wasn't typed on Will's machine, that means we are still looking for our murderer.'

Two of the cyclists had vacated their table and were filing past her at that moment, their shoes clicking on the pavement. The word 'murderer' was still ringing in the air when they stopped and looked down at her.

The one in front frowned. She knew that frown. He was trying to square the elements in front of him, to connect the retired lady sitting in the tea shop with her Labrador, with the sentence that came out of her mouth. She met his eyes. He looked away first.

27

'Let's have our coffee outside,' Julia said, opening the kitchen door, and stepping out to take a deep breath of the cool air, filled with fragrance and birdsong. 'It's so perfect out.'

'Goldilocks conditions. Not too hot; not too cold. Just right,' Sean said, following her out, a mug in each hand. He put them down on the little mosaic-topped table, and they sat down.

Summer was coming. The early-morning sun was gentle on her shoulders. In pots on either side of them, the delicate white bells of the lily-of-the-valley shivered in the lightest of breezes, giving off a sweet scent that mingled with the basil in the herb garden and that of the wisteria that grew over the door, dripping with the heavy purple blooms.

'Your garden is looking wonderful, Julia. You've got a green thumb.'

'I don't know about that,' she said, holding up her regular old pink thumbs, 'but I do love it. I love learning about plants and trying things out and seeing what works. It's creative, and nurturing.'

'Like you are.' He took her hand.

'Thank you, kind sir.' She felt the heat of the blush on her cheeks. She wasn't very graceful in the face of a compliment. 'The only trouble with gardening is that you are constantly looking for things that need doing. You can't enjoy your morning coffee in peace, you're always thinking, "The lawn could do with a cut," or "Gosh, I need to stake the tomatoes," which, actually, I *will* have to do tomorrow.'

'Luckily, I'm not burdened with that urge to improve anything in your garden. I can relax and enjoy it just the way it is. You should try it! Once you've got the hang of it, you'll never look back.'

Sean had come for supper and stayed the night. Leo had come too, and the two dogs were lying companionably on the grass, each chewing on a bone saved from last night's chop dinner. Henny Penny, who was less sure of Leo than she was of Jake, kept to the shrubbery. In between looking for snails, she glanced her beady black eye in the direction of Leo, who could not have been less interested in her presence.

The dogs would keep each other company when Sean and Julia went to Eve Davies' memorial. The thought of what lay ahead of her took the gleam off the perfect morning, but Julia knew she had to go.

'What time do we need to leave?' Sean asked, reading her mind.

'It's at eleven, so around ten fifteen? It's best to be there a bit early.'

'I should imagine there will be quite a crowd. She was well known and well liked.'

'Yes, and she had all these different aspects to her life. The veterinary practice, all the committees and boards, the animal charities and so on, the Padel, and then of course her friends and family.'

'Yes, I suppose that's why it's being held in the function room at The Swan. Plenty of room.'

They were right, as it turned out. The car park was half

full of cars, with more arriving in a steady stream. Sean parked, and joined the people walking towards the big old ivy-clad manor house that had been converted into a hotel, restaurant and conference venue. They walked past the covered terrace with its smattering of late breakfasters, into a room set up with rows of chairs. At the back was a table of eats, covered with a cloth to indicate they were for after the service. The room was half full and filling up rapidly. Julia knew quite a few people and recognised more. Many of them were local dog owners who she'd crossed paths with regularly. They looked strange without their dogs. She couldn't quite place, for example, the very familiar young woman who nodded and greeted her, until she realised she was the owner of Sammy, the clever border collie. And Mrs Furnivall looked completely naked without her Great Dane.

Kay Davies came in precisely a minute before eleven, on the arm of a man of similar age, with exactly the same features – a brother, presumably, or perhaps a cousin. Kay wore a dark grey dress and a black jacket, stockings and black court shoes, which seemed like a lot of clothing for a warm day. The man escorted her to the front of the room, where two chairs awaited them. Kay looked as if she'd collapse without him holding her up. She sat, while he stood at a small podium and introduced himself as Eve's uncle – Julia had surmised correctly – and welcomed the crowd.

'Eve was a woman of great principle. She had so much love – for people, for animals, for nature – but she was also a fighter. She wasn't afraid to stand up for what she believed was right.'

There was some nodding and muttering of agreement.

'Many of you knew her through her work, either at the veterinary clinic, or in one of her volunteer positions. Her many... *many*...' there was a ripple of quiet laughter '... volunteer positions.'

The woman next to Julia, who had been sniffing into her

handkerchief, shook her head and said quietly, 'A hero, she was, that woman.' Julia gave her a sympathetic smile.

Eve's uncle continued to enumerate Eve's causes, projects and good qualities – she was, apparently, also a whizz at the fiendishly difficult *Financial Times* crossword puzzle, and a good baker – with Kay Davies nodding silently at his side. Julia felt quite inadequate by the time he'd finished, what with her modest volunteering at Second Chances, her Wordle obsession, and her very average baking.

He handed over to Kay, who looked frail and nervous, almost colourless with her pale face and grey-toned outfit. A brooch glinted on her lapel. The only spot of brightness on the poor, grieving mother. Squinting, Eve saw that it was the shape of a Scottie dog, gold, with a tiny red stone for the eye. She remembered seeing Eve wear it. It was all so terribly sad. Julia felt a wave of something more than sadness, a kind of despair in the world that would take this woman's daughter. Sean must have intuited as much. He leaned in to her, his shoulder pressing into hers, and took her hand. He squeezed it gently.

'Thank you all for coming to honour Eve,' Kay said, her voice trembling, and so quiet that Julia held her breath and leaned forwards. 'She was a good girl. A very good girl. I don't know what I'm going to do without her.'

Kay stopped on the brink of tears. She managed to gather herself together enough to say a few more words.

'If anyone would like to make a donation in Eve's name, we would be most grateful if you would support the RSPCA, or the Adopt-don't-Shop campaign.'

Julia's neighbour muttered 'Thank you', nodded vigorously. Turning to look at her, Julia saw that she was wearing an Adopt-don't-Shop badge on her T-shirt, on which were printed the words 'I'm a rescue mum' and a cartoon picture of a dog which was stretched by her generously upholstered bosom, resulting in a rather strangely shaped hound with a too large head. Her black trousers were lightly covered in fur, as if she'd recently had a cat on her lap.

Kay spoke again, 'Eve was very much in favour of the shelters. The rescues. She always said everyone deserves a second chance. People and animals. She certainly gave me many chances.' She stopped, sniffed loudly, and continued. 'And that other poor girl. Olga. Can we take a moment for her too. A bad business. Really.'

Kay sat down heavily in her chair. Clearly, she had reached the end of her stamina and courage. Her brother closed the proceedings and invited everyone to stay for tea.

'Lovely words,' Julia's neighbour said. 'Eve Davies was a fine woman.'

'She was. She was a wonderful vet. She looked after my dog with such care.'

'A good vet, and a good person. She did good work for our organisation. Raising awareness about why people should get rescue dogs. She even helped us shut down some dodgy breeders, if you can even call them that. Puppy farms, is more what they were. The last one had twenty puppies, and three poor mother dogs who were kept constantly pregnant. Eve spayed them without charge, and they found good homes. She will be missed.'

'I'm sorry for your loss.'

The neighbour thanked her and stood up from her chair. She squeezed out of the row and headed surprisingly nimbly for the food table.

'How are you?' Sean asked gently.

'Oh, you know...' she said with a sad smile.

'I know.'

They sat for a moment. One thing she'd learned in life was that there was seldom a need to rush to the food table.

When they reached the table, there was, as predicted, plenty left. It was classic funeral fare – sausage rolls, little sandwiches, cream scones, a chocolate cake. As they left the table with a sampling of each, Julia wondered how the standards for such things became the standard, and then an immutable law of the universe. She would have made this observation to Sean, who enjoyed her strange thoughts on mysterious ways the world worked, but it seemed rude to analyse the food at such an occasion. Especially when you are eating it, she thought, biting into a still-warm sausage roll. Flakes of butter pastry scattered onto her plate.

Sean and Julia stepped away from the table, and found themselves alongside Hamilton Cunningham-Smythe, in conversation with Dr Ryan. Julia introduced Sean, experiencing a moment of complete panic when Hamilton's real name escaped her – in her mind, he would always be the Frog Dude. Fortunately, his name came back just in time.

'A tragic loss. She was a fine chap,' he said, raising his teacup in a sort of toast. Not an easy manoeuvre, as he also had a plate loaded with three cream scones. 'Remarkable, what a contribution she made.'

Surprisingly deftly, he leveraged one of the scones into his mouth.

'Indeed, and a fine colleague,' said Dr Ryan.

'Awful for you. To lose Eve and then Olga, so soon after. It must feel terribly sad at work.'

'It is, Mrs Bird,' he said sadly. 'I've got a temp in for the phones. I don't know what will happen about another vet. And to top it all, I have Olga's cat with me at the office as a constant reminder.'

'The black-and-white one?' she wracked her brain for the name. 'Chaplin.'

'Yes. Chaplin. I've taken him in temporarily.'

'Well, he's a lovely chap.' Good lord, she thought, Hamilton's speech patterns were starting to rub off on her.

'Oh, he is. Just lovely. Very friendly. He really needs to go to a home, though. I can't have him at my place – one of my dogs isn't good with cats I'm afraid.' He paused. 'Wait. I don't suppose you would consider adopting him, Mrs Bird? He's wonderful.' Dr Ryan's eyes brightened at the prospect.

'That he is. But no, I really can't.'

Julia felt an awful hypocrite. Here she was at Eve's memorial, admiring all the work Eve did for animal adoptions, and when the opportunity came for her to make a contribution, she baulked.

She said, a little lamely, 'I would, but I've got Jake.'

'Jake would get used to him quickly, I'm sure. He's a softy. Labs are known to be good with cats, you know. Gentle dogs.'

The young vet reminded Julia of the salespeople she'd encountered at flea markets the world over, who pounced at the tiniest glimmer of interest in their products.

'He is that. He lets one of the chickens sit on him. He doesn't move until Henny Penny vacates her position.'

They laughed, but not too loudly. It was a memorial after all.

'He'll be fine with the cat in no time.'

'I'm not worried about him hurting the cat. I'm worried about *him*. I don't think he could cope with being subjected to a cat in his own home. Weirdly, Jake's scared of cats. He can't meet their eyes. He actually *slinks* when he has to pass one in the road.'

'All the better,' Dr Ryan said. 'I tell you what, I can help you socialise the two of them. There are proven methods.'

'Oh I...'

'Think about it!' he said, stopping her before the word 'No' could exit her mouth. 'Sleep on it and we'll chat in the morning.'

28

The *Southern Times*, the local paper for the region, had joined the twenty-first century two decades after its start, and now had a website and an emailed newsletter. So it was that Julia discovered that she, herself, was in the news, that Monday morning.

She was in the kitchen, dogs fed, eggs collected, breakfast made and dishes washed up. The second cuppa of the day was at her elbow, on a coaster on the desk. When she picked up her phone to do Wordle, she found a news alert from the *Southern Times*. This in itself was unusual. There wasn't a great deal of news in the local paper that was alert-worthy. This was, though. Very alert-worthy, as it turned out. Especially for Julia Bird:

S.T. JOURNO FINDS SECOND BODY ON HILL PATH

All thoughts of Wordle vanished from her mind. She clicked through to the article, which was flagged with a red banner that said SOUTHERN TIMES EXCLUSIVE! And there she was, in the intro paragraph:

Southern Times' *own investigative reporter* **Jim McEnroe**
describes how he and a Berrywick local, Julia Bird, were out on
a country walk when they found the body of Olga Gilbert, the
second death in as many weeks...

The aforementioned 'Berrywick local' liked to keep a low
profile, and was not thrilled to find her name in the paper. She
clicked through to the full story, which was Jim's dramatic
account of their 'grisly find', and a recap of the recent 'tragic
loss' of the local vet. There was little information that was new
to her, given that she'd personally found both bodies and done a
fair amount of snooping and sleuthing. She was interested – if
not exactly surprised – to read, at the bottom of the third paragraph, that *Berrywick police have reopened the inquiry into Eve*
Davies' death. Investigation into both deaths is ongoing. Detec-
tive Inspector Hayley Gibson confirmed that the deaths are being
treated as suspicious.

She also learned that *Local residents are up in arms at the*
slow progress from the Berrywick police in these cases.

At the bottom of the article was a link to an opinion piece,
written by the editor herself, headlined:

Are our coppers up to the job?

Short answer, if the writer was to be believed, was No. She
had Berrywick residents backing up his view:

'Seems to me like they're sleeping on the job,' said Hubert
Humphry, a lifetime resident of Berrywick, and a respected
local cobbler. 'People don't feel safe anymore, what with people
being pushed off hills left right and centre, and all the bodies
piling up.'

'The village has also been terrorised by a peeping Tom,'
said Martha Grounds of Windfall Lane. 'He's been sneaking

*around for weeks, and what's been done about it? Nothing,
that's what.'*

The writer concluded:

*Superintendent Roger Grave from regional head office
promised to go down to Berrywick and personally supervise the
investigation. We can only hope that he gets the results that
have heretofore been sorely lacking.*

Julia's heart sank at the last paragraph, and it wasn't only
because of the use of the word 'heretofore', which in itself was
enough to ruin your morning. The primary cause of her distress
was the imminent arrival of the superintendent. Poor Hayley
would not be happy to have the man she called Shallow Grave
breathing down her neck, and grandstanding for the cameras.

And on the subject of not being happy, she was building up
quite a head of fury at Jim for *one* putting her name in the
article without asking, and *two* not even alerting her to the fact
that the story was coming out. She knew Berrywick well enough
by now to know that every one of her friends and acquaintances
would phone, message or stop her in the street to discuss it.
Right now, a message popped up from Tabitha, and at the same
time, the phone rang.

'Hello, Jim.'

'Julia, how are you? Not too early, I hope. Are you free for a
quick chat?' He spoke with a heartiness that was not his usual
tone. She wasn't in the mood to let him off the hook easily.

'Maybe we should have chatted yesterday. I see I'm in the
paper. A heads-up would have been nice.'

'That's why I'm calling. I'm sorry. My editor went nuts on
the story and rushed it through. It's not often we get a big scoop
at the *Southern Times*. And having the only first-hand

account... Well, nuts. As I say. I should have warned you. I'm really, really sorry.'

Julia sighed.

'Was there any other reason that you called?'

'I just wanted to tell you how I'm really sorry.'

Julia knew she would forgive the young man, but right now, she didn't feel like talking.

'I have to go. Bye, Jim.'

As predicted, her phone was rapidly filling up with messages. Tabitha and Dr Ryan had both called, but neither had left a message. There was a voice note from Hayley: 'You're in the paper I see. Me too, but inadvertently. Bloody Jim McEnroe. Bloody Roger Grave. I had a question for you, but I'll phone you later. You won't get me. I'll be out on the road with Walter all day. We're starting from scratch on the investigation. Family and friends of the victims. There must be something we're missing. Later.'

Julia did her best to ignore the messages. She intended to have a day entirely free of murders, investigations, questions and newspapers. Monday was washing day and the weather was perfect for it – warm and sunny with a small breeze. She stripped the linen off her bed, and bundled it into the washing machine with a week's worth of dirty clothes. The whole lot only made up one load. Not like the days of Jess's school uniforms and Peter's work shirts. One a day, but at least he ironed them himself.

She had no sooner set off the washing machine than the doorbell rang. It was a bit of a formality, ringing the doorbell, because Julia – like everyone in Berrywick – left her front door unlocked. She opened it to find Jim, half obscured by a big bunch of flowers.

'Gosh,' she said.

'This is how sorry I am. Even sorrier, actually,' he said,

handing them over with a rueful smile. He looked like Jake when he had 'accidentally' eaten her slipper.

'They are very lovely,' she said grudgingly, taking them in both hands. 'Peonies are my favourite. Ooh, and the smell of those freesias.' The bouquet was a gorgeous, soft and springy country arrangement from her favourite florist, Blooming Marvel.

'Well come in then, let's put them in a vase.'

'Thanks.'

Julia could never hold a grudge for more than a few minutes, even if, like now, she was actively trying to. He followed her into the kitchen.

'Could you pass me the vase?' she said, pointing to a tall glass one on the top shelf above the fridge. She might as well make use of his height. Save her fetching the kitchen steps.

He took it down and to the sink, where he filled it with water. She unwrapped the flowers from their brown paper and put them in, fluffing them a bit.

'Lovely,' she said, putting them in the middle of the kitchen table. 'Tea? Or I've got lemonade, home-made.'

'Thank you,' said Jim, sounding relieved. 'Lemonade, please. And again...'

'No need. You were just doing your job.'

She made a tray with a jug, two glasses, and a plate of cheesy crackers. Jim carried it to the outside table. Naturally, Jake behaved as if he'd been locked in a bunker in solitary confinement for a year and Jim was the first human he had encountered since his incarceration.

'Okay, Jakey, settle down. Enough with the whining, now. Sit!'

He stopped leaping about and plonked his bum on the ground. She tossed him a biscuit from the stash she kept in a tin outside. The trainers recommend you reinforce good behaviour with treats, but she sometimes felt Jake had trained *her*. Trained her to give him treats.

'Full disclosure, I'm working on a follow-up story.'

'Of course. Your editor must be chomping at the bit.'

'She is. And Hayley Gibson isn't returning my calls.'

'I doubt you'll get her today. She's out doing interviews. Friends and family of both victims. Starting afresh.'

'Makes sense.'

'Besides. I shouldn't think she's very happy with you.'

'Just doing my job,' Jim said with a shrug. 'And my editor wants a more personal piece on the two victims, as well. Their place in the community. How much Dr Eve will be missed. That sort of thing.'

'That'll be easier to come by. Eve was well known and well liked.'

They sipped their lemonade in companionable silence, each in their own thoughts.

'There was a list,' said Julia, eventually. 'With your name on it. That Olga wrote.'

'What?' Jim sat up, and started patting his pockets as if looking for a pen to write this down.

Julia raised her eyebrows. 'This is why nobody wants to talk to you, Jim. You regard everything as material for an article. I'll tell you, but it's off the record for now. But you can use it for your follow-up story when I say so.'

Jim sighed a sigh heavy with the sheer unfairness of life.

'Fine,' he muttered.

Julia told him about the list that she found at Olga's, and how she thought it was the list that Olga wanted to share with her, of people who had bought dog treats. But Jim said he'd never bought the treats, and Will Adamson didn't even have a dog yet.

'So, if you didn't buy the dog treats, and Will Adamson

didn't buy dog treats, it's not a list of dog treat buyers. So what is it?'

'My question exactly. Why am I on a list?'

'Let's look at the names, take them one by one, and see what we know about each. What connects them to each other and to Olga.'

Julia pulled up the photograph she'd taken with her phone the day she had gone to Olga's house to find her. Under the heading 'April' was a list of five names.

'Well, there's me...' Jim said. 'A patient, yes, but no treats.'

'And then there's Will Adamson, the last name on the list. He doesn't even have a dog yet, so he didn't buy treats and he's not a patient of Dr Eve. I can't imagine why Olga would have him on a list. Do the two of you have anything in common?'

'Me and Will Adamson? Male. Berrywick. I've met him once or twice. Interviewed him for a story I did a couple of years ago on the new shopping centre. I guess we might have some acquaintances in common. He's older though, so...'

'Okay, park that. Let's see. I don't know Moira Walker. But I do know Robert Benjamin. I had some dealings with him when his wife, Ursula, died last year.' She did not add that Julia herself found the woman in the centre of a maze at the village fete, but Jim obviously recognised the name because he said, 'Oh, yes, gosh... Well, let's see what we can find about him.'

A Google search wasn't helpful, and he wasn't on social media.

'We'll come back to Robert Benjamin.' Jim leaned in to look at the list. 'Gina McFarlane.'

'I know her a little. I met her at the pub quiz. She's in one of the teams, and a patient of Sean's, too.'

'What's she like?'

'Blonde. Chatty.'

Jim laughed. 'Doesn't sound as if you like her much.'

'I don't know her well, but she seems nice enough.'

Julia was not going to share her instinctive response to Gina, which was irritation. The woman was all over Sean like a rash with her James Bond jokes. 'Ooh, Dr O'Conner – or should I say – Mr Connery!', and her nudging, and the flicking of her golden hair. Sean, of course, behaved entirely appropriately, perfectly polite but distant, with the occasional mild outbreaks of blushing. She suspected that he secretly enjoyed being likened to Sean Connery, whom he did somewhat resemble in appearance and in voice.

'How about a bit of online stalking?' Jim said, already tapping at his phone, while Julia did likewise. 'Ah, here we go. Gina's on Facebook.'

Gina, unsurprisingly, was a compulsive oversharer, posted multiple times a day, and had zero privacy settings. Anyone in the world could see what she made for lunch. Her latest post was a photo labelled 'the girls' at someone's fortieth. It put Julia's teeth on edge.

The other thing she loved to share was her dog. It was a shaggy blonde dog, half grown, with a sweet if rather dim face. Gigi was her name, and she was clearly much beloved. There were multiple posts about the naughty cute things the pup had done. And many, many pictures of the two golden ones.

Jim flicked at the screen and stopped with a snort. 'Here's a small spat about where the correct name for the golden retriever/poodle cross was goldendoodle or a groodle.'

'They missed a trick not going for catchypoo,' said Julia, eliciting a guffaw from Jim.

'It's funny. The dogs people choose,' said Jim. 'This one is, like, a perfect match. Gina and Gigi. They have the same colour hair. The same vibe. Do you think she chose this dog because they are so similar?'

'Maybe. And then there are opposites. There's a huge

fellow around here, looks like a real bruiser, who walks his teacup Yorkie about on a fancy designer lead every evening. The Yorkie's name is Precious.'

'No.'

'Yes. I kid you not. Sean and I have a running list of the bizarre names people give their dogs. The other day we heard someone in the park calling for Petrarch. I mean, what comes over people? Why would you name your dog after a Renaissance poet?'

'Heaven knows. What breed?' Jim asked.

'Dalmatian.'

For some reason, that made them laugh. It settled the air, brushed away the crossness and the awkwardness. Jim sent Gina a message via the Facebook app, introducing himself and asking her to please get in touch.

'And now I wait... We haven't made much progress, though,' Jim said glumly. 'I was thinking...'

'Hmm?'

'I need to go and find these people in person. Chat to them for my follow-up story. When you say I can write it that is,' he said, catching a glimpse of Julia's frown. 'I need to find out what connects them to each other and to Olga.'

'It's the obvious next step, I must admit.'

'Why don't you come with me? You know a couple of them already. You're good at asking questions.'

Julia considered the offer. She had no official position, absolutely no right to go snooping around. She wasn't even a social worker anymore. After a few entanglements with the investigations of the Berrywick police station, she had resolved to remember that it wasn't her job to solve every problem.

But she would like to help. And – let's face it – she was already deeply involved, having found the two bodies. She would like to solve this particular little aspect of the mystery: What did the people on Olga's list have in common?

'Julia?' Jim prompted. He was eager to get going, now.

'Okay, I'll come.'

He stood up.

'But first you have to help me hang up the washing.'

29

Jim drove to Robert Benjamin's house. Julia remembered where he lived. She also remembered that at the time of Ursula's death, he had recently retired from his job as an accountant. She hoped they'd find him at home, doing whatever it was that widowed, retired accountants did with their time.

In between giving Jim directions, she checked her phone. Of course, *everyone* had seen the *Southern Times* article, and *everyone* felt the need to tell her so. There were six or seven messages from friends and acquaintances, most of them delicately hovering between curiosity and concern: 'Just checking in to see how you're doing...' and 'Poor you, what a thing...' and 'If you want to talk about it...'

She responded only to Tabitha, who had weighed in more heavily on the 'concern' side of the equation, with a message: *Just phoning to see how you're doing. I see you made the news. Not your favourite thing. Hope u OK. Chat later.*

Julia wrote back: *Thanks. Saw your call. I'm out on a mission. Ph you when I'm back. Xxx* and put her phone away.

'Left here,' she said, and then. 'Pull over. This is it.'

It seemed that what widowed, retired accountants did with

their time was meticulously clip the edges of the lawn and rake the paths within an inch of their lives. The garden was every bit as neat and tidy as you would expect the garden of an accountant and a maths teacher to be. Even if the maths teacher had passed on. She wondered how their son Luke was doing. The poor young man had a difficult relationship with his mother. In Julia's experience, having a difficult relationship only made death harder on the bereaved. As well as the loss of a loved one, there was often guilt and regret to deal with.

'Coming?' Jim said. He had got out of the car while she mused on Luke's emotional state.

'Yes, sorry. Just thinking.'

They walked up the gravel path, their feet crunching in time. Julia hung back, walking behind, letting Jim take the lead. It was his idea and his story, after all. She was just... What was she doing here, actually? She had resolved to quit poking her nose into police matters, but the urge to solve a mystery, to get things settled and sorted, was so strong in her – and reinforced by years as a social worker – that it was impossible to resist interfering, or helping as she preferred to think of it.

Jim rang the bell, which elicited a deep bark; an articulated *woof, woof,* that sounded almost like a human imitating a dog bark. It wasn't, they discovered with some relief, when Robert Benjamin opened the door. It was a big Doberman, with an energetic puppy jumping up at it, alternately yapping and trying to catch the bigger dog's tail.

Robert Benjamin positioned his leg to prevent the dogs' escape. Julia hadn't seen him since his wife's death – he wasn't one to frequent the local spots or events – and she noticed he'd aged a little, his hair paler than when she'd last seen him, more silver than steel. If anything, his narrow face was thinner, more drawn.

'Hello. Can I help you?' he asked Jim.

'I hope so. Jim McEnroe, *Southern Times.*'

'Oh, I don't need...'

He spotted Julia behind Jim, and interrupted himself to say, 'Oh', in a rather confused tone. 'Mrs Bird?'

'Hello. How are you? How is Luke?'

'Well, thank you. He's away at uni. I got this little rascal to fill the space a bit.' He indicated the puppy as he said this. 'He's a real live wire, he is.' He looked down at the dog, who was butting his head against his leg, trying to get past him to greet the exciting new visitors. Robert seemed to be wondering what on earth he'd let himself in for. 'Now, Charlie, calm down, old chap, get down.'

'He'll certainly keep you busy! Robert, Jim is a friend of mine, and, as you know, a journalist. He's writing about the two women who died recently, Eve Davies and Olga Gilbert.'

'I saw in the paper that you found them. As you did Ursula. Uncanny, isn't it?' Julia couldn't quite read Robert's tone as he said this.

'I did. It was a bizarre coincidence. Not one I relish.'

Jim could see that Julia felt a bit uncomfortable, and stepped in. 'I'm working on a story about the deaths. I'd appreciate your input, Mr Benjamin. I've got one or two questions you might be able to help me with. It won't take a moment.'

'Oh, well, I don't think I can be of much help there,' he said sadly, as if he was sorry to disappoint. 'I don't know anything about that.'

'It's background information, really. Nothing very specific. Would you mind?'

Robert made a non-committal sort of muttering sound, which Jim decided to take as affirmative.

'Great. I believe you were a patient of Dr Eve? Or, to be more accurate, these chaps were?' he indicated the dogs.

The big dog had calmed down, but the little one was now jumping up at Robert's leg, which was acting as a barrier between the dog and the great wide world. Perhaps because of this, Robert didn't invite them in.

'Yes. For many years. Well, not many years for Charlie, she's just a puppy. But Bounder has been a patient for years.'

'Did you know Eve well?'

'Quite well, in a long-term professional relationship sort of way, through the dogs, but not social friends, no.'

'And Olga?'

'Again, only through her work, but she was a helpful sort. When I had concerns, or needed information of any sort, she was very willing.'

'The thing is, Mr Benjamin. There was a list of names on Olga's table the day she died, and yours was on it. I'm wondering if you know why that might be?'

'A list? No idea. I was at the vet a few weeks ago, with Charlie, for his injections, so perhaps it's something to do with that? People to schedule appointments for, or to phone back. Something like that.'

Charlie, perhaps at the sound of his name, renewed his bid for attention, abandoning his jumping in order to wrestle Robert's shoelaces. He growled like a mad thing, his whole body writhing around on attack.

'Charlie, leave it!' Robert Benjamin made an ineffectual attempt to loosen the dog with little flicks of his foot. 'Sorry.'

'Don't apologise. I've got a puppy too, I quite understand. Mr Benjamin, the police are treating these deaths as suspicious. Do you know any reason why anyone would want to harm either of the women?'

'Good heavens no!' He sounded quite appalled. Julia feared the conversation had triggered thoughts of his own wife's violent death. 'Really, I can't help you further. I don't know anything that would be of any use to you for your story, Mr McEnroe. Now, I must be getting on. Charlie!'

And he closed the door.

Gina phoned as they got into the car. She had got Jim's Facebook message and didn't seem to have any concern about responding to a stranger reaching out to her on social media. Jim put her on speakerphone, although Julia had no desire to make herself known to Gina. Gina was no more helpful than Robert Benjamin, although rather more eager to chat. She brought her elderly cat Thunder (*such* a darling!) and her new puppy, Gigi, to the vet. She didn't know either of the women personally, but liked them both and was most upset by their deaths. She had no idea why she'd be on a handwritten list.

'Okay, last on the list is Moira Walker.' Jim turned to Julia expectantly. 'Now, where do we find her?'

'The obvious place. On your computer.'

'Facebook?'

'Try that first.'

'Fifteen Moira Walkers!' Jim said irritably.

'Presumably they don't all live in the Cotswolds.'

'No. This one does, though.'

Jim handed his phone to Julia.

'Oh, I recognise her! She has a clever and well-trained border collie called Sammy who runs at heel off-lead. I see them all the time on the paths and parks.' She gave Jake a pointed look, to indicate that he might be more aspirational in this regard.

'Where does she live?'

'I don't know!'

'Oh,' Jim sounded surprised and disappointed by this failure on her part. 'You don't know?'

'I don't know the address of every person in the village, you know, Jim. I know where we can find her this afternoon, if that helps. She's bound to be on the path by the river. We pass each other almost every day just after four.'

Jim looked at his watch. It's three now. What do you say we

swing past my place to fetch Moxy, and we take to the river path?'

'Okay. I was going to take Jake out anyway. Let's go.'

'And, Julia, if you could complete the walk without finding any of the residents of the Cotswolds deceased along the way, that would be super.'

'I'll do my best, Jim. I'll do my best.'

30

Moxy and Jake were the very model of Good Dogs, trotting along side by side on their leads.

'Remarkable,' said Jim, incredulous. 'Just remarkable. Jake is such a good influence.'

'Oh yes, that's my Jakey.'

Jim and Julia tried to behave like normal people and discuss matters other than murder as they walked the dappled path beneath the chestnut trees, alongside the river. Julia asked Jim about his plans for the summer holidays. Jim was going to France to visit his sister. He asked about her plans. Julia and Sean would take a dog-friendly local trip, perhaps with Sean's son Callum and his girlfriend, on their visit from Vietnam. They gave it a go, but their hearts weren't in it, and after the cursory answers, they lapsed into silence.

Julia was the one to break it, and of course, her thoughts had turned to the murder. 'I've been wondering about Olga's job,' she said. 'Remember when Eve died, I overheard Olga comment on the phone that at least her job was safe with Eve gone. Something along those lines. I never found out for sure what the trouble was. Why her job was under threat. I thought it was that she'd claimed to be sick but gone off to play Padel. But that makes no real sense, because she only did that on the afternoon that Eve died. There wasn't time for her to be in trouble. She must've done something to upset Eve before that.'

'Do you think that it could be related?'

'It bothered me – that Olga, who seemed so bereft – was actually relieved on some level that Eve had died. It seems like it might be related.'

'Could be. You could ask Dr Ryan if he knows anything.'

'I think I will. No harm in asking. I'll phone him when I get home.'

A figure appeared in the distance. They squinted eagerly, hoping to see Moira, but it wasn't her – there was no dog at her side. The far-off figure resolved into someone older and much, much slower than Moira. The tottering gait gave her away – it was Edna.

'And then there were two little fellows,' she said, ignoring Julia's hello, and bending down to address the dogs. 'Twins, twins. Black and black makes black, Jack.' She cackled at her own humour. As always, it made little to no sense to anyone else.

'Hula hooping snoopy snooping sleuthy sleuthing,' she said, straightening up and looking Julia in the eye. 'Ups and downs. Down down down. Take care, now. Take care.'

With a final nod to the dogs, she tottered past.

'That woman gives me the creeps,' said Jim with a shiver.

'Oh, she's harmless enough.' Julia said this breezily, although she understood Jim's point. Edna often made her feel weirdly seen, and sometimes judged, and a little bit nervous. On a few occasions, her nonsense seemed to be less nonsensical, and almost – in a way she didn't understand – profound. 'Let's move on.'

They'd taken only a few steps in the direction Edna had come from when they saw another figure coming towards them. This time, the figure was moving fast and fluidly, and it was accompanied by a dog.

'That might be Moira,' Julia said.

'I see black and white, that must be her with the border collie,' said Jim, who was younger and had better eyesight. Julia missed the perfect vision of her youth. It was one of the more annoying side effects of getting older. Now she seemed to have an ever-narrowing range of good vision. She had to take her glasses to the shops to read the labels, and she couldn't make out a border collie at a distance.

'It's her all right. She's got two dogs with her.'

They came closer, Moira walking briskly with a little dog on a lead, and Sammy the border collie trotting neatly at heel.

They didn't even have to hail her to a stop. She halted in surprise.

'Goodness!' she said, looking down at Jim's little Moxy.

'Blimey!' said Jim, looking down at Moira's dog. They looked back and forth from one to the other, noting that each was a dead ringer for the other.

'They're like the same dog,' said Julia, rather unnecessarily, for they were, in fact, identical. The soft blacker-than-black fur. The bright eyes. And they were exactly the same size.

The two puppies sniffed and nuzzled at each other. Jake watched them, bemused. One small shiny black thing is fair enough, he seemed to be thinking, but two? And are there more where these came from? Will the madness never end?

'This is Moxy.'

'This is Penny.'

'They must be siblings, surely,' said Julia.

'Did you get Moxy from George Mullins?' Moira asked Jim.

'I did. About three weeks ago.'

'Well that explains it. Julia's right. They must be related.

The same litter, presumably, like twins, because I got Penny at around the same time. Mid April. I'm Moira, by the way.'

'I know.'

'Have we met?' she asked in surprise.

'No, Julia mentioned your name. I'm Jim McEnroe.'

'How are you coping with your little one?'

'Ah, love the little gal. A lot of work, though, aren't they, puppies?'

'They certainly are. Gosh, the energy in this one. Yesterday, she destroyed a whole bath mat in the five minutes it took me to pop out and post a letter.'

'Oh, yes, the chewing! My Moxy...'

'Twins! Aunt Edna!' Julia blurted out, interrupting the exchange of puppy tales. 'That's what she was talking about. That weird nonsense she was saying about twins. Two fellows. Black and black makes black.'

'She said that? How strange. I saw her on the path. She played with Penny for a bit. She's a bit of a mystery, is Aunt Edna.'

The two puppies were gambolling and wrestling like a small black whirlwind with strings attached. The leads quickly became entangled. Moxy yelped in panic, and pulled away, yanking Penny with him. She scrabbled to get away. Sammy, the sensible border collie, looked at Moira in alarm. Julia quickly knelt down and grabbed both puppies, holding them to her so that they couldn't worsen the situation. 'It's okay, chaps, let's sort this out for you,' Julia said. She clipped each lead from its collar, freeing them instantly. The little things wriggled in delight, rubbing their silky fur against her face. She inhaled their milky puppy smell, the best smell in the world, and it only lasted a couple of months.

She took another deep sniff, enjoying their smell and their softness, and popped them down. 'There you go, pups.'

The owners clipped the leads onto their respective dogs.

'Quick thinking, Julia,' said Moira.

'Yes, good save.'

'Make sure you each get the right one!'

'I'd better get on with my walk. Penny and Sammy will be wanting their supper. Nice to meet you, Jim.'

'You too, Moira.'

'Good luck with Moxy.'

'Bye then.'

'Goodbye.'

Instead of moving away, the two of them lingered there smiling. Feeling like a spare wheel, Julia stepped off the path and made a show of examining a patch of bluebells bobbing under an oak tree.

'Perhaps we could walk them together some time,' she heard Jim venture.

'A playdate for the dogs. That will be good for their social skills.'

Julia could actually *hear* the beaming in his voice. 'I'll phone you to set it up. What's your number?'

Julia turned, and watched the exchange of numbers, which carried with it an undercurrent of flirtation and a dash of awkwardness. The dogs were all quiet and still, as if they wanted to do nothing that might derail this whole business.

Having sufficiently noted the magnificence of the bluebells, Julia rejoined the little knot of people and dogs to say her good-byes to Moira and her dogs. They parted company, Julia and Jim back to the car park, Moira to complete her circuit.

As soon as they were out of Moira's earshot, Julia grinned at him and spoke. 'Well, *that* was very interesting.'

'Ah, it's only a walk, Julia. For the dogs,' Jim said, blushing. 'Don't give me that look.'

Julia ignored his stammering, and continued. 'Don't you see? Jim, that list that Olga was writing at the time she died, the one I found on her kitchen table. It's not about the dog treats, it's about the dogs... Everyone on that list has recently bought a puppy. Or, in Will's case, is about to get one. *That's* what they have in common.'

'So Olga's list is a list of puppy owners?' Jim said, eager to move on from any embarrassing discussion of his intentions around Moira. 'Seems a bit random. I can't see how that could have anything to do with Olga's murder.'

'Nor can I,' Julia said. 'But it seems that's what connects them.'

'They must have something else in common,' Jim said.

'Well, they were all patients of Dr Eve, I presume. Since Olga knew them. But how that ties in...' she gave up in frustration.

Jim clicked his fingers. 'I don't know if this will be helpful, but if I'm not mistaken, we all got our puppies from the same breeder. The Mullinses. I know that Moira and I did. Penny and Moxy both came from there.'

'And Will Adamson too,' said Julia. 'That was his alibi for the afternoon of Eve's death. He was visiting the puppy place when Eve was killed. Hayley checked his story, and it was true.'

'I bet the Mullinses will be able to help us figure this out. If we have a chat with them for the story, see if they have any details or colour – I bet they've even met the murderer!'

'It sounds like rather a long shot, Jim.' Julia was starting to worry that the younger man had a bit of an overactive imagination.

'Those are the best shots!' Jim said, all fired up now that he had a lead to work on. 'Coming?'

Julia didn't have much choice, seeing as they had come together in Jim's car. Besides, they'd come this far, she might as well stick with Jim. See what the Mullinses had to say about the puppy list.

She opened the back door, and patted the seat. 'Come on then, Jake.'

He leapt in, and Jim lifted Moxie in next to him.

Julia slammed the door and opened the passenger door.

'Let's go.'

31

'Shouldn't you phone and see if they're there?' Julia said, as Jim started the car.

'Nah. Never give up the element of surprise, I say. Even for random witnesses and people you hope will provide background colour. If you give them notice, they'll have prepared the whole story in their heads already. It's better to come at them fresh.'

'That makes sense. In fact, I've seen the same thing happen in my work. There's a version of what's going on in the family, or the relationship, and that's what gets trotted out every time.'

'That's interesting. You mean in your social work?'

'Yes. You have to work hard to build trust if you want to see deeper, or you want things to change. Or, as you say, a surprise turn of events can bring out some new information or response.'

Julia didn't mention that the surprise turn of events in her line of work was often quite traumatic. A crisis or a disaster. In his too, presumably, although not in this case. It was more likely that this would be a dead end, that the Mullinses would have nothing useful to add. No insight into the list. No colour for Jim's story.

Jim drove smoothly along the country roads, keeping precisely to the speed limit, leaning gently into the curves and turns. Julia sat in silence, enjoying the ride, admiring the view. 'Only a few weeks ago I was here to pick up Moxy. Funny that,' he mused.

'And Eve and Olga were still alive.'

'You know, Olga was the one who put me in touch with George and Debbie in the first place. She recommended them when I said I was considering getting a puppy. Told me to say that she'd sent me.'

'That's so strange to think about, isn't it? How things can change, just like that. In just a few weeks.'

'It is. Strange and horrible.'

'What do you plan to ask, exactly?'

'I want to ask about Eve, just for background for the follow-up story. Her place in the community, and so on. And about Olga too, although I don't know if they'd have known her personally. Maybe ask them about the other people they've dealt with. Maybe someone in the puppy community had something against Eve and Olga. Maybe ask them if they noticed anything about the people on that list.'

'Heck, I forgot to phone Hayley back,' Julia said. 'She wanted to ask me something. I'll give her a quick call.'

'Go ahead. We're nearly there. In fact, I think this is the edge of their property.'

Julia couldn't see much behind a thick, tall hedge. She phoned Hayley, who answered almost immediately, but her voice was so broken up she couldn't make out what she wanted.

'... ask you for... dog... shshshshhs... where... you?'

'I can hardly hear you. I'm on the road, near the Mullins' puppy people... Yes, I said *puppy* people. The phone signal is bad here. I'm with Jim... I said... Yes, we're in Edgeley. Jim wants to see...'

There was more muffled crackling that interrupted Julia, punctuated with occasional words that made no sense.

'Hayley, I can't hear you. This isn't working. I've got a stop to make here with Jim, then home. I'll call you when I'm back in Berrywick.'

She ended the call. 'No luck,' she said to Jim. 'I don't know what she wanted. It was like shouting into a hurricane. We can try to get hold of her later.'

'Okay,' Jim said. 'And here we are.'

Jim slowed and turned into an entrance. The high hedge was broken with a big wooden gate, which was closed but not locked. Julia opened it, noting the well-kept little house ahead, at the top of a small rise. There were banks of hydrangeas on either side.

Jim drove through. 'I'll walk,' she said, when he drew up next to her. 'It's only a few yards.' He nodded, and drove off slowly. She closed the gate and walked after him.

Jim had to park in a small clearing on the other side of the driveway from the house, next to a small old fashioned VW Beetle. Beyond it, under the trees was another car with a tarpaulin thrown loosely over it.

Jim climbed out of the car and walked up to the front door with Julia. The door was opened by a woman who must have been a few years older than Julia, in a well-worn summer dress. She had a pleasant, homely face, plump and pink-cheeked. Her grey hair was held in a long plait that draped over her shoulder.

'Hello,' she said. Julia recognised the uncertainty in her voice – she knew Jim's face, but couldn't quite place him. Being increasingly afflicted by the same vexing problem, Julia felt sympathy for the woman.

'Hi, Debbie. It's Jim McEnroe. I got a puppy from you? Little black girl, Moxy, the Schnoodle?'

'Oh yes. Of course! How is the dear little thing?'

'She's just lovely. And this is my friend Julia, she loves dogs too.'

'Hello, Julia. Anyone who loves dogs is all right in my book. I remember you now,' she said, looking at Jim. 'You're the journalist.'

'Exactly, with the *Southern Times*. That's kind of why I'm here. I wanted to ask you a few questions, if that's okay.'

Her sunny face clouded over. 'Oh, I don't know about that. I'm not much one for that sort of thing, and I don't think George would want me chatting away and getting in the paper.'

'Oh, it's nothing controversial,' said Jim. 'Just a bit of background for a story I'm doing on Eve Davies and Olga Gilbert, and what they meant to the animal-loving community of the area. You would have known Eve and Olga, I believe?'

'Ah, well George would be the one for that,' she said, looking worried. 'He'll be back soon, he's just out doing a delivery. Will you come in?'

They followed Debbie into the house, to a sunny kitchen. The already full table was covered with the necessities for baking – a deep glass dish, a big glass jar of sugar, another of flour and a bowl of apples sat next to a cutting board, with a sharp knife lying ready for use. A huge dresser on the far end held antique kitchen implements, stoneware, jugs and bowls. A pair of ancient binoculars balanced on a typewriter. Decorative tins commemorating various royal occasions.

'Don't mind the mess, I'm making an apple pie.'

'I hope we're not disturbing you,' Julia said. 'Coming by unannounced.'

'No matter. I was about to have a cup of tea, in fact. You'd be welcome.'

'Thank you, if you're sure,' said Jim.

Debbie nodded and turned on the gas under the kettle on the stove.

'Have a seat.'

Julia took a seat at the table. As she lowered herself to the cushion, she heard a funny noise, a sort of high-pitched growl, and stood up in alarm. She looked down. The noise appeared to be coming from the cushion.

'Noodle! Heaven's alive,' cried Debbie, confusingly.

'Goodness me, you silly boy, you almost got yourself sat on!' Debbie said, rather more understandably, as the cushion squirmed to reveal a small dog, the same honey brown as the cushion, and showing a snarl of tiny white teeth.

She scooped the tiny bundle up into her arms. 'This is Noodle, my Yorkiepoo.' She kissed the little face. 'He was the runt of one of our litters. We never thought he'd live, but I bottle fed him day and night, and he did, he pulled through. I couldn't let him go after that, and now he's the Lord of the Manor, aren't you? The King of the Castle.'

'Oodles of Schnoodles and Noodles and Yorkiepoos!' Julia said with a laugh.

'Well, we do specialise in the poodle crosses,' Debbie said, rather earnestly. 'They're so lovely.'

'They are. And they're very popular, I know a few Labradoodles, too. And who did I meet recently with a cockapoo?'

'It was Robert Benjamin,' said Jim.

'Oh yes,' said Julia. 'That's who it was.'

'One of ours,' said Debbie proudly.

'Really? Well, that's a coincidence. I wonder...'

Julia's wondering was interrupted by the sound of boots scraping on a mat, and the opening of the kitchen door.

The man who stepped inside was vaguely familiar to Julia. He was tall, and thickset, and his nose veered off at a slightly strange angle, as if it had been broken and not set properly. Julia knew she'd seen him somewhere recently, in passing, but couldn't place him.

'George!' Debbie said. 'You remember Jim? He adopted one

of the Schnoodles, the most recent litter, remember? A dear little black one, a feisty girl.'

'She is that,' Jim chuckled. 'Got me round her little finger. Paw, I suppose. Or toe?'

'And this is Julia.'

'Hello, I think we've met. You look familiar.'

George ignored her and turned to Jim. 'You're the journalist.'

'That's right. The *Southern Times*.'

'What do you want?' Unlike Debbie, George did not seem at all pleased to see Jim and Julia. His tone was sharp, making Julia think of how her mother used to deal with encyclopedia salesmen knocking on the door.

'Now, George! Is that any way to speak to our customers?' Debbie said it with a little laugh, to make it seem jokey, but Julia saw that she was embarrassed and annoyed at her son's rudeness. The man looked furious, his lips pursed, his face red. Debbie was such a dear, and he looked a right grump – must have got his personality from his father, Julia thought.

Jim, meanwhile, spoke in a friendly, placating tone. 'As I said to your mum, I'm doing a story on Eve Davies and what she meant to this community. The people of Berrywick and Edgeley, and the dog-loving community. It's a background piece. Human interest, you know? Just thought you might have an anecdote or a comment, seeing as so many of their clients seem to have got puppies from you. You must have met many people who knew them both.'

'I don't have anything to say.'

Julia had been staring at George while Jim spoke, and suddenly something about the angle of his head made everything fall into place.

She knew where she'd seen him before. He'd been a lot friendlier then. But it wasn't how he was behaving that was the important memory. It was *where* she had seen him. She glanced from him, to the typewriter on the table amongst the baking stuff.

Julia felt a prickling fear. She stood up.

'Come on, Jim, we'd best be on our way. Let the Mullinses get back to their business. This was just for some colour – no need to pester these nice people. They're not involved in any way.'

Jim shot her a quizzical look, and continued. 'It's just that I know you knew the veterinary practice, because Olga recommended you to me when I was looking for a dog. She couldn't have been more complimentary, said I must drop her name, so I assumed you were friends, or that she knew that you were good breeders. Perhaps she'd been out here, seen your puppies?' Jim had a friendly expectant look on his face; a bit like a Labradoodle himself.

'You assumed wrong. Hardly knew the woman,' George said gruffly, then added, 'May she rest in peace.'

'Thanks for the tea, Debbie. We won't bother you further. Jim, these nice people don't know anything useful to you. Come *on*, Jim,' Julia said, heading for the door. She took a few quick steps out the front door and towards the car. Jim was following her now, keeping pace. He had finally realised something was up. When she turned round and caught his eye, she could almost see he was trying to work out what it was, but trusted her instincts enough to follow her lead. They each opened a door of the car and got in. Julia felt an enormous sense of relief as the doors closed.

'What's going on?' Jim said, starting the engine.

'I recognise George Mullins. You won't believe this, Jim, but George was in the car park the day Eve died. He had two poodles with him, and Walter asked him to watch Jake and Eve's dog, Fergus.'

'That's extraordinary. But what do you think that means?' Jim asked, reversing the car to point it towards the gate.

'I don't know exactly how it fits together, Jim, but George Mullins was on the scene at Eve's murder. And he owns a typewriter. The police spoke to all the people seen on the walk – but we all forgot about him.' Julia paused for a moment, thinking. 'Someone dropped some treats on the hidden path near where Eve died – and that could very likely be George. And everyone on Olga's list got a puppy from George Mullins.'

'On Olga's recommendation, I assume – seeing as that's how I came to him.' Jim had reversed successfully out of the parking space as they spoke. He put the car in first. 'She was actually a bit weird about it, now that I think about it. Slipped me a note when she heard me asking Eve about puppies, and was very insistent that I tell them that she sent me.'

Julia paused, thinking, while Jim carefully negotiated the car back around the tree.

'Jim, I think she was running a side hustle! Getting commission from referring buyers!'

'And that explains what you overheard!'

'I need to phone Hayley,' Julia said, her eyes on the phone already in her hand as she spoke, a steady stream of words coming out quickly as she put it all together. 'George Mullins is involved somehow. Eve must have found out that Olga was in cahoots with breeders. And what if the breeders were not legit, what if they were...' She found the most recent call, and hit 'redial'. The car came to a sudden stop, and Julia looked up. They were at the gate, where George Mullins was standing, barring their way.

'Damn,' said Jim quietly.

George slipped a padlock onto the bolt of the gate and locked it. He walked slowly to Jim's window.

Jim rolled it down an inch or two. 'Come on now, George. What are you doing?' he said in that matey tone of his. 'Just let us be on our way. We understand that you don't want to be interviewed. No hard feelings, mate.'

'You're not going anywhere. We need to talk.'

Julia glanced down at the phone. She could see that either Hayley or her answering service had picked up the call.

'George Mullins, I must insist that you allow us to leave your property,' she called loudly, across Jim, in the direction of the open window. She hoped that the phone lying on her lap was picking this up and that either Hayley or her answering service was getting the details. 'We are being detained at your house against our will. Unlock that gate and let Jim and me out.'

'Not happening,' he said, and he wrenched open Jim's door.

32

Debbie Mullins must have followed them all down the driveway, because she drew up next to George and looked at them aghast. Julia and Jim were out of the car, each next to their open car door, with George Mullins between them and the gate.

'George, good heavens. What do you think you're doing?' she said, her voice pitched high with shock. 'Don't be mad, now...'

'It's okay, Mum, it's a mistake. There's been a misunderstanding. I just need to explain. It's not what it looks like. I'm not... what did she say?... I'm not *detaining* anyone. I just want to talk.'

Debbie lowered her voice and spoke calmly to her son. 'Now, George, you open that gate right this minute, and we can all go about our business as if this never happened. Come on now.'

'No, Mum. I mean yes, I will. But I need to sort this business out first.' He passed his hands over his face, leaving a streak of dirt across his forehead. He clutched his hair, pulling at the tufts. 'Just let me think.'

'You mustn't think badly of George,' said Debbie. 'He gets a bit carried away at times, but he's a good lad. Everything will be fine.'

'It will *not* be fine unless he opens that gate right now,' said Jim, taking a couple of steps forward, squaring up to George, who stood his ground. Men could be quite tiresome, really, Julia thought, looking at them chest to chest like two cockerels. Or one turkey and one cockerel, really, George being significantly larger than Jim.

'Right, well if you won't open it, I'll do it myself.'

Jim stepped around George, in the direction of the gate. George grabbed his arm.

Jim pulled his arm away and squirmed to free himself. His longish rather scraggly hair and slim build gave him a laid-back appearance, but he was wiry, and stronger than he looked. Still, Julia wouldn't back him in a fight with George Mullins. She seriously hoped it wouldn't come to that. 'You don't want to be doing that, George,' she said calmly, walking towards them. George kept his hold on Jim, but loosened his grip. Julia could see he was anxious and undecided as to what to do next. She felt that she could talk him down. 'Let's take things down a notch. No one wants things to get out of hand, do they, George?'

Jim looked as if *he* wanted things to get out of hand. In fact, he looked as if he wanted to punch George Mullins in the face, rather than take things down a notch. Jim's own face had turned an interesting mix of ashen, speckled with large red blotches. His free arm hung at his side, and his hand clenched into a fist and relaxed, clenched and relaxed. Yes, Jim might be her bigger problem. He was also scared and angry.

'Jim,' Julia said, 'why don't we—'

Jim was in no mood for listening, he wrenched his hand away from George and gave the big man a shove, two hands flat against his chest.

George stumbled back in surprise, and then leapt forward nimbly, grabbing Jim by the shoulders. He spun him around, so he was holding him in a bear hug, his thick arms around Jim's chest.

'If you could just be still and let me think,' he said. 'I can explain.'

Julia was still trying to salvage the situation, keeping her voice steady, as if the man didn't have her friend in a stranglehold, and her friend didn't look as if he was having the air squeezed out of him. 'It's okay, George, why don't you explain. That's a good idea.'

Debbie, who had been rooted to the spot in horror, came to life and cut in, 'George. Hold your tongue and let that man go.'

Julia looked from Debbie to George and back.

'I'm sure there's really nothing to explain,' she said, in her calmest voice. 'Just let Jim go.'

'I'll tell you what's happening,' said Jim, undeterred by his status as George's prisoner. 'The two of you are running an illegal puppy farm. One of those puppy mills. We've done some articles in my paper.' Julia really, *really* wished he hadn't said anything.

'No, no. Puppy farm? That's such an ugly term.' Debbie seemed genuinely affronted. 'We are a specialist dog breeder. We take good care of all our dogs. Not at all like those dreadful places.'

George nodded. 'Mum loves the puppies, and they're all good dogs.'

Julia kept up the calm, matter-of-fact tone she had used so successfully for scared runaways and belligerent drunks. What Peter used to call her 'social worker voice'. 'I can see that the dogs are well cared-for. Moxy is lovely. And so are the other puppies of yours we've seen. I think we can all agree that this is no puppy farm. So if you'd be so kind as to release Jim and open the gate, George, we'll be on our way.'

'Just trying to make an honest living. But the licence, you know it's not easy. The whole country's turned into a nanny state,' George said, his voice a bit calmer, more of a defeated grumble than an aggressive stance. He no longer looked as if he might swing a punch. He loosened his hold on Jim, and gave him a gentle push away from him, in the direction of the car. Julia almost felt sorry for George, shaking his head sadly at the state of the world.

Instead of taking the gap and moving further away, Jim took his phone from his pocket, where he had obviously been recording the whole conversation, held it up to George and said:

'And Eve Davies got in your way, is that it? She threatened to report you to the authorities? Did you kill her, George?'

Julia could willingly have punched Jim herself, at this point. What was he thinking, riling the man up, just as she'd started to calm him down?

'She shouldn't have interfered,' yelled George, making a lunge for Jim's phone, but Jim was off. He made off round the car, with George lumbering after him. When they stopped, they were on either side of the car. Jim moved left, George moved right. Jim moved right, George moved left, the car between them. At one point, Jim missed a step and ran into the open car door. It was like some farcical scene from a pantomime, except for the fury on George's face.

'Oh, for heaven's sake!' Debbie had clearly had enough of her son's antics. She turned and marched quickly back to the house.

Julia would rather have been somewhere else herself, but here she was, watching the two men lunge and feint. Left and right, back and forth. And then George upped the stakes, dashing away from the car to pick up a heavy rake that was lying against the fence. Its metal parts were rusted and sharp tipped. He resumed his position at the car – Jim moved to keep the car between them – and reached over the top of the car in a stabbing motion.

'Stop that! Put it down!' shouted Julia, as the lethal-looking rake came alarmingly close to Jim's face. Even if he avoided losing an eye, or getting impaled through a vital organ, the rake was so mucky and rusty, a nick would be dangerous – he'd likely get tetanus, by the look of it.

Up until now, Jake and Moxy had been sitting calmly at the back of the car, observing the inexplicable ways of the humans. But now, alarmed by the panic in Julia's voice, Jake shot out of the open door, barking. He surveyed the scene, and despite being somewhat dim, extremely placid, and unschooled in the ways of violence, seemed to realise that George was the threat. He lunged at him, barking ferociously, and snapped at his legs.

George kicked in his general direction, missing him, thank goodness. He was still stabbing at Jim over the top of the car, and kicking at the air where he imagined Jake might be. The multitasking was too much for him. He tripped over the jumping, excitable Jake and went sprawling to the ground. Jake looked down at him in surprise. It reminded Julia of the time that Jake, having spent a year chasing the pigeons that roosted in the neighbours' garage and came down to eat his morning dog biscuits, actually caught one. He had held it gingerly in his mouth and looked at Julia pleadingly as if to say, 'A bit of help here please?' Julia had gently opened his jaws to release the bird, which flew off without any sign of injury.

This time, Jake stood next to the fallen man, and looked up at Julia, as if for guidance. George pulled himself up onto his hands and knees, and Jake gave a low, threatening growl.

George, who had hesitated in a kneeling position, must have decided to take his chances with Jake. He got to his feet, picked up the rake, and lunged at Jim again, who now took off at a run. George set off after Jim. Jake, assuming that things had now taken a turn for the playful, bounded after him, jumping and barking. Moxy shot from the car to join in, her high-pitched yaps tearing through Julia's last remaining nerves. Moxy followed Jake's lead, jumping and barking at George, who was falling further behind the more nimble Jim, who was unencumbered by the canine chorus.

'Jake. Moxy. Come!' called Julia, eager to remove the dogs from the confrontation, for their own safety. Jake slowed, torn between the chase, and his mistress's instructions. Moxy followed his lead.

'That's enough! Nobody move.' Debbie's voice came from the direction of the house. Julia turned towards her, and was alarmed to see the older woman coming up the path with a long gun held aloft. Julia was no expert in firearms, but the thing looked antique. The sort of thing Debbie's grandfather might have used to hunt rabbits. Both men stopped at the sight of the gun.

'Mum!'

'Shut up, George! Put that rake down right now. Don't make me ask you twice.'

'Mum, I have to—'

'You have to do what, exactly? Kill someone? Someone *else?*' Debbie's voice broke, as she asked softly, 'Did you kill those two women, Georgie? Did you?'

George looked at her, tears in his eyes, his mouth opening and closing, as if he was trying to find just the perfect words to make it all make sense to himself and his mother.

No words came, but Debbie knew the answer. She seemed to lose her will. Her whole body slumped, her head bowed, the rifle hanging from her limp arm. 'Oh, George. Why?'

Whatever George's answer might have been, Julia didn't hear it. She was distracted by the sound of tyres on gravel, and a car squealing to a halt at the gate. DI Hayley Gibson emerged from the driver's side, and with a speed and grace that surprised Julia, climbed over the gate. Walter Farmer followed, slower, and less elegantly.

'This is the police,' Hayley said, authoritatively.

The three participants in the drama stood stock-still, in a

strange little tableau. George with his rake, Debbie with her rifle, Jim at the edge of the house, poised ready to disappear around the corner. Even the dogs stilled at her tone.

'Drop your weapon,' she told Debbie Mullins, then turned to George. 'And you too. Put that rake down.'

'Oh, this?' Debbie lifted the rifle and looked at it as if she'd never seen it before. 'It's not a *weapon*.' Debbie started poking and pulling at the gun as if in illustration. 'It's not even loaded. It's my grandfather's old rabbit shooter, it's just a...'

An almighty crack rang out – a gunshot, for sure, Julia thought – followed quickly by the blood-chilling sound of a terrible wailing cry.

33

A small, whining snore came from the back seat of Sean's car. Julia turned in the passenger seat and smiled at the sight of Jake dozing, exhausted by a long hard day of heroics. The back of Sean's car was already fitted out for canine passengers, with a rug to protect the seat. Sean had left a fleece hoodie on it, which Jake had somehow scrunched up into a comfortable pillow, on which he rested his head.

Julia envied Jake his little nap. She was exhausted herself, but exhausted in that adrenaline-fuelled state that meant she'd be awake until midnight, tossing and turning, running a home movie of the day's dramatic activities.

The dramatic day wasn't over. They were on their way to the police station, where Julia would give a statement, along with all the participants and witnesses of the scene in the Mullins's driveway. Sean had come dashing over when she'd phoned him to tell him what had happened at the Mullinses, and insisted on driving Julia and Jake to the station. DC Walter Farmer had left just ahead of them with George and Debbie, in a van with the uniforms. Jim had followed in his own car, with Moxy.

A couple of crime scene chaps had been left at the scene, finishing up the job of bagging up the weapons and clues under DI Gibson's watchful eye. She would be minutes behind them, she said. The RSPCA was there to decide what to do about the four dogs and seven puppies on the premises.

'I wonder what will happen to the poor puppies. Maybe Debbie will be home to take care of them. She won't be held, will she?' Julia asked. 'She didn't commit a crime, after all. As far as I can tell, she had nothing to do with either of the two women's deaths. Didn't have any inkling of what her son had done. That's all on George.'

'There's the small matter of discharging a firearm. An *unlicensed* firearm,' said Sean. 'She was reckless. It's a miracle no one was hurt.'

'By the look of it, that old thing had been on top of a cupboard for decades.'

'It could have exploded in her hands. Believe me, I've seen a couple of accidents with guns and it's not something you want to...' Sean let the sentence trail off, and shook his head. 'Thank goodness it didn't.'

'Isn't there some saying about God looking after fools? My gran used to say that.'

'Yes. It was fools, drunkards and babies, that he was watching over, if I remember correctly.'

'Thank heavens there were no drunks or kids in the mix this time. More than enough fools, though.' Julia's sigh carried the hint of a smile in it. 'Plenty of those.'

They drove on with just the sound of the tyres, and Jake's gentle snoring. It was quite pleasantly peaceful, driving slowly along the country road in the dusk. If only they weren't going to the police station.

'So tell me what you think was going on there,' Sean said. 'They are running an illegal dog breeding operation?'

'Yes. I looked it up online,' said Julia. 'Anyone breeding and selling three or more litters of puppies in a year has to have a licence. I'm sure the Mullinses were over that limit. Breeders must meet certain conditions. Hayley will look into that side of things, but it appears the place was unregistered and illegal.'

'I've seen a few stories about that in the newspapers. There's been a big crackdown on it recently. Two women went to jail a few months ago, if I'm not mistaken.'

'That's what I saw when I looked it up online. Puppy farms, they call them. Some of them are awful, and the dogs are neglected, but the Mullinses took care of their dogs, even if they had too many of them.'

'So where did Eve and Olga fit in?'

'Eve had realised that they had too many puppies coming through the practice, I think. She must have threatened to go to the police, and George panicked. When I saw her the day before, Eve talked about not being sure about what to do about something. I think that she knew that they weren't bad people, but also that they weren't keeping the rules.'

'I don't know why George Mullins didn't just do the necessary paperwork and get a licence and stick to the rules.' Sean, himself a man who stuck to the rules, sounded utterly perplexed.

'Greed, I suppose. He wanted to sell more puppies. And believe me, these special hybrid dogs are not cheap. Depending on the cross, more than a thousand pounds.'

'A thousand pounds?' Sean's perplexity was even deeper. 'For a dog?'

'Sometimes more. Two thousand for some exotic cross.'

'What's it crossed with, a unicorn?'

She laughed and rested her hand on his thigh. He took one hand off the steering wheel to cover hers and said simply, 'I'm glad you're okay.'

'I am too, Sean. Thank you. Anyway, it seems like Eve was onto them. I presume she was threatening to turn them in to the authorities. End of profitable unicorn puppy business. That's why George killed her.'

'But what about Olga? Why did he kill her?'

'Olga was making a bit of extra money by sending buyers to the Mullinses and getting a commission. Remember, there was something that she was in trouble about at work, that Eve's death resolved. I think that Eve knew about her side hustle, and was cross. When I overheard her, I think she was talking to George – she said that Eve's death solved both their problems. Of course, she didn't know that George had killed Eve.' Julia paused, thinking about Olga. 'She must have known that the Mullinses weren't keeping all the laws, but she was making commission on the puppies. It wasn't the kind of money that would draw attention – enough for a few treats, trout for lunch at the Buttered Scone – but once Eve's death was being treated as a crime, that changed. When I asked about the treats Olga must have made the connection. She drove to the Mullinses, and confronted George. He must have killed her.'

'And then typed a suicide note and placed her at the foot of the cliff, to try to make it look like she had jumped. Like a copycat suicide,' said Sean.

'Exactly. Jim and I even saw her car parked at the Mullinses when we arrived, and didn't realise what we were seeing.'

They drove in silence for a few moments, when Julia suddenly said, 'Slow down!' although they were already going slowly, it being a narrow and poorly lit road. 'Look there.'

Ahead, a dark figure had one foot up on a low garden wall, and was reaching for the roof of the garden shed on the other side of it.

'What's he doing?' Sean asked, slowing to a stop.

'It must be the peeping Tom! That or a cat burglar. Come on...' She opened the door.

'Julia,' Sean hissed. 'Don't be crazy. Let's just call the police.' As she walked towards the wall, she heard the sentence finish in a sigh, as he opened the door, got out, and went after her.

'Thank you,' she said, when he caught up with her.

They peered over the wall, trying to make out a figure in the gloom. Visibility was poor, and not helped by the dense foliage of the border, the well-established trees, and the garden shed which partially blocked their view. There was no sign of the mysterious man – at least, Julia assumed it was a man.

'We'll have to go in,' Julia whispered, turning to walk along the length of the wall to the gate.

'Have you not been sufficiently imperilled for one day?' Sean asked tiredly. 'The rusty rake, the musket.'

'I don't think it was a musket... And I won't confront him. I'll just peer round the gate, see what I can see. Someone might be in danger.'

'We shouldn't be sneaking around other people's gardens in pursuit of possible criminals. We should phone the police.' Sean was exasperated. And also, probably right. But Julia was by now firmly in the grip of her curiosity and her concern for the house's inhabitants.

'Good idea. You phone the police while I take a peek.'

'I'll phone, then I'm coming in after you...'

Julia continued along the wall in an awkward crouched position. It was hell on her knees, and not very easy on her thighs either. Not to mention her back. Her sprained wrist was starting to hurt again as she balanced herself by holding the wall. She really must sign up for that online Pilates that Tabitha had been raving about and nagging her to join. Tomorrow, she told herself, straightening behind the cover of the gatepost and surveying the scene.

There he was, the sneaky bugger, standing a little way away from the house, peering up at the upstairs window. Julia was no stranger to the broad and creative badness of humanity, but honestly, the way some people got their kicks. It was most peculiar.

The man took a step onto the sturdy, square plinth that held up a large pot planted with the happiest hydrangea Julia had seen in a long while. He was of small build, and managed to perch there, holding onto the pot while he craned his neck for a better view. Quite what he could see was a mystery. From where Julia stood, it seemed the curtains were completely closed. There was barely a sliver of light showing between them, let alone a sliver of whatever it was that dirty bloke was hoping to see. Still, he seemed intrigued, shifting about for a better view, turning his head, searching into the gloom.

He craned his head to the left, giving Julia a quick view of the side of his face, under a cap. The light from a bulb at the front door briefly illuminated it.

She recognised that face. And that cap, in fact.

'Sean!' she shouted.

The reply came not from Sean O'Connor, but from DI Hayley Gibson, who shouted, 'Police, don't move.' For the second time that day.

34

'Bats?' Hayley repeated weakly. She looked just as tired as Julia felt, and pretty grumpy to boot. She had, after all, worked a full day, and now been intercepted on her way back to the office from the crime scene. 'Bats? The little flying mammals?'

'Yes, bats. Marvellous chaps, and very important in the ecosystem. They are under great threat. Fortunately, they have adapted well to the semi-urban environment, and often nest quite happily in residential properties.'

'Well, that's nice for them, I'm sure, but you're trespassing.'

'Officer, I must apologise. I should never had come onto private property. It was most irresponsible. I don't know what I was thinking.'

'Well, I was thinking that you were a peeping Tom. Or perhaps breaking and entering.'

'Good heavens. I didn't think. I just saw the bats fly in and I followed. I didn't break anything. Or enter. I've been observing the bats of Berrywick for some weeks now. Lovely chaps. Vital.'

'It's all right,' said the homeowner, an exhausted-looking young mum who was already in her pyjamas when she came outside to investigate the commotion in her garden. She carried a baby on her hip, and a little girl of three or four clung to her leg, looking nervously at the adults gathered there in the dark. 'Look. It was a mistake. I'm not pressing charges or anything. If you all just move along, we can say no more about it, and I can get these two to bed.'

'Well, the police were called, so I'm afraid there's paperwork...'

It was a toss-up as to who would cry first, the woman, or the little girl. Hayley looked pretty wiped out, too. Julia felt for them all. She had an idea. 'It was more of a personal call though, really. We'd left our previous engagement at the same time, so I knew you were minutes away. I asked Sean to phone you on your personal mobile, just as a friend, you know.'

'That's true,' Hayley said, her demeanour lightening as the paperwork fluttered away into the distance. 'I would say that as a person just helping out a friend, perhaps I don't really need to do any paperwork at all.'

'Well, in that case, goodnight,' the woman said, firmly. She took the girl's hand, hoisted the baby up a notch on her hip, and turned for the door.

'You're free to go,' Hayley said to Hamilton Cunningham-Smythe. 'You're very lucky I'm not bringing charges against you. Trespassing. Wasting police resources. I'm sure I can think of a few more.'

'Again, ma'am, my sincerest...'

'Just go.'

Sean, Julia and Hayley watched him scuttle rapidly away, like one of the small nocturnal critters he so loved, then followed in the same direction.

'Thanks, Julia. Your quick thinking saved me a tonne of paperwork.'

'You're welcome. I'm more than happy to be of assistance in the worthy cause of less paperwork.'

The three of them leaned against the low wall, unwilling to move. Julia's day seemed to have been a hundred hours long. She had no doubt Hayley's had been just about as taxing, and it was far from over. The DI would be at the station for hours yet, processing the Mullinses.

Hayley seemed to have read Julia's mind.

'Lord help me, the paperwork from this afternoon's antics is going to keep me busy for a week,' Hayley began to count on her fingers. 'Unlicensed firearm...'

'She didn't know it was loaded,' said Julia, who found herself rather protective of Debbie Mullins. She felt she wasn't a bad woman.

'I didn't know that at the time. Neither did Debbie Mullins, I suspect. That gun was covered in an inch of dust. I reckon it had been stashed for years. But no matter, it's an unlicensed firearm. That means paperwork. Forms and forms.'

She counted off the second offence, 'Firearm pointed at another person.'

'Yes, but...'

Hayley ignored her. 'And number three, firearm discharged. Both of those are serious offences which means investigation, and...'

'Paperwork.'

'Right. And we haven't even got to my paper-worthy actions – discharging a taser.'

'You had to use the taser on George. He'd turned on you. It was absolutely necessary. Who knows what might have happened if you didn't. And lord, who knew that a man could scream like that?' Julia shivered at the recollection. 'Anyway, that taser put an end to a protracted standoff that might have been a lot worse.'

'Even so, paperwork. And that's before we even get to the forensics, crime scene, interviews...'

Sean chipped in, 'On the bright side – well, the bright-ish side – it looks like you have solved two murders.'

'With your help. Thank heavens you had the presence of mind to phone me and keep the line open and drop some information about your whereabouts. That was very clever of you, Julia.'

'Ah, well, a bit of luck too.'

'You'd mentioned earlier that you were near the Mullins farm. So when you called, I could figure things out fairly quickly.'

'You arrived just in time. Things were getting a bit hair-raising.'

'Success all round,' said Sean. 'Everyone's safe, and – if all goes well – two crimes solved.'

'Three, in fact. Don't forget about the feared peeping Tom of Berrywick!'

'Or as we now know him, the Batman of Berrywick.' Julia's little joke lifted everyone's spirits, and stirred them into action.

'True. That's one thing off my plate. Speaking of my plate. More will be piled upon it as we speak. I'd best get to the station.'

'Good luck, Hayley. I hope it all goes smoothly.'

Julia took Sean's hand and together they watched Hayley's tail light disappear into the distance, until they were two tiny red pin pricks, and then nothing at all.

Julia stood up from the wall. 'I've an idea.'

'You have?'

'Two ideas, in fact.'

'Let's hear them.'

'First idea: half a cold lager. Second idea: a chicken and mushroom pie.'

'A quick sojourn at The Topsy Turvy Inn?'

'It's only half a mile away. And we haven't had supper. And they take dogs.'

'Julia Bird, you are a genius amongst women.'

'I have my moments of brilliance.'

He turned her towards him, and looked into her face with his bright blue eyes, doing that crinkly thing that made warm prickly waves in her tummy.

'Just one of the reasons that I love you, Julia Bird.'

A LETTER FROM KATIE GAYLE

Dear reader,

Katie Gayle is, in fact, two of us – Kate and Gail. We are so grateful to those of you who have read all of the Julia books so far, and to those who have just discovered her. We hope that new readers have enjoyed life in Berrywick and will read the whole series! And we hope that those who have already read the series enjoyed this one as much as the others. We feel that Jake rose to new levels of heroism in this story – what a Good Boy!

We've definitely got more adventures planned for Julia and Jake and the characters of Berrywick. If you want to keep up to date with all Katie Gayle's latest releases, just sign up at the following link. Your email address will never be shared and you can unsubscribe at any time.

www.bookouture.com/katie-gayle

You can also follow us on Twitter for regular updates and pictures of the real-life Jake! (What a Good Boy he is!)

We would be very grateful if you could write a review and post it on Amazon and Goodreads, so that other people can discover Julia and Jake too. Ratings and reviews really help writers!

You might also enjoy our Epiphany Bloom series – the first three books are available for download now. We think that they are very funny.

You can find us in a few places and we'd love to hear from you:

Katie Gayle is on Twitter as @KatieGayleBooks and on Facebook as Katie Gayle Writer. On Twitter or X or whatever you want to call it, you can also follow Kate at @katesidley and Gail at @gailschimmel. Kate and Gail are also on Insta and Threads, and Gail, for her sins, is trying to figure out TikTok!

Thanks,

Katie Gayle

facebook.com/KatieGayleWriter
x.com/KatieGayleBooks

PUBLISHING TEAM

Turning a manuscript into a book requires the efforts of many people. Katie Gayle and the publishing team at Bookouture would like to acknowledge everyone who contributed to this publication.

Audio
Alba Proko
Melissa Tran
Sinead O'Connor

Commercial
Lauren Morrissette
Hannah Richmond
Imogen Allport

Cover design
The Brewster Project

Data and analysis
Mark Alder
Mohamed Bussuri

Editorial
Nina Winters
Ria Clare

Made in the USA
Las Vegas, NV
07 September 2024

94918259R00146